Also by R. Cameron Cooke

ROME

DEFIANCE OF THE LEGION

This is a work of fiction. The names, characters, places, and incidents are either products of the author's imagination or are used fictitiously. Any resemblance to persons, living or dead, events, or locations is entirely coincidental.

ISBN-9798668535804

ROME

DEFIANCE OF THE LEGION

By

R. Cameron Cooke

"It was scarcely believable that the obscure and humble Eburones had dared make war on the Roman people."

- Julius Caesar

I

Drums beat outside. The war cries of the Belgic brigades grew to a deafening roar as thousands worked themselves into a frenzy. The attack was nigh. The warrior did not have much time.

He took great care as he wrapped the delicate papyrus in oil cloth, then wound it tightly about the shaft of the javelin, securing it with coils of fine black wool. A breath of the chill air outside gusted past the elk-skin flap drawn across the doorway and invigorated the small cooking fire in the center of the dank, smoky hut. The warrior took a few moments to admire the marvelous weapon, the light of the flames twinkling along its polished shaft and within the facets of its fine point. He knew the art of the javelin well, and this one was not easily cast away. It had been cut from an oak sapling, chosen for its pliability and straightness, and sanded to perfection. The air would flow unhindered across its smooth edges, allowing it to travel much further than other missiles of similar size and weight. The blue peacock feathers adorning its tail would give it stability in flight, but they also served another purpose. They had been especially chosen for their exotic design, kept pure and unspoiled, as vivid as the moment they had been plucked.

They were intended to catch the eye, to be noticed.

He checked the binding once more, confident the message would not fall off, even after the hardest impact. He must not be found out. Surely, he would suffer the grisliest of executions should any of the howling warriors outside discover the letter. Most would not be able to read it, but a few would recognize the characters as Greek.

Ducking out of the hut into the frigid air, he joined the mass of warriors forming for the attack, just another skirmisher in a host of thousands.

The host advanced on the Roman fort in the dark, trotting at first, and then breaking into a run when they passed into range of the Roman throwing machines. Several warriors tripped in the darkness and were instantly trampled by the surging ranks behind them. No man wished to stop whilst in the deadly space, for many had witnessed the horrors wrought by the Roman engines in previous attacks.

Tonight's horror was about to begin.

A ball of fire rose from the fort, sluggishly arced across the night sky, and landed amongst the onrushing Belgic host, scattering flaming pitch in all directions. Men were consumed in fire, some flailing, some crying out in pain, some merely crumpling to the earth to die. The aroma of seared flesh filled the air. As the host drew closer to the fort, a hail of fiery missiles spat from the Roman towers, shedding light on the massed warriors below. They were the heavy darts of the Roman ballistae, and they came down like lightning from the sky, skewering men indiscriminately, sometimes two or three on a single missile.

But the Belgae had brought their own flames to the fight, dancing flames amongst the horde, tall torches whipping in the brisk wind. The bearers of these flaming standards became the chosen targets of the Roman projectiles, for their purpose was to bring fire to the fort. Belgic bowmen flocked to these cauldrons to ignite their pitch-tipped arrows. A few fires became many. Then the fires began to dance across the night sky as the bowmen loosed their arrows. Soon flaming missiles were travelling in both directions above the heads of the charging warriors. Though the Belgic arrows were sent by the hundred, most stuck harmlessly into the walls which the Romans had packed with mud and snow for just such an occasion. Only a few arrows surmounted the high parapets to start fires within. But the Belgic arrows were meant only as a nuisance, a distraction to keep the defenders occupied while the spearmen closed on the walls.

Like all Roman forts, this one was surrounded by a ditch. As the sprinting warriors approached the escarpment of this obstacle, the men in the front ranks felt sudden shooting pains in their feet, having inadvertently charged headlong into an area sown with thousands of knife-like barbs. Buried just beneath the snow, the finger-long spikes pierced feet and became imbedded in the soles of boots, each agonizing step driving the spike further into the foot. Again, the stumbling unfortunates were trampled over by their comrades until a carpet of pulverized corpses afforded a way over the field of barbs to reach the ditch.

The base of the ditch was covered in ice, its true depth difficult to judge, and when the Belgic warriors leapt into it, many found themselves crashing through into neck-deep water. Roman helmets appeared above the parapet, and soon a flurry of pila rained down from the ramparts, piercing flesh and turning the icy water black red. Men screamed in terror and lashed about but found no way out of this hell they had stepped into. For the far side of the ditch was slick with icy mud and too sharp to ascend, as was the side from which they had jumped. They were trapped in a pit of ice, frozen blood, and corpses, and had no choice but to await their own deaths as they were pelted with stones, darts, excrement, and any other object the Romans above had devised to further their torment.

As the Romans on the wall delighted themselves at the sight of the carnage below, the javelin man found a good position from which to throw his weapon. He had not gone down into the ditch with the others, instead crouching at the escarpment, darting in and out of the shadows, looking for just the right place to deliver his javelin. And he found it – a Roman tower rising just beyond the wall, atop which two shadowy Roman legionaries discharged missile after missile from a ballista.

It was the perfect target. The tower supports were behind the wall, so the javelin would only be withdrawn by someone on the inside. It would not be an easy throw. The pylons were some fifty paces away, and his missile would have to clear the wall as well, but he was no novice. He had been specifically chosen for this task.

A man to his right was climbing out of the ditch, the infernal pit of hell. He reached out to the javelin man for help, pleading with him for a handhold that would remove him from the disaster that had befallen all the others. The javelin man ignored him, instead judged the distance to the tower. He withdrew the leather strap from his girdle and looped it around one end of the shaft. It would give the dart another thirty paces. He rose from his spot, stepped to the top of the berm, drew back the javelin, and then, with every bit of strength he could muster, sent the missile flying toward the target, giving the strap a final jerk as the weapon left his hand. The javelin sailed through the night, its tail feathers twinkling in the light of the fires. It flew over the ditch, easily cleared the wall. The javelin man gave a triumphant shout when he saw it strike the tower's stanchion square in the middle, firmly embedding itself there. He had accomplished his mission.

The next moment, a flaming bolt shot out of the darkness. The giant ballista bolt struck the javelin man squarely in the chest, splitting his chest cavity open to the spine, killing him instantly and setting his twitching body alight.

Atop the tower, the Roman legionary manning the ballista followed the flight of his missile as it ran true to its target, skewering the Belgic skirmisher below. The legionary watched with indifference as the blue-painted warrior dropped to the ground, the flaming pitch setting fire to his clothing and hair.

The other legionary on the platform with him turned and grinned beneath his helmet. "Good shot, Lucius!"

The grinning soldier was Legionary Jovinus. He held a giant elliptical shield pierced by a dozen arrows that would have otherwise found their way to the engine or the man who worked it.

"That bastard had a good arm, Lucius," Jovinus continued. "But he won't be tossing any more darts our way."

Lucius Domitius made no reply to his elated comrade but simply cranked on the wheels of the engine to prepare it for another dart. Though both men were legionaries, Lucius was much taller and more powerfully built than

Jovinus. Any observer who happened to miss the broad chest beneath the stretched coat of mail would certainly not fail to notice the massive forearms that now rippled as they pulled on the wooden spokes. Normally, it took two men to fight against the tightly wound coils of hemp, and a slave had been assisting Lucius up until a few moments ago. Now, that slave lay in a pool of his own blood, pierced through the eye by a barbarian arrow, and so Lucius turned the spokes alone. The straining engine creaked and whined, but it slowly succumbed to the greater strength of its master.

"Look lively, Lucius." Jovinus peered over the edge of the tower to the mass of shadows and flames below. "There are some bastards with a ladder down there. Do you see them?"

After at last attaining the rewarding click of the engine's final gear, Lucius looked where Jovinus pointed. A mass of Belgae waited in the darkness beyond the ditch, just out of javelin range. As he watched, the enemy ranks parted to allow a giant ladder to pass through. The ladder was wide enough for two warriors to climb up its length side-by-side, and it must have been immensely heavy, because it was borne by some two dozen warriors who staggered beneath its weight. These men were surrounded by others holding shields to protect them from the Roman arrows and stones, and the whole group moved along slowly but steadily toward the wall, encouraged by those behind who incessantly hammered spear against shield. The ladder was obviously constructed for surmounting the battlements, but it was clear to Lucius that the men below intended to use it to bridge the ditch.

"I see them," Lucius said as he rotated the man-sized engine and lowered the elevation to its lowest setting. Judging the ladder-bearers' path, he aimed for a point well ahead of them, grabbed up a pitch-coated dart, and quickly set the missile alight from a nearby brazier. He then waited for the right moment, ever mindful that the burning missile might set fire to his own engine were he to wait too long. Finally, he pulled the lever, releasing the coiled energy in a single instant. The recoil of the engine shook the entire tower as the flaming dart sailed into the darkness with the strength of twenty bows behind it. The missile flew true to its target, striking the ladder like a meteor from the sky. The impact shattered one of the main supports, coating it in burning pitch, and still the missile retained enough energy to vivisect the third man from the front, forcing those behind him to let go of the ladder for fear of being impaled themselves. This caused the rest to lose control of their unwieldy charge, and the whole teetering group tumbled to the ground. With the ladder damaged and ablaze, most of the bearers chose to flee for the rear. A few of the braver ones scooped up handfuls of mud to douse the flames, but the archers on the battlements quickly brought these down in a hail of arrows.

"Go back, you lily-livered curs!" Jovinus shouted. He plucked a Belgic arrow from the post beside him and hurled it in the direction of the fleeing enemy. "Go back to those open-legged whores you call your mothers!" Grinning weakly, he turned to Lucius who was already rewinding the engine for another shot. "They've had it, I think, Lucius. They won't come at us again this night."

That was good, Lucius thought, since he counted only two darts remaining in his stash. If the Belgae kept up the attack, he would soon have nothing to send at them but insults and curses.

But Jovinus's words proved true. The attack faltered all down the line, where other enemy hordes had been beaten off in a similar fashion. The Belgae had managed to escalade the battlements in only one spot. From his high vantage point atop the tower, Lucius could see that the wall there had already been retaken, and the hundred or so barbarians that had infiltrated the fort were now being hacked to death by the flying century. The blades of the savaging gladii flashed brilliantly in the light of the fires, unyielding amid the pleas of mercy from the trapped foe.

A horn trumpeted in the distant enemy camp, a few sour notes that Lucius and Jovinus, and the rest of the besieged Romans, had heard many times over the past several days. It was the Belgic signal for withdrawal. Soon after it sounded, the few remaining shadows in the field began to dissolve and creep back toward the distant tree line.

The battle was over, but the barbarians would come again. If not later tonight, then tomorrow. Out there, across the open field, in the dark forest beneath the stars, the flickering campfires of the enemy host reminded the defenders that they were severely outnumbered, and that their defeat was only a matter of time.

"Their witches will be brewing up a new prophecy for tomorrow," Jovinus said, as if echoing Lucius's thoughts. "That druid magic will get them all stirred up, and they'll have another try at us." He sighed. "At least we can relish one more night in the land of the living, eh, Lucius?"

"Relish?" Lucius chortled grimly, pulling the cloak around him to keep out the freezing wind that seemed to blow harder now that the attack was over.

"Aye, you're right. Death would be a welcome mercy next to this. I must admit, old friend, I never thought I'd meet my end in such a forsaken place, shivering inside my armor, skulking behind a rampart. It's no way for a soldier to die."

"One place is as good as another," Lucius replied evenly. "And there are worse ways to die. Ever seen what the

Belgae do to their prisoners?"

"That's little consolation, Lucius."

Jovinus looked over the edge of the tower and called down to the men lining the battlement below. "What's the count, Decimus?"

"Three dead, sir!" came the reply from one of the upturned helmets. "Five wounded. Arrow wounds, sir!"

"I've told that bastard never to call me that!" Jovinus grumbled to Lucius, after waving an acknowledgement to the young legionary below. "I've told him a dozen times if I've told him once."

"What do you expect? You're the cross-plumer, now. Our centurion."

"Juno's tight arse, Lucius, I am not!" Jovinus retorted as if even the notion of the office were a curse. "I am the signifer of this century, nothing more. I'm simply filling the role while Centurion Silvanus and Optima Avitus are down with the fever. Believe me, once Silvanus is back on his feet, I pick up my standard and leave this foul position to him. I want nothing to do with it." He caught sight of the snide grin on Lucius's face and added. "And you damn well know it, you mule turd!"

Lucius chuckled. He had marched with Jovinus long enough to know how to get under his skin. They had served together for many years, ever since the Seventh Legion left Spain to come to Gaul. Jovinus was a good soldier, a loyal friend, and Lucius would wish for no other man to stand beside him in the battle line, but Jovinus was no leader. He was a simple man without ambition, no desire to attain any rank above signifer. Even that rank had been thrust upon him against his will.

Lucius, too, had avoided promotion over the years, although for different reasons. He wished to remain a nameless spear among thousands, and that had become harder to do of late, as disease and battle thinned the legion's ranks.

Four years ago, the Seventh Legion arrived in Gaul to join the army of the proconsul Gaius Julius Caesar as he made war on select tribes of Gaul and made peace with the rest. The proconsul had conquered in the name of Rome, and Lucius and Jovinus had played a part in that conquest. For the last four years, they had fought one tribe after another, each conflict seemingly more desperate than the last. Those tribes subjugated by Caesar were placed under his protection, which meant the tribes were at the mercy of Rome, which meant they must allow Roman armies to cross their lands, and worse, Roman colonists and merchants.

Caesar always claimed to respect the local cultures, but it was clear to Lucius that the very presence of unclean Romans, like him, was an affront to these druid-led people, an abomination to their old gods. Most accepted the change, knowing that resistance was a hopeless endeavor. The might of Rome was infamous the world over, and tales of what that great empire had done to other, greater nations, had reached even these cold northern lands. The city of Carthage, down on the African coast. The great city of Corinth in the Greek lands. All knew the fates of these two once-mighty kingdoms. Those wars, fought over a hundred years ago, still evoked fear whenever the legions were on the march. In more recent memory, the great Roman general Marius had dealt stunning defeats to a collection of Gallic and Germanic tribes, but Marius had returned to Rome after those victories. Caesar had come here to stay, and had conquered so many lands so quickly, that he did not have enough legions to secure all of it.

This year had proved particularly trying since the harvest had been bleak and Caesar had found himself without enough food to feed his troops. As winter came on, instead of returning the legions to plentiful Italy and Spain, he had brashly posted them far and wide, across all of Gaul, and in so doing had spread them too thin. The winter forts on the border with Germania were the most at hazard, a hazard that manifested itself when the tribes of the Belgae unexpectedly rose in revolt. The remotest of these forts was three days' march east of the battlement on which Lucius now stood. It had been manned by General Sabinus and the Fourteenth Legion and was suspected to have been the first casualty of Caesar's brazenness, the first victim of the Belgic army that now surrounded the camp of the Seventh. Rumors of a great defeat were still trickling in, rumors of an unprecedented disaster. If true, somewhere out there, in the cold forests of Belgica, the entire Fourteenth Legion had been annihilated and General Sabinus slain.

A pack of wolves howled in the distance, accented by the beat of a blacksmith's hammer. In the barbarian camp, armor and weapons were being repaired. The mortally wounded littering the field had not yet expired and the enemy was already preparing for tomorrow's attack.

Lucius glanced at the dead slave lying at his feet. Gorton had been a loyal and trustworthy servant. Lucius had won him months ago, while on campaign in Britannia. The lad had needed some instruction at first, but he had proved useful, and Lucius had started to grow accustomed to having him around. He had been toying with the idea of keeping Gorton and not selling him to the eastern traders come the spring. The lad had died fighting against a people that were much like his own, and Lucius wondered whether his gods would forgive him for such a betrayal.

This was a strange place, where ally and foe looked much alike, a wild land far from Rome and his native Spain. Though he had said otherwise, Lucius, like Jovinus, did not wish to die in such a forsaken place.

II

A golden dawn broke over clear blue skies, and with it came gusts of wind that heaped snow against walls and partially buried the dead. Upwards of three hundred bodies lay frozen in the desolate field, beards frosted with ice, stiff arms raised, some still clinging to sword or spear, some burnt beyond recognition. A haggard flock of black carrion braved the cold to feast on the night's harvest. Like winter lilies, Roman arrows and javelins littered the ground, many frozen so firmly to ice or corpse that the slaves and legionaries now casing the field were forced to leave them behind. A full cohort stood under arms just beyond the praetoria gate, while the scroungers salvaged the valuable shafts.

"Death descended on this place yester night," Jovinus

said, watching the scavengers. Beside him, along the battlements, the other men of the century huddled inside their cloaks trying to escape the bitter wind. "The bloody Belgic gods welcome many a warrior to the afterlife this day."

"Warriors?" Lucius replied. "I was down there earlier this morning retrieving darts. I got a good look at some of those blue-painted bastards. Many of them had yet to see their first shave. An untrained rabble of boys and old men assailed us last night – simple farm folk. Not warriors."

"There is no doubting their valor, eh?" Jovinus offered.

"What use is valor when it results in slaughter?"

Across the field, before the distant tree line, hundreds of Belgae toiled like an army of slaves. They dug trenches and erected earthworks stretching for miles in either direction, only their heads and arms visible above the freshly upturned earth. They used short swords as their tools – gladii recovered from the slaughtered Fourteenth Legion. The Belgae worked diligently to complete a wall of circumvallation around the Roman camp, and though their progress was much slower than it would have been had they been legionaries, it was clear that the wall was only days away from completion. After that, nothing, not even a stray deer, would enter or leave the Roman camp.

"I wonder who taught them how to do that," Jovinus said, adjusting the frost-coated hood of his cloak such that it would not get caught up in the fangs of the wolf-head adorning the crest of his helmet.

"Perhaps our old comrade Vitalis." Lucius said, referring to a centurion of the Seventh who had disappeared in Belgica some years ago.

Jovinus looked at him and laughed. "They'd better work faster than that if old Vitalis is in charge. He'll have that vine branch of his singing across their backs."

Lucius smiled at the memory of his friend, but the fond memory brought to mind darker recollections as well – their last campaign together, the last time the legions faced the Belgae in bloody conflict, when tens of thousands of Roman and Belgic warriors met their fates at a ford on the Sabis River. That battle seemed like a lifetime in the past, yet it had been only three short years ago.

"They'd do better to go back to their fields," Lucius said solemnly.

"Who can blame them, Lucius? They've no choice, or at least they think they don't. They had a poor harvest this year. Here come our legions, bivouacking in their lands, demanding a quarter of their hard-won grain – grain meant to get their families through the winter. I sometimes think I'd do the same, were I in their place." He brushed snow from the parapet before resting his hand there. "Still, it is unusual, Lucius, to see these people so organized, so bent on a common purpose. We've both been in these parts long enough to know it takes a leader to stir them to such actions, and whoever leads the host yonder must be a great man – perhaps one to rival Caesar himself. Those bastards come at our walls, night after night. What kind of a man can inspire men so?"

"Perhaps the same man who would do that?" Lucius said bitterly, pointing to the far side of the field, where five bloated bodies stood impaled on high stakes. Though the bodies had turned blue, the cuts and bruises of their long torment were still visible. They were what remained of the messengers that had been sent to seek out Caesar and alert him to the destruction of the Fourteenth Legion and the plight of the Seventh. The poor souls had been captured, tortured, and placed in the space between the camps in clear view from the walls, that the men of the Seventh might be constantly reminded of their peril.

They were isolated and alone. No one was coming to their aid, nor was Caesar even aware of their dilemma. Rumor had it that Caesar was hundreds of miles away, perhaps already across the Alps, taking his winter repose in the milder climes of northern Italy, where he could better monitor the political affairs in Rome.

"You're supposed to protect the damn thing, not use it as a shield!" An irate voice called above them. Lucius and Jovinus looked up to see a scowling centurion descending the tower. He appeared twenty years older than either of them, with skin like wrinkled leather, but he spryly jumped the last few feet skipping the final rungs of the ladder. "Seventeen, Legionary Jovinus! Seventeen!" the centurion said, his hands stretching a vine branch tight between them. The centurion's mail shirt was adorned with an array of iron discs of various design, each one a badge of honor won in battle. "I counted seventeen fresh arrowhead marks on your engine, many of them dangerously close to the springs."

"Apologies, Centurion Deodatus," Jovinus said, meekly.

Deodatus was the centurion of the legion's artillery, and treated every one of the legion's engines like they were his own children, taking great offense if they were not well cared for. "Just how much spare sinew rope do you think we have within these walls, Legionary Jovinus? Cut that cord and the whole engine is useless. I've already got six ballistae ruined by the man-apes working them last night setting the bloody things on fire, or over-torqueing the springs. I won't have any more lost to stupidity."

"They're just soldiers, sir," Jovinus replied defensively. "If we had more engineers, then perhaps –"

"Did Mucius Scaevola stop pumping the stump, or did he learn to use his left hand?" Deodatus interrupted. "We work with what we have, Jovinus. If I find any further damage to your engine, I'll see that your name is known to the primus pilus. Is that understood?"

"Yes, Centurion." Jovinus cast a weary glance at Lucius, the dislike of his temporary position as leader of the century evident on his face. Lucius gazed back with amusement from behind Deodatus.

After another threatening glare at Jovinus, Deodatus made to leave, but then stopped suddenly in his tracks. Something on the tower had caught his eye.

"By Juno!" he said, holding up one hand to shield his eyes from the morning sun, the previous ire gone from his tone entirely. "Now that's a pretty thing! I've never seen the like."

Lucius followed the centurion's gaze up to a javelin lodged in one of the tower's main support posts. The shaft had been polished to a fine shine such that it now gleamed in the sun. The blue feathers adorning its tail gave the weapon a more ceremonial aspect than a warlike one. It was clearly not the type of weapon one would throw over an enemy's wall to be forgotten.

"Perhaps, sir, you wish to see it?" Jovinus said, now eyeing Lucius vengefully. "Allow me to send Legionary Domitius up to fetch it."

"Yes," replied the centurion, not taking his eyes off the weapon above. "Yes, Jovinus. Send Legionary Domitius up there at once. I wish to see this barbarian craftsmanship up close."

Lucius shot a grudging look at Jovinus, but doffed his cloak and helmet and began to climb the ladder. Lucius was quite dexterous for his size, but he came near to slipping several times as he crept out onto the ice-covered cross piece, and each time shot a condemning glance down at Jovinus. For his part, Jovinus appeared quite entertained by the spectacle. Lucius made a mental note to wait until his comrade was no longer acting centurion before plotting his own revenge.

The weapon must have been thrown with incredible force, because Lucius's first attempts to free it failed. He could see that the point of the weapon was nearly half-buried in the post, and it would take a long effort of wiggling it back and forth to dislodge it. A thought came to mind of simply breaking the shaft, but the artillery centurion below seemed to read his thoughts and called up to him.

"I want it intact, Legionary Domitius!"

As Lucius held on with one hand, he used his other to move the weapon minutely back and forth, and slowly his great strength managed to free the head. But just as he tucked the weapon beneath his arm, he noticed a piece of canvas that had been carefully wound around the middle of the shaft. It piqued his curiosity enough to pause for a moment to examine it further. With as much care as his frozen fingers would allow, he untied the cord and removed the canvas from the shaft. Inside it, he found a sealed message, written on papyrus with a simple Greek inscription on the outside.

"What is it?" the centurion demanded, when Lucius finally descended to the battlement carrying both the dislodged javelin and the message. "Let me see it."

Lucius handed the centurion the ornate weapon, but kept the message, a reluctant look on his face.

"What's wrong, Lucius?" Jovinus said. "Give him the paper, too."

"I'm sorry, sir, but I can't."

"You can't?" Deodatus said incredulously. "And just why in Pluto's realm can't you?"

"The inscription on the outside, sir," Lucius replied. "It states the finder is to take it directly to the general, and to no one else."

"A message from the Belgae?"

"I don't think so, sir. It's written in Greek."

The three men stared at the paper in Lucius's hands for several long moments.

"Come now, Lucius," Jovinus said finally. "Give it to Centurion Deodatus. It's more appropriate that he goes before the general –"

"On second thought, Jovinus," Deodatus interjected, turning the javelin over in his hands as if he had lost all interest in the message. "Let Legionary Domitius deliver it. I haven't the time, nor the inclination to see Cicero right now. Our inattentive general has been all too careless of late, and those of us who have not yet given up hope must pick up the slack of those who have. There are more engines to inspect." He eyed Jovinus harshly one last time. "Remember what I said about yours."

"Yes, Centurion."

Deodatus marched off to confront the next century further down the battlement, twirling his newly attained keepsake, obviously pleased to avoid any audience with the general, leaving that unpleasantness for Jovinus and Lucius to sort out.

"Any excuse to get out of the wind, eh, Lucius?" Jovinus said finally. He glanced at the orderly rows of log huts within the confines of the walls, a myriad of snow-covered roofs turned gray by belching chimneys. Crimson banners fluttered over a rectangular structure in the center of the fort. "It appears the general is at the praetorium."

"Is he ever anywhere else?"

"Do not tarry long, Lucius. None of your tricks this time. We have much work to do."

"Yes, Centurion." Lucius replied light-heartedly, reveling in the frustration on his comrade's face.

Then, with message in hand, Lucius headed for the ladder, looking forward to even a few moments out of the biting maw of the wind.

III

"And just how did you come by this?"

Lucius stood at attention under the glare of a portly, balding man with bulging eyes who reeked of wine and who now sat on the edge of a large cot. The man was naked but for a blanket draped over one shoulder. The room smelled of herbs and perspiration.

"It was thrown over the wall, sir. Last night," Lucius answered, wishing now that he were back on that wall with Jovinus and the rest of the century.

General Quintus Cicero, legate of the Seventh Legion, regarded Lucius with something akin to disgust as his pudgy hands picked away at the remnants of the wax seal. He then shooed Lucius away as one might a nosey dog, before opening the letter to read it.

Cicero struck an unimpressive figure as he sat there,

examining the letter, unconsciously scratching at an itch on his bare chest. The general was in his late forties, though his sagging features and half-inebriated state made him look much older. Lucius had seen the general many times before the siege, strolling about the camp with his entourage in tow, but this was the first time Lucius had ever seen him like this. It was said that Cicero had once been propraetor of a province in the east, but now Lucius was having a difficult time imagining him in charge of a latrine detail.

A collection of blank-faced tribunes and adjutants stood along the side of the room, waiting silently and patiently for their general to finish reading. A handful of bearded Gauls were there, too - nobles from the few tribes that had chosen to stand with their Roman allies rather than take part in the revolt. One of the tribunes, a gentle-eyed man with a crop of gray-blonde hair, smiled at Lucius appreciatively, as if sympathizing with his discomfort.

Lucius could count on one hand the number of times he had visited the praetorium, and while it was true he felt somewhat out of place in this sanctum of senior officers, where a man's pedigree and wits carried more value than his skill with the sword, what made him more uncomfortable was the playful stare of the young woman whose nude, curvy form lay amidst the rustled furs on the general's bed.

She must be Belgic, Lucius surmised, judging by the tattoos that adorned her body. She lay on her side, seemingly aware that the perfect shape of her pale, tattooed buttocks was entertaining the eyes of every man in the room. All but Cicero's, who seemed to have trouble focusing on the letter in front of his face. The woman stared at Lucius over her bare shoulder, a dark-eyed, challenging stare, as if to peer into the inner recesses of his soul and expose his wildest fantasies. Her eyelids were tattooed a deep blue, much darker than the woad often worn by her people, and the shadow gave her green eyes an infinite, all-knowing aspect, as if she belonged here – indeed, as if she commanded here. Her ink-black hair was tousled from a recent romp with the general, which had been vociferously in progress when Lucius had arrived. Lucius had been made to wait outside for a long interval before being admitted, but he had heard enough to feel that he already knew this woman better than he wanted to. He had not eaten for some time, but the thought of that fawn of perfection with the bulbous general made his stomach churn.

A loud belch emanated from Cicero when he had finished reading the letter. He turned the paper over in his hands several times, as if doing so might reveal more lines than the scant few that were there.

"*Expect succor.*" He read out loud, his speech somewhat slurring. "Is that it? *Expect succor.* What in Pluto's name does that mean? Was there nothing else with this message?"

"No, sir," Lucius replied. "It was attached to a javelin we found stuck in a post. It wasn't there before. One of the enemy warriors must have thrown it during the night."

"One of Caesar's agents, more likely," Cicero retorted, yawning and groggy-eyed. "It bears his mark. It seems your man made it through, Vertico." This last was said to one of the Gallic nobles in the room, to which the Gaul merely nodded in concurrence.

"Your pardon, General," the light-haired tribune spoke. "Would it not be wise to ask the woman to leave?" The tribune eyed the reclining woman with suspicion, and Lucius gathered from that one look that he did not approve of her – now or ever.

"What did you say, Honorius?" Cicero said, looking up from the letter.

"The woman, my lord," Honorius said with forced patience. "She should not be here. These are sensitive matters."

"Oh, you mean…" Cicero's voice trailed off as he glanced over his shoulder at the woman. She smiled back at him innocently, then blew him a kiss. The general's face instantly transformed into an eager-to-please smile, like that of a tamed dog. "Erminhilt is harmless, Honorius. You well know she comes from a friendly tribe, one of the few who have sent warriors to man our walls. She serves me. And very well, I might add." Cicero proceeded to laugh uncontrollably, until his face was red, and though his humor was repulsive to most of the others in the room, it was met with coos and caws from the overly placating Erminhilt.

"My lord," Honorius continued, clearly annoyed by the general's behavior. "If it was indeed Vertico's servant that reached the proconsul with news of our situation, then Caesar will be operating on old information. He will know nothing of the thousands of fresh troops we observed arriving in the enemy camp yesterday."

The woman continued to nudge Cicero with her feet under the furs, which he slapped at playfully, as if he had not heard a word Honorius had said.

"My lord!" the tribune exasperated. "Your soldiers need leadership!"

"Do not lecture me, Honorius!" Cicero turned on him, his face suddenly red with anger. "I grow weary of your manner and your tone. The situation is untenable. This king of the Eburones, this Ambiorix, has managed to rouse nearly every Belgic tribe within a hundred leagues. We are surrounded by thirty thousand savage barbarians who, mere days ago, annihilated Sabinus and his legion. What makes you believe things will be different here?"

"If the reports we received are true, sir, General Sabinus allowed his legion to be caught in the open. He did not remain within the protection of his walls." The tribune then pointed at the letter in Cicero's hand. "Nor did he have a message from Caesar promising relief. It seems clear that if we hold out longer, we –"

"Yes, yes, if Caesar is indeed coming!" Cicero said hotly, his jowls shaking as he moved his jaw. "But this letter tells me very little, Honorius. How far away is he? How many troops does he bring? This letter does us no good. In fact, the more I consider it, the more I am convinced it is a trick, a ploy by our enemies. Caesar could not have written it, for the simple reason that Caesar is now in Italy. Have you forgotten? He will have crossed the Alps by now, for his winter holiday, leaving the rest of us to freeze and starve in Gaul!"

"But it bears Caesar's mark, sir."

"A forgery, no doubt. No, my dear Honorius, I am afraid Caesar has pushed his fortune too far this time. It is hopeless! Perhaps tonight, perhaps tomorrow, your severed head and mine will adorn the Belgic pikes to be paraded triumphantly through their villages. Until that time, I say let each live as he will. You and the others may order the camp and play the loyal soldiers of Rome to the end, if you like, but I prefer to go out enjoying the simple pleasures of life, and to complete my great works." Cicero gestured to a table in the corner littered with pens, an overturned ink pot, a half-unwound roll of papyrus, and a small ivory figurine carved into the shape of a sphinx. "The tragedies and poems I have penned will be my legacy, Honorius. My gift to posterity. You, too, may spend your final days as you wish."

Lucius had heard about the general's recent fixation. Aside from fornicating with the Belgic woman, he was obsessed with finishing a collection of writings, convinced they would be his crowning achievement in life. It was obvious Honorius was exercising extreme restraint with the forlorn general, holding back his true opinions.

"My lord," Honorius started with the calm respect of one accustomed to serving under an eccentric. "I believe this message is legitimate. It makes no sense otherwise. Why would the enemy feed us with false information that only encourages us to hold out longer? If we consider that the message might have come from Caesar's hand, and that the proconsul himself is at this very moment marching to relieve us, I would ask that you consider my earlier request regarding Sabinus's Legion. We have a duty to see that the silver does not fall into the hands of our enemies."

At the mention of silver, Lucius's ears perked up. He also noticed the woman's playful smile fade nearly imperceptibly. Evidently, she, too, had an interest.

"Silver, silver, silver! Is that all that matters to you?" Cicero grumbled. "You cannot take one denarius with you to the afterlife. Were I you, Honorius, I would focus the energies of my final days on something more momentous, something more enduring. Have you ever penned a poem?"

"With all respect, my lord, I do not wish to take the silver with me to the afterlife, or anywhere else. I wish to see it returned to Caesar."

"Caesar, again," Cicero guffawed. "I thought we had settled that. This message is a forgery, Honorius. Tell me, why would Caesar take such risk to send this letter, and then convey so little information with it?" Cicero slapped the paper with the back of his hand. *"Expect succor! Expect succor!* What in Juno's bosom does it mean? What purpose does it serve, when I can do nothing but sit behind my walls and wait?"

There was a silence after this, and before Honorius

could reply, Lucius suddenly spoke.

"Maybe Caesar wishes to give you hope, sir," Lucius said with unintentional sharpness. "Perhaps you should share his message with the legion, to give them hope as well."

It might have been the cold, or his lack of sleep, or his frustration with this worthless general who seemed intent on his own destruction as well as that of his men. Whatever the reason, Lucius had said it. He had voiced his opinion, quite inappropriately, an egregious offense from a common soldier, and now a hush descended on the room like that following a sentence of death handed down by a magistrate.

Cicero's cylindrical head turned to face him wearing a smile that held no merriment.

"What did you say, legionary?" the general said, as a spider might lure its next meal into its web.

There was no turning back now, Lucius thought. He might as well jump in with both feet. "With respect, sir. The lads would fight with more vigor if they knew Caesar was coming."

Cicero's smile faded, his face turning red with rage, his hands almost to the point of shaking, and Lucius now regretted ever having spoken at all, or having seen that damned message tied to the javelin.

"Has the great Hector returned from the underworld to grace us with his wisdom?" Cicero said poisonously, through gritted teeth, looking at Lucius as if he might march over and strangle him. "Or did some drudger of the muck just tell me my business?"

"I am sure the legionary meant no impertinence, sir," Honorius tried to intercede, but Cicero ignored him.

"By Hercules, do you know who I am, you mule-brained oaf? Curse your impudence! You stand before a man who was once propraetor of Asia. I had power over countless cities and towns. A million souls rose and slept under my purview, bent to my will, and mine alone! I've sent hundreds to the gallows better than you." Cicero hurled his half-filled cup across the room. Lucius did not flinch as the cup struck his mail shirt and its remnants splattered on his face. The woman on the bed seemed mildly amused.

"To think that I would be lectured by some ape of the trench," the general continued, his drunkenness more evident the angrier he got. "Did I ask for your opinion, legionary? Did I indicate in any way that you had permission to speak? Why, I should have you flogged for this insolence! Damn you! What is your name?"

"Lucius Dom-"

But Lucius was interrupted by Honorius who quickly took him by the shoulder and began directing him toward the door. "It is not important who he is, my lord. He is one of your loyal legionaries and he will return to his post at once. Do not concern yourself with him."

"Get him out of my sight! Out of my sight!" Lucius heard Cicero shouting even after they had left the room. "I want him flogged, do you hear!"

After quickly escorting Lucius out into the antechamber, Honorius pulled him aside and gave him an apologetic look. "Say nothing of this to anyone, legionary. Neither regarding the message nor the general's unfortunate outburst. Is that understood?"

Lucius nodded. "Yes, sir."

"You made an excellent suggestion. As you said, the men need something to hold onto. They need to have confidence in their general, even if that confidence is unfounded." Honorius smiled at the look of surprise on Lucius's face. "What is your name, legionary?"

"Lucius Domitius, sir."

"Return to your century, Legionary Domitius, and do not worry about the general. You have my word you will not be punished."

"Honorius! Honorius!" Cicero's voice boomed from within the quarters. "Where in Pluto's name are you?"

The tribune sighed heavily, smiled once more at Lucius, and then returned to the general's quarters.

Lucius stepped into the snow-lined street corduroyed with logs, pausing for a moment to ponder all that he had just witnessed. He had never felt inherently inferior to men like Cicero, and, thus, the upbraiding did not weigh heavily on him. Indeed, there was a time when Lucius himself might have worn the plume of a tribune, instead of the horsetail of a common legionary. But, such were the fates. They teased a man, held fortune and happiness before his nose that he might savor the sweet aroma, and then abruptly dashed any hopes of ever attaining them.

But money could help a man decide his own fate, and Honorius's mention of silver had aroused Lucius's interest. How much silver? It must be a large amount to be of any concern at such a time as this. The legionaries of the Seventh had not been paid in months. Were there any substantial amount of silver within the fort, Lucius was certain he would have heard about it. Honorius had spoken of the silver as if it were something not yet attained, something that needed to be secured and kept out of the hands of the enemy. If it was not within the walls of the fort, then where was it? And what of the captivating woman, Erminhilt? Did she have an interest in the treasure beyond that of an opportunist strumpet?

Lucius partially understood Cicero's fascination with her. She had an alluring beauty that left a man pondering her long after leaving her, and it was obvious she knew it all too well. Lucius had managed to tear his eyes away from her pleasing figure long enough to observe her as she gazed around the room, looking gratifyingly at Cicero, scornfully at Honorius, contemptuously at all the others, and at Lucius…How had she regarded him? Was it lust, amusement, condescension? She was indeed as attractive as the rumors about the camp had suggested. Whatever her true intentions, Lucius could not imagine a world in which a woman of such enthralling beauty would willingly give herself to a pathetic wretch like Cicero, no matter his rank or station. But after spending only a few moments in the woman's presence, Lucius understood why the tribune Honorius did not approve of her presence. Lucius had been with his share of women over the course of his travels. He had encountered all types. Enough to know, this one was not to be trusted.

Across the street, a crow lighted on a charred wooden beam, the blackened remnants of a barracks burned to the ground by a clay incendiary thrown over the wall several nights ago. The croaking bird stirred Lucius from his thoughts. Perhaps it was an omen. Whether good or bad, it reminded him that he must return to the wall.

He sighed as he pulled his cloak about him and marched briskly through the slush.

IV

The camp horns sounded the start of the next vigil, stirring the relieving centuries from their barracks to replace those on the wind-bitten battlements. Cooking fires crackled beneath bread ovens and stew pots as weary legionaries placated their gnawing bellies with half-rations, their weapons and helmets stacked nearby, never far out of reach.

It had been another long night on the wall. The Belgae had attacked again, in the early morning hours, just before the dawn. This time they had brought with them two siege towers, crudely constructed, but an unheard-of feat for the Belgic tribes. A moment of shock and disbelief overcame the legionaries who witnessed the two wheel-borne monsters emerge from the darkness bristling with sword warriors and archers. But the attack had been poorly coordinated, and neither tower reached the wall. Upwards of a thousand Belgic footmen rushed forward bearing brushwood and tools for filling in the ditch, but they had arrived on the scene too late, and the paused towers became targets for every Roman engine that could bear. Within moments, both structures were ablaze, the towering infernos quickly becoming crematoriums for the screaming Belgae within.

The gray dawn had broken to reveal the towers' smoking skeletal remains, surrounded by scores of the fallen. The enemy assault had failed. Again, the Belgae had suffered the worst of it, but arrow and stone had claimed some of the defenders, too, losses that could not be replaced.

Lucius sat on a log fashioned into a stool as he and the other sixty-two men of the century ate their meager breakfast. They lounged outside their barracks, an orderly row of thatched-roofed huts where they might spend a few cherished hours out of the wind with aching feet thawing near smoldering braziers. The icicles skirting the barracks dripped in the morning sun like some bothersome drummer counting the interval until they must return to the wall again.

It had been two days since Lucius had been expelled from the general's quarters, two days during which there had been no punishment handed down, indeed no mention of the incident. The tribune had been true to his word.

The putrid stench lingering about the interior of the fort spoiled the savor of Lucius's breakfast. With the gates closed up, and rotting garbage and dung piled high in the central square, it had grown more foul each passing day. The fort housed the nearly five thousand soldiers, slaves, craftsmen, horses, mules, and vehicles of the Seventh Legion, many ill and many wounded. It was a miserable existence. They lived in a world devoid of vegetation, passing their time between the mud and slush of the streets and the cramped confines of their quarters. Except for those freezing moments spent on the battlements, their view in every direction was limited to walls and towers. Like the malodor, a foreboding sense of doom hung over them, as if this fort were a prison, and each awaited execution.

Lucius glanced down the street where a score of wounded soldiers lay propped on the portico of the hospital, waiting to be seen by the camp surgeons. As Lucius watched, Jovinus emerged from the building and marched toward the barracks. He wore a forlorn expression, and Lucius quickly surmised the reason for it.

"What news, Jovinus?" Lucius handed his friend a half-loaf of warm bread.

"Silvanus is dead," he said despondently. "Succumbed to his fever in the night."

"That is unfortunate," Lucius said, his suspicions confirmed. "And Avitus?"

"Optima Avitus is still very ill. It is possible he will not survive the day."

"I am sorry, Jovinus. For Silvanus, and for you."

Jovinus nodded, but said nothing. The other men of the century close enough to have overheard did little more than raise their eyebrows at the news. They were either too tired or beyond the point of caring. Silvanus and Avitus were just two more faces to add to those that had faded from memory over countless campaigns.

Lucius sensed Jovinus did not wish to discuss it further, and, after clapping him on the shoulder, rose to retire to the barracks.

"Your respite can wait, Lucius," Jovinus said with mock authority. "I'm in need of another strong back. I've a long list for the armory."

Lucius had been looking forward to a few hours of sleep, but kept his curses to himself and accompanied Jovinus.

The armory was only a short walk from their barracks. It was an exceptionally long structure near the center of the fort, and as far away from the walls as possible to minimize the hazard of enemy incendiaries. Lucius and Jovinus entered the building and joined the line of soldiers formed before the storekeeper's counter, behind which a half dozen slaves moved from one bin to another sorting and organizing everything from boots, to woolen cloaks, to leather belts. The slaves moved under the direction of an irate clerk who seemed displeased with everything they did, launching into one tirade after another. The clerk was a slightly built man, with a weak jawline. A tuft of long hair at the top of the clerk's round head reminded Lucius of those he had once seen worn by a band of mercenaries from a certain region of Illyria. There were several dozen scribes and clerks attached to the legion, to maintain the books and manage the day-to-day inflow and outflow of supplies, but, in all his time with the Seventh, Lucius had never seen this one before.

"No, no, no! This is all wrong!" the clerk demanded while inspecting a stack of several hundred pila. "Where did these come from? What cohort do they belong to?"

"They were retrieved outside the walls, Master Diogenes," an apprentice answered meekly. "They come from many different cohorts."

The clerk snatched up one of the javelins and read out loud an inscription carved into the wooden shaft. "*I am for Odin's arse.*" He then picked up another and read it. "*Belgic cocks are diminutive.*" And another. "*Use this in your wife's...*" the clerk stopped abruptly, his face red with frustration. "The pilum is a weapon of war, not a conveyor of lewd messages. Where did you obtain such base practices in the Seventh?"

"Master Faustas never made an issue of it, Master Diogenes."

"Yes, I am learning that Master Faustas did very little during his tenure as chief stores clerk. I shall make a full report to the primus pilus about that, believe me." Seeing the vacant look on the apprentice's face, the clerk sighed, and then abruptly changed his tone to that of a mentor. "Each shaft must be marked with the name of the legate and the legion – nothing else. Otherwise, how do you expect accolades to be appropriately distributed after a battle? Have you not read the wars of Marius, young man? Did you not read of the battle against the Cimbri, in which the legions of both Marius and Catalus were engaged? When the javelins were plucked from the enemy corpses and tallied, more were found bearing the name of Catalus than Marius. Thus, Catalus snatched the victory away from the great general simply because his pila were properly marked. Do you not see?"

The apprentice stared back at him blankly, appearing no less confused than before.

"Oh, for Juno's sake," the clerk said, exasperated. "Scratch out these vulgar idioms and replace them with the name of Cicero. Is that understood?"

"Yes, Master Diogenes."

The servants scurried away to avoid the glare of their master who checked off another item on a wax tablet he held in one hand. Meanwhile, the counter was left unattended with no indication that anyone would be helping those in line anytime soon.

Jovinus cleared his throat loudly. "Bother with your cataloging fancies on your own time. Do you not see there are fighting men waiting?"

The clerk slapped his stylus onto the tablet, turning abruptly to face the waiting legionaries. He sneered as his eyes darted from one to the other, seeking out the offender. Eventually, they settled on Jovinus.

"Jovinus, isn't it?" The clerk said his name as if it were an obscenity. "Yes, I am quickly learning the names of the rabble-rousers in this legion. I know your kind well, Jovinus. Those who believe battles are won by the thrust of sword and spear alone. Well, my uneducated friend, I regret to inform you they are not. Battles are won by the storekeeper's ledger, the number counters who ensure you and your comrades are clothed, fed, armed, and sheltered. Without these cataloging fancies, as you call them, you would have none of it. And then where would you be, in your hack and slash world? I'll tell you. You would be no different from those barbarians out there. Now, you will just have to wait your turn, like all the others."

The clerk went back to reproaching the slaves while Jovinus stewed in silence.

"Who is that bugger?" Lucius asked under his breath. "I've never seen him before."

"You've heard of him, though probably not by name," Jovinus replied dourly. "His name is Diogenes, but you know him as the only known survivor of the Fourteenth Legion."

"Him? A bloody clerk?" Lucius had heard of a refugee from the massacre who had arrived just before the siege, and who had been the chief source of information regarding the fate of General Sabinus and his legion.

"I've no idea how he escaped the slaughter, Lucius, but, Jupiter help me, I'd be glad to strangle him myself to make it a clean job. If there was anyone I wished the Belgae had skewered, it'd be him. Never trust an only survivor. You remember Faustas, the old storekeeper?"

Lucius nodded. "Died of the fever a few weeks back."

"That's right. Well, someone came up with the bright idea to put this Diogenes in his place, I suppose to make use of him. If you ask me, they never should have opened the gates for the unpleasant little bastard."

The door to the armory opened admitting a blast of cold air that stoked the embers in the braziers. A man entered wearing the fine cloak of a tribune. Pausing to stomp the mud off his boots, he looked around the room and finally pushed back his hood. Lucius saw that it was Honorius, the tribune he had seen in the general's quarters. Honorius flashed a smile to the legionaries, apparently not noticing Lucius, and then moved to the front of the line.

"I see you are busy, Diogenes," Honorius addressed the clerk. "Getting used to your new billet?"

The clerk's face instantly transformed into the most amicable grin, his former sourness all but vanished. "Never too busy to assist an officer, sir. How can I assist you? A new pair of boots perhaps?"

"No, nothing like that." Honorius gestured to an uninhabited corner of the room. "Might I have a private word with you?"

"Certainly, sir. Anything for you, sir."

The clerk came out from behind the counter and followed the tribune to the corner, where the two began to discourse in low voices. Lucius thought it curious, blithely wondering what matter might be so sensitive that it could not be discussed openly. Were supplies running short? Had the food reserves spoiled? Or were the two simply sharing thoughts on the change in the weather?

Whatever they discussed, the clerk seemed nervous, the tribune guarded.

"Just look at him, Lucius," Jovinus whispered in a tone

of revulsion. "Standing there like an owl turd on Minerva's left shoulder, eager to lick any officer's arse. I wonder what favors he's promising the tribune. I tell you that bugger's not to be trusted."

But Lucius was not sure Diogenes was promising any favors. His manner was not obliging, but anxious, and seemed to grow more so as the conversation progressed. This prompted Lucius to listen intently amid the din of the other voices, and to focus on the clerk's lips. Lucius was certain he saw, and perhaps heard, the word *silver* mouthed several times, each time followed by a nervous glance around the room. Lucius immediately concluded that it must be the same silver Honorius had mentioned in Cicero's quarters.

If so, then where was this secret fortune, and what did the peevish clerk have to do with it?

Like any legionary with hardly twenty denarii to his name, Lucius could not help but fixate on it. Mulling over a dozen different explanations, Lucius continued watching Diogenes, hoping for some other clue, but the private meeting ended before he could glean anything further. Diogenes gave a respectful nod to Honorius, as if their business was not done, only adjourned, and returned to the counter. In an ostentatious fashion that was entirely disingenuous, the clerk immediately began attending to the first man in line, behavior that could only have been for the tribune's benefit.

Honorius lingered only long enough to impart a few encouraging words to the waiting soldiers, and then made to leave. But before he pulled the hood back over his head, he suddenly noticed Lucius.

"Legionary Domitius!" the tribune said jovially. "I thought I recognized you. How are you, man? Not thrown from the Tarpeian Rock yet, I see."

"No, sir."

"I told you nothing would come of it. Did I not?"

"Yes, sir. Thank you, sir."

"You know, the general hasn't forgotten about what you said to him." Honorius eyed him cunningly.

"He hasn't, sir?"

"I've even reminded him a few times, myself – leaving your name out, of course. If it's any consolation to you, you were right. The general knows it, too, though you wouldn't have guessed it from his behavior that day." Honorius looked at him approvingly. "We need more soldiers like you, Legionary Domitius, men who are quick with their wits, as well as their swords."

Jovinus cleared his throat, evidently troubling to hold back laughter at the notion, but the tribune did not seem to notice.

"In any event, I would advise you to watch and wait, Legionary Domitius," Honorius said finally. "Watch and wait, and I believe you will be pleasantly surprised."

"Yes, sir," Lucius replied. He did not have the slightest notion what Honorius was referring to, nor did Honorius shed any more light on the matter. With a casual smile, the tribune donned his hood, pulled his cloak tightly about him, and left.

"Well, aren't you the tribune's play pretty," Jovinus commented, clearly amused by the whole scene. His merriment, however, was short lived. The door had hardly shut before Diogenes dropped the façade and returned to his former obstinacy. The miserly clerk left the counter and went back to berating his servants, leaving Lucius and Jovinus and the others to wait indefinitely.

V

In the few hours remaining before the century would return to the wall to stand the vigil, Lucius could not sleep. Whether he was simply too tired to sleep, or his mind too fixated on the events in the armory, he could not tell, but he donned his cloak and ventured outside the barracks into the cold air of the early evening.

The night was quiet, save for the foreboding thump of the distant Belgic drums. Somewhere on the other side of the camp a dog barked, answered immediately by the whinny of a horse in the stables. The streets were nearly empty. There had been no attack all day, and most of the legion had retired to their barracks to take advantage of the rare moment of calm.

As Lucius pondered the mystery of the silver, wondering

whether he would learn more before the Belgae broke through the walls and made the whole issue irrelevant, he caught sight of a cloaked man walking up the street. The man was alone, and moved with some degree of urgency, taking short quick steps, not the steady gait of a legionary. He crossed to a small brick and mortar shrine, where candles flickered amid an assortment of small wood and ivory figurines. The shrine held household idols of soldiers, placed there as a precaution should an enemy incendiary burn their barracks to the ground and destroy the precious carvings. Lucius assumed the man intended to add his own idols to the collection, but was surprised when he instead pushed back his hood and knelt to pray. Even in the dim lighting Lucius recognized the distinct oval head and tuft of hair. It was Diogenes, the master clerk from the armory. He prayed fervently, seemingly oblivious to Lucius standing in the shadows some thirty paces away. In contrast to his earlier bombastic manner, the clerk now appeared supplicant, almost repentant, mumbling some invocation of gratitude or entreaty to his deities. When he finally rose from his prayers, he seemed somewhat nervous, glancing up the street in either direction before donning his hood again and leaving the same way he had come.

It was almost as if he expected to be assailed at any moment. Lucius thought this odd – that is, until he saw two figures emerge from the shadows of a nearby building and begin following the clerk. They remained just far enough behind to go unnoticed. Both wore hooded cloaks. One was of large stature and had the deportment of a soldier, while the other was more slightly built. Lucius instantly concluded that the clerk was in imminent danger, and before he knew it, he was following, too.

There had been many nights in Gaul and Britannica during which Lucius's survival had depended on his

moving unseen past barbarians close enough to smell.
Thus, he had no trouble following without being seen or
heard. Diogenes walked quickly, never looking behind him,
and the two figures shadowed his every move. At one
point, the clerk abruptly turned off the main thoroughfare
and disappeared. Lucius surmised he had headed down a
dark alley between two barracks. It was, perhaps, the
shortest path to the armory, but a poor decision, all the
same, since such alleys were poorly lit and seldom
frequented. Seeing their opportunity, the two pursuers
quickened their pace, and soon disappeared around the
same corner. By the time Lucius reached the alley, there
were sounds of a scuffle in the darkness. Drawing his
sword, he dashed towards a cluster of shadows and came
upon the two cloaked men wrestling Diogenes to the
ground. The clerk seemed half-unconscious, presumably
knocked on the head, and put up a flimsy resistance as the
other two attempted to bind him. They were too busy with
their prey to notice Lucius's approach, and he would have
taken them completely unawares, had he not stepped into a
gap between two logs on the corduroyed path and tumbled
into the mud. By the time he regained his feet, the two had
turned to face him. The shorter of the two said something
in the Belgic Celtic tongue, a high-pitched voice that
sounded like that of a woman. The larger one complied
with this order, immediately. Leaving the clerk on the
ground, he produced a dagger that glimmered in the
moonlight and faced Lucius. Then, with the dagger raised,
he then rushed forward haphazardly, evidently not
anticipating the gladius Lucius held beneath the folds of his
cloak. At the last moment, Lucius flung back his cloak and
delivered a lightning quick stroke that clanged off his
attacker's wrist and sent the dagger twirling off into the
darkness. Had the man not been wearing some kind of

metal bracer, the hand would have flown off as well. Still, he clutched at his wrist as if the bone had been broken. The other one saw this and shouted something in frustration, again the high-pitched voice. He – or she – left the clerk where he lay, and both attackers fled the scene, turning the corner of the barracks into another dark alley. Lucius chased them only long enough to ensure they were gone, and then returned to the side of the disoriented clerk.

"Wh-What happened?" Diogenes said, blinking several times.

"You were waylaid," Lucius replied.

"Who are you?"

"Just a soldier, who hates an unfair fight."

"Please. Help me get to the armory. I'll be safe there."

"If these two men mean you harm, and I believe they do, that's the first place they'll look for you." Lucius saw an opportunity to clear up the mystery once and for all, and he took it. "You will come to my barracks. I'll have no arguments. Come get patched up and out of the cold, and you can return to the armory in the morning."

Even if he wanted to, the clerk was in no shape to argue. He simply nodded, allowed Lucius to help him to his feet, and then leaned on him as Lucius led him back to the barracks.

Once in the relative warmth of the tiny room and seated at the makeshift table with a thinly-laced cup of wine before him, Diogenes seemed to gather his senses, enough to study Lucius's face inquisitively.

"You were the one with Jovinus this afternoon," Diogenes finally said, his speech still unsteady. "I despise that man. Always making demands, like he's Agamemnon reborn." He took a long drink and then gestured to the legionaries snoring in the bunks around him. "I sincerely hope he is not one of these?"

"One of these?" Lucius said with a smile, refilling the clerk's cup. "No. These are just my tent mates. We're just common soldiers here. Jovinus sleeps in the centurion's quarters."

"Does he now?" Diogenes seemed disgusted by that. His unpleasant manner was returning along with his senses. "A man like that would never have made centurion in the Eighth Legion."

"The Eighth? I thought you were from the Fourteenth."

The clerk shot him a guarded glance. "I expect you know of my recent past then?"

"Only rumors really." Lucius shrugged. "I heard you were the only survivor of the Fourteenth."

Diogenes chuckled quietly, a humorless laugh, more apprehensive than sadistic. His eyes narrowed at Lucius. "Like the moans of a harlot, rumors are often specious. I would not be surprised if you heard such prattle from your friend Jovinus."

When Lucius did not reply, instead doing his best to appear innocently ignorant of matters above his station, the clerk's demeanor seemed to soften to the point of appearing somewhat embarrassed.

"I must apologize. I am forgetting myself. There is no telling what those two brutes would have done to me had you not come along when you did. What is your name, legionary?"

"Lucius Domitius."

"Well, Lucius. You saved my life, surely. I am grateful to you for that, and for your hospitality."

"Do you know who they are?"

Diogenes shook his head as he gazed into his cup. "No. Some miscreants of the camp, I suppose."

"They wore the garb of legionaries, but spoke in the Belgic tongue. They must have been from one of the auxiliary units."

"Very likely."

"Why would they assault you?"

"Who knows?" Diogenes shot Lucius a suspicious look, as if uncomfortable at the direction the conversation was taking, then added sardonically, "Perhaps, like your Jovinus, they do not approve of the way I run my shop." The clerk went back to his wine, and made no effort to expound on the subject.

Lucius sighed inwardly. He was getting nowhere. Refilling the clerk's cup again, he decided to try a different tack.

"It's a shame," Lucius said glumly.

"What?"

"That you were not at the massacre. I was hoping you might have news of some old mates of mine in the Fourteenth."

"I was there," Diogenes said bluntly. "I witnessed the whole dreadful affair."

"But you said the rumors were false."

"That I come from the Fourteenth Legion, yes." At the look of confusion on Lucius's face, Diogenes added, "The Fourteenth was not the only legion present. There were also five cohorts of the Eighth under General Cotta. I served Cotta."

"I would be most grateful, if you could tell me what happened."

Diogenes eyed him quizzically. "And why would you wish to know that?"

Lucius assumed a melancholy fashion. "Ever since I heard the news of the disaster, I have grieved for my old comrades. My thoughts fixate on their unknown fates, and I can scarcely think of anything else. I cannot sleep, which is why I was strolling the camp this night and was fortunate enough to happen upon you before those two made off with you. In any event, I expect I shall someday meet with the kin of my old mates, and I should like to impart the true story of how they met their end. Are they not entitled to at least that?"

"It is a long tale, one that I wish I could forget." Diogenes appeared somewhat annoyed at first, as if he were about to say something spiteful, but then, as Lucius watched, the clerk's petulant exterior melted away. Whether it was the effect of the drink, the ordeal in the alley, or the scars left by that tragic day, Diogenes lost all composure, sobbing with his face buried in his hands. It was a long, uncomfortable moment before he could speak again. "The gods saw fit to spare me, Lucius Domitius. I do not know why? Whatever the reason, I will carry this burden to the end of my days. To the end of my days! Do you understand?"

Lucius persisted, though in a more sympathetic tone. "I would consider your debt to me repaid in full, were you to tell me the whole story."

Like a man who had just been dragged behind a cart, Diogenes sat back in his chair, slumping, no resistance left in him. After another long drag on his cup, he finally sighed and nodded.

"Very well, Lucius Domitius. The whole story."

VI

Lucius poured another drink as he waited patiently for Diogenes to speak. The clerk gripped the cup firmly, like one mustering the courage to walk over a bed of hot coals bare-footed. After a long moment of silence, Diogenes stared at the flittering flame at the tip of the candle and began his tale.

"To tell you how the Fourteenth met its fate, I must first tell you how I came to be there. I am a freedman, born of slaves. I was sold into the army when I was but a lad and have served the legions ever since, in Gaul and many other places. Those over me saw little use for my slight build digging trenches, so I was relegated to the storekeeper's service, where I developed quite an astuteness with numbers, and a reputation to go with it. Years ago, in the campaign against the Helvetii, my path crossed that of

General Aurunculeius Cotta, who had learned of my meticulous skills and desired I bring his accounts back into order, which had been sorely neglected by his former bookkeeper. The assignment was only meant to be temporary, but it wasn't long before General Cotta came to rely on me. He eventually purchased my freedom, the gods bless him, and placed me under his employ, taking me with wherever he went." A rare sorrowful expression crossed his face. "General Cotta was a good man. I can say, without hesitation, that I have never served under a better man."

He paused, and appeared to steel himself mentally, before continuing. "As you already know, the Fourteenth made its winter camp nearly sixty miles east of here, deep in the country of the Eburones, as ordered by Caesar. General Sabinus, the legate of the Fourteenth, was in overall command, with my master, General Cotta, who commanded a supplemental force of five cohorts, serving as his second. My master's troops were intended to bolster the camp and to serve as a deterrent against any trouble from the local tribes. The camp was, after all, further east than any other Roman outpost, and thus the most susceptible to being cut off should the tribes rebel. But I can safely say, from my daily proximity to the generals, that no one expected any trouble, especially not after the warm reception we received upon entering Eburones land. The Eburones king himself, a man by the name of Ambiorix, met our column on the march, welcoming us with smiles and bringing with him cartloads of provisions. You have heard of him, by now, surely. He is the same Ambiorix who now leads the armies arrayed against these walls, but at that time he displayed nothing but a friendly and accommodating disposition. I saw him on many occasions. An impressive man. A leader more by intellect than brawn, one might guess from his demeanor. He was young, perhaps in his late twenties, with a head of long chestnut hair to match his beard. He wore a green patterned robe that looked as though it had just been woven the day before, and a bronze band around his temples. He was powerfully built, but wore no armor, carried no sword, and looked like he had just come from a matrimonial feast. He spoke Latin fluently, as if he had dwelt in Italy all his life, and proceeded to use his disarming smile and devil's tongue to charm his way into our generals' confidence, heaping accolades on both. He told them how overjoyed his people were to have the legion there, that its mere presence would dissuade the German raiders who often preyed on Eburones villages in the winter. Receiving these flatteries with a measure of caution, General Cotta advised General Sabinus to politely send the Eburones king on his way, but Sabinus would have none of it. Thrilled at having his ego stroked thus, Sabinus accepted everything Ambiorix told him as the truth and slowly lowered his guard. When the overly accommodating king suggested a site for our winter camp – a beautiful spot on a level field overlooking the Mosa, with easy access to the river for trade and communication – Sabinus embraced the idea, disregarding the protests of Cotta who eyed with prudence a nearby wooded hill that had complete command of the place. Sabinus chastised my general for being too cautious. After all, this same Ambiorix owed a debt to Caesar, did he not? The proconsul had graciously negotiated the release of several of the young king's kin, held hostage by a neighboring tribe. Ambiorix's considerate behavior was nothing more than a king fulfilling his obligations, a loyal vassal of Rome returning Caesar's generosity with kindness. Sabinus went so far as to invite Ambiorix to dine with him each night, casually sharing information about the disposition of the legions across Gaul to the point that

Cotta refused to attend. Finally, after observing the sighting of the camp and the initial construction of the ditches and palisades, the Eburones king finally took his leave of us, promising to deliver more provisions as the winter months progressed."

Diogenes pursed his lips in frustration. "We know now, of course, that Ambiorix was playing the charlatan, and intended our destruction all along. The gods curse the day he was born! Juno help me, he passed no more than an arm's length from me, on several occasions. I am no soldier, but I wish to Mars I had snatched up a weapon, any weapon, and run the snake through. So many would still be alive.

"I have often wondered why Ambiorix did not attack us before the fort went up, and have concluded that he was not ready to attack us then. Perhaps his army had not yet assembled. Indeed, I believe he was not yet ready to assault the camp when a happenstance, undoubtedly unforeseen by him, forced his true intentions into the light.

"A fortnight passed without event. The construction of the camp was nearing completion. Sabinus offered this period of tranquility as proof of Ambiorix's good will, but General Cotta's suspicions never abated. If anything, they increased in the days since the Eburones king had left. The countryside was too quiet, too devoid of travelers, for we had not been visited by a single merchant in all that time. Cotta continued to eye the wooded hill with suspicion, though several patrols there had turned up nothing. After much pleading, he managed to convince Sabinus to strip the hill bare, since it held such a prominent position over our northern wall and could provide cover for enemy engines. And it was when our work details began chopping down the trees that the Eburones suddenly attacked. A troop of barbarian cavalry came whooping out of the woods with spears leveled, riding down our men as they made a desperate dash for the fort.

"I believe now that our work detail took the enemy by surprise, that the enemy horsemen were only an advance party tasked with watching the fort, but when they saw the legionaries removing the forest they would need to hide their army, they panicked. In any event, Cotta was no fool. He was ready for them, and had century of Spanish horse in the saddle before the horns could stir the legion to arms. These burst from our gates at full gallop and sent the enemy horse fleeing back to the woods.

"Of course, every man in the fort was alarmed by this turn of events, not the least of which Sabinus, who, several hours later, gaped with astonishment when an enemy host no less than fifteen thousand strong appeared on the crests of the surrounding hills. The green banners of the Eburones fluttered distinctly over the helmeted heads of the enemy ranks, and all doubt as to Ambiorix's treachery vanished. Baffled and disheartened, as a man who woke to discover the sky above him was purple, not blue, Sabinus fell into a stupor, leaving it to Cotta to bolster the moral of the legion. Cotta assured everyone that no fifteen thousand Belgae alive could defeat a Roman legion entrenched behind the robust walls of a winter camp.

"Undoubtedly, Ambiorix had concluded this, too, and chose to pursue other methods. The devious king appeared at the head of a delegation, no longer in the dress of an emissary, but bedecked in full battle armor. Ambassadors were exchanged and Ambiorix immediately set about undermining the will of Sabinus. Claiming that his tribesmen were responsible for the attack, and that they had forced him to comply with their will, Ambiorix once again pretended to be Sabinus's friend. He stated that his people were mad to think they could take on the might of Rome, and that they themselves had been manipulated by other Gallic tribes who demanded that all tribes rise up and attack the Roman garrisons on this day. He understood the folly of sending poorly armed men against the well-defended Roman walls, but that an army of veteran German warriors had been paid to join the rebellion. The Germans had just crossed the Rhenus, and were but two days' march away. Once they arrived, he would not be able to restrain the belligerents among his warlords. They would force him to attack, and, though he would lose many warriors, the fort would certainly fall. In the interest of preventing such a tragedy, he offered safe passage to the nearest Roman camp if the legion would only quit the fort and depart Eburones lands. They would be allowed to march under arms and take with them every soldier, servant, slave, and pack animal. None would be molested in any way. Ambiorix vowed this upon his honor.

"It goes without saying that Cotta saw through this. He implored Sabinus to refuse, assuring him that the legion could hold out for weeks, even months, if necessary. Relief would surely come before the provisions ran out. But the conviction and vigor that guided the soul of Cotta were entirely absent in Sabinus. The timid general could do nothing but despair of all that might happen if the Germans were indeed coming. The heated debate lasted well into the night, but Cotta finally capitulated. What choice did he have? Orders were issued to the cohorts, and the legion spent the dark hours of the morning preparing to march. Though he vehemently opposed it, General Cotta played the part of the loyal lieutenant, overseeing the preparations as if the idea to abandon the fort had been his own. It was during those hasty preparations that he told me to...," Diogenes paused, a flash of apprehension crossing his face as if he were about to mention something he should not and caught himself just in time.

"Told you to what?" Lucius prompted, in an attempt to keep the clerk talking, for this was precisely what he had been probing for.

"Nothing," Diogenes said dismissively. "It is not important."

He took a sip of wine and then continued in a tone that was not quite convincing. "I was about to say that Cotta told me to remain close to him. I normally marched with the impedimenta, but he wanted me nearby, certain that we would meet with some mischief.

"We set off at first light, seven thousand men, carts, and animals, quietly marching in a long column that stretched two miles behind the eagle at its head. The enemy camp was clearly visible, with bands of spear-wielding warriors watching us curiously in the distance. But watch as they might, the Eburones exhibited no hostility towards us, and the consensus among the ranks was that Ambiorix had been true to his word. How wrong we were.

"Our path took us to a narrow valley, the same valley we had traversed weeks before when entering that country. The forest was thick on both sides, each side a sharp slope of bare sticks so dense you could have hidden an elephant at fifty paces. It was so infernally quiet, a silence that disturbed the soul, with no sounds but the gentle clink of armor and the tramp of legionary boots in the soft earth. Down the line, all chatter ceased, as if every man felt some looming threat. Fearing ambuscade, Cotta suggested deploying centuries to scout the flanks, but Sabinus would not have it. He believed such a disposition risked opening a skirmish with the enemy patrols, which might set off a general engagement, for not even Sabinus doubted the enemy was watching our every move. But such precautions were pointless when Ambiorix never intended to keep his word. The consequence of our general's ill-placed trust in the Eburones king was soon to manifest itself.

"The valley descended gently for more than a mile, such that when the head of our column reached the floor, the rear cohorts had yet to start their descent. As I said, I was at the head of the column, with Cotta, so I did not see the first missiles fly. The enemy assailed the rear of the column first, attacking the impedimenta from both sides and quickly throwing the cohorts there into disarray. The attack had been well-timed, perfectly executed, such that the cohorts at the front had to fight their way uphill to come to the aid of those at the rear. Many legionaries fell in this exertion. They faced a wall of spears and shields drawn up across the valley to bar their passage and divide the column. Several disjointed attempts were beaten back, some cohorts nearly annihilated in the process. The men looked to Sabinus to coordinate their efforts, for only a proper placement of the cohorts could break through the Belgic ranks, but the general was not up to the task. Even then, he believed the ambush was a misunderstanding, a mistake by Ambiorix's reckless warlords which the Eburones king would surely stop at any moment. Our soldiers began to despair. Some fled into the woods, and many more would have followed, had not General Cotta taken charge. He directed that the cohorts discard any notion of flanking the enemy line. Instead, he bad them punch through the center in an overwhelming rush of shields and gladii, and this tactic finally succeeded. The elation at this small victory, however, was short-lived. When we rejoined the rear of the column, we found that the cohorts there had suffered terribly. Half their number had been slain. The barbarians had lost many, too, but their attack only seemed to strengthen.

"Placing the eagle in the center, Cotta ordered every

man to compress into a great orbis about the eagle. This we did, though with much despair, since all knew it was the formation of last resort. With shields and pila facing outward on all sides, we withstood one attack after another, breaking wave after wave of the screaming devils until every blade was dressed with gore and the ground churned into a crimson mud. After countless failed attempts, the Belgae grew timid over their losses and finally drew back. We rejoiced at the reprieve, but it was only temporary. Originally expecting to assault our fort, the enemy had brought missiles in abundance, and these they began hurling into our compact mass. By sheer numbers alone, the deadly missiles found the gaps between our shields, and our men began to fall. It was near impossible to return the volleys. Any man rising from the protection of the shields was instantly spiked with a dozen feathered shafts. It seems impossible now when I think on it, but we stayed in that dismal formation well into the afternoon, suffering many casualties. One century, resolved to die fighting, broke formation and charged but were instantly surrounded by a storm of thrusting spear points and butchered to a man. This ill-fated foray left a gap in our ranks, and General Cotta, seeing the danger, pulled units from the opposite side to fill it." Diogenes paused, his face grave. His voice broke slightly when he continued. "It was while General Cotta was directing these dispositions that he fell, struck in the mouth by a stone that shattered the teeth from his skull. As he clutched his bloody mouth, I helped him retire to the protection of the raised shields, but then lost him in the tangle of men and shadows. The storm of missiles beat like hail above us. Men were dying all around me in that horrible space, and I felt certain one of the enemy arrows would eventually find me. But then, the enemy fire abruptly stopped.

"I heard the trumpet of a Belgic horn, and, like many others imperiled myself to look and see what was amiss. What I saw made me question my own sanity. Beyond the roof of spiny shields, at the edge of the orbis, General Sabinus and several of the officers were leaving the formation. They stepped out onto the field littered with corpses and assumed a dignified manner as they walked toward the trees. It was clear they intended discourse with the enemy. I thought this madness, and was relieved to see that Cotta was not in the delegation, though nearly every other officer above centurion rank was. Descending the wooded slope to meet them was an equal number of Belgic knights led by Ambiorix himself, conspicuous in his ornate war helmet the crest of which was shaped like a falcon's head and adorned with many feathers. Sabinus saluted the Eburones king in a most servile manner and began pleading for terms of surrender. In an amenable fashion, Ambiorix directed Sabinus and the officers with him to drop their swords, which they reluctantly did at Sabinus's prompting. Once again, that fool Sabinus had believed the Eburones king, and no doubt expected clemency. But, he was tragically mistaken. No sooner had the Belgic knights gathered up the fallen swords than a cry of elation erupted from the enemy ranks. Even from where I stood, I could see the confusion on Sabinus's face. Even then, he seemed to hold out some hope for mercy, and he did so right up to the moment that he and every one of his officers were slaughtered under the blades of the Belgic knights.

"All of this happening within clear sight of the legionaries, and it sent a wave of panic running through the formation. They were incapable of stopping the next charge. The Belgic warriors were emboldened and the legionaries exhausted. The cohorts came apart like dandelions in the wind. They broke and scattered, some choosing to fight, some fleeing in the direction of the fort, but most were run down and butchered like animals.

"In my own terror, I took up a fallen pilum and defended myself as best I could. I am no soldier, but I sent at least one of those barbarian bastards howling to the rear with a pierced thigh. With the battle lost, I saw no reason to die needlessly, so I decided to make my escape. I ran up the slope and into the woods as fast as I could, found a hollow beneath a fallen tree, and hid there under a blanket of mulch.

"I waited there for hours, barely allowing myself to breathe for fear of discovery, but I was never found. I clearly heard the battle raging below me, the cries of hundreds of men being butchered, the victorious howls of the enemy as they ransacked the dead. On one occasion a bloody legionary stumbled past me, not twenty paces away. I considered calling out to him when a band of Belgae suddenly appeared and ran him through with a dozen spears. I did not stir from my hiding place until the last glow of the setting sun had left the western sky. I could hear the bands of enemy warriors in the distance, could see the light of torches and bonfires through the trees, but encountered no one as I crept through the forest. I was faced with two choices, neither appealing. I could travel south to Labienus's winter camp, or I could come west to Cicero's. Both were an equal three-day journey, but I knew the forest stretched off to the west, while the way to the south descended to fields and valleys. There was certain to be enemy horsemen patrolling both paths come morning, so I chose the route with more cover. I was surprised the woods were so devoid of the enemy that night, but the reason for this became evident when my path took me to the summit of a hill from which I could look back and see the fort we had recently abandoned. It was far away, but I could see that fires raged within the walls, and the tiny fireflies of flaming missiles filled the sky above it. I realized that some of the legion must have fought their way back to the fort and were putting up a spirited defense. But it was clearly a lost cause. Soon, the whole fort was ablaze, with flames rising like the opening of a great portal to the realms of Hades. I knew that no man could have withstood those flames, and I was truly alone.

"I will not bore you with the tale of my journey to this camp, but it was not uneventful. Needless to say, by the grace of the gods, I reached the protection of these walls and made a full report to Cicero. The general received me with great generosity, and appointed me to fill a vacancy supervising the armory."

"And then the army of the Eburones arrived, close on your heels," Lucius said, as if to finish the tale for him.

Diogenes nodded dismally. "I've fallen out of the fire and into the flame. It is all in the hands of the fates now."

He tipped the cup back to finish the remnants of the wine, and a long silence presided between them.

"What of Cotta?" Lucius finally asked. "Did you see him fall?"

The same look of apprehension that had crossed the clerk's face before was suddenly there again. He appeared hesitant to respond, as if Lucius had just questioned his sister's virginity.

"Yes," Diogenes replied, in a manner suggesting he chose his words carefully. "I was near him when he died. He died like the great general he was, with the blood of a dozen Belgae on his sword."

Again, the clerk stopped, as if fearful of saying something he should not.

"Did he tell you anything?" Lucius pressed him.

"No! He said nothing!" Diogenes said, suddenly angry.

He scrutinized Lucius's face, as if to determine whether the question had been innocent or clever. But, after a moment of unease, he appeared to have decided on the former, and smiled amiably. "My apologies, Lucius Domitius. I meant no wrath toward you. You will understand if I am still a bit shaken by the whole ordeal."

Lucius nodded casually, as if unfazed by the outburst.

"And now, I really must be going," Diogenes said, rising abruptly. "Do not worry, I will be fine. I'm sure those ruffians, whoever they were, have found their fingers cold, as well as the trail, and have long since given up." He extended a hand, and gave the closest thing to a warm smile his harsh features could manage. "My thanks to you, again, Lucius Domitius. Should I ever see you again in the company of that scoundrel Jovinus, I shall not hold it against you. Fare thee well."

After the clerk had left, Lucius smiled and drained the remnants of his cup. For he had a fair notion about the silver now, where the clerk fit in, and why Honorius had such interest in him. The rumors shared among common soldiers were often light on truth and heavy on fantasy, but those threads of truth were useful at times. If Lucius's assumptions were correct, then that miserable bastard Diogenes was the most valuable item within these walls. Perhaps the enemy knew it, too. Certainly, the two men in the alley had known it, and would they not try again, when so much was at stake?

Reaching for his cloak and sword belt, Lucius ducked out the door into the cold night. He would shadow the clerk, just to be safe.

VII

No attack came that night.

As the light of dawn touched the field, it revealed three Belgic knights sitting astride their mounts and just beyond the range of the Roman artillery. One held a black standard, indicating their intentions. This was a delegation, and they wished to parley.

With earlier Belgic treachery fresh in their minds, Cicero and his senior officers were immovable. They sent out a single tribune on horseback to inform the three knights that any conference they wished to have would happen within the walls of the fort, and that only one ambassador would be given admittance.

In the time it took to convey this reply, the legion was turned out in full armor and arranged in ranks along the principal street running down the center of the fort. This was done to impress the ambassador of the Belgae, perception being nearly as important as reality in such situations, but also to ensure the enemy agent did not deviate from the path chosen for him. The praetoria gate was opened, allowing the single mounted knight holding the banner of truce to enter the fort. The knight glanced casually at the blank-faced legionaries lining the street on either side of him as he made his way to the plaza. There, he was met by four cohorts drawn up in perfect order, standards held high, painted shields removed from their leather covers. A pathway ran between the assembled troops, at the end of which sat Cicero and Honorius, mounted, bedecked in plumed helmets and flowing crimson cloaks, and flanked by their adjutants. Behind them stood the eagle of the Seventh Legion surrounded by a squad of decorated centurions in cross-plumed helmets.

Lucius was among the thousands standing at attention. His century was close enough to the front ranks that he could observe the Belgic knight clearly. The warrior wore a black cloak which was thrown back over one shoulder to reveal a shirt of polished mail armor beneath. His open-faced helmet was plain and devoid of ornament, apart from a large dent on one side. Braids of blue hair dyed with woad extended beneath his helmet to match his blue-dyed beard. He was unarmed, aside from a sheathed sword and the pikestaff holding the banner.

"You may stop there," Honorius said with little courtesy, and on that queue, five members of the general's bodyguard advanced with javelins raised to bar any further encroachment. "State your name and your business."

The warrior reined his horse to a halt and took a long look around him, at the walls, at the assembled legionaries. His eyes rested resentfully on the collection of armed Gauls standing in Cicero's retinue, no doubt viewing them all as traitors. As the knight's gaze moved around the assemblage, Lucius saw him pause, and his face soften, almost imperceptibly. The moment passed in the blink of an eye, the knight turning his attention elsewhere, but Lucius was curious. What could have captured the man's attention so? Lucius looked to where he judged the warrior had been gazing and was astonished to see the woman Erminhilt standing with her bodyguards in the front ranks of the command staff. Had the enemy warrior been looking at her? It had certainly not been a look of hatred.

Smiling confidently, the warrior finally raised a hand in salute. "Hail, Cicero, commander of the Seventh Legion," he spoke in Latin. "I come in the name of Ambiorix, king of the Eburones."

"It was my understanding that Cativolcus was king of the Eburones," Cicero said tersely. "This Ambiorix, you speak of, is a man without honor. He is not worthy of the title."

Cicero struck a much different appearance than when Lucius had seen him last. Undoubtedly at the prompting of Honorius, he had taken great care to appear every bit the confident Roman general. He even appeared to be sober.

"I stand here for my lord Ambiorix," the knight said firmly. "He commands the host before you."

"Host?" Cicero scoffed. "I see nothing but a band of brigands led by a liar — a liar who answered Caesar's good will with the poisonous fangs of a serpent."

The warrior continued to smile, but when he spoke again his tone was thick with scorn. "Perhaps General Cicero gazed over his walls yesterday. Perhaps he observed the two additional bands of brigands that joined forces with my king — the Nervii and the Aduatuci. Thirty thousand spears my king now commands, and many more are coming. Word of his victories spreads like the spokes of a thunderbolt. The Centrones, the Levaci, the Geiduni, the Pleumoxii, the Grudii – all are sending more warriors to join him. Soon, all of Gaul will rally to his banner. They call my lord Ambiorix – Savior of the Belgae, Savior of Gaul."

"They will soon curse his name, when they are forced to reap the harvest he has sown," Cicero replied contemptuously. "In any event, not all Belgic tribes have sworn allegiance to him. I have, within these very walls, many Belgic warriors who have wisely chosen to remain loyal to Rome. Your king, as you call him, is suffering from delusions."

The warrior smiled. "You have never met my lord, have you, General?"

"I have no desire to meet him, or to bandy words with you. Now, get on with your business, or be off."

"Very well," the warrior replied, no longer smiling. "I have been instructed by my lord to convey this. He does not wish this tragedy upon himself or his friends the Romans. He has been catapulted to greatness through little choice of his own, but when called to serve his people and the people of Gaul, his noble blood will answer as the gods intended. He does not bear any ill-will toward the Romans, but he must adhere to his people's demand, that no legions bivouac in Belgic lands. Your presence here is an affront to them, and to their gods. Sadly, the legion of Sabinus did not listen to his pleas, and were thus destroyed. And, just yesterday, the legion of Labienus, in the land of the Treveri, met its own tragic doom." The warrior paused to allow this statement to have its effect, and it did. An audible murmur moved through the assembled troops. It was common knowledge that Sabinus's legion had been massacred, but this was the first they had heard of the fate of Labienus, whose legion had its winter camp fifty miles to the south. With Labienus gone, the nearest legion was that of Fabius, in the land of the Morini, at least a week's march away. A harsh look from Cicero silenced the hum, and the Belgic knight continued. "The destruction of Labienus's legion was not the work of my king, but that of an army of German mercenaries, who come seeking nothing but blood and pillage. Those same mercenaries are heading here, now. They will arrive within two days. It is uncertain my king will be able to restrain them. Therefore, to avoid the bloodshed that will surely come should you continue in your obstinacy, he begs you to consider his terms."

"Terms?"

"My lord does not wish your destruction, only that you depart this country. Thus, he grants you safe passage to the land of the Aedui, or any country you wish, so long as it is not Belgic land. You may take with you all weapons, pack animals, and baggage. You may even put the fort to the flames when you leave, that my lord might not benefit from its use. He only desires that you do this before the sun sets on the morrow. These are most generous terms, are they not?"

"Given by an enemy under arms, and in the process of circumvallating our walls?" Cicero replied with a mirthless laugh.

"I warn you, General. If you refuse my king's benevolence, the alternative will be quite the opposite. No quarter will be given, not to any Roman." The knight glared at the Gallic nobles. "Nor to any who stands with them. Every man within these walls shall die under our blades. They will know unimaginable pain. They will be flayed alive and their skins used as flaps for our tents. Their severed heads will be piled in a great heap that all who see it may know what happens to invaders of our lands."

Cicero gave no response, but simply glanced at Honorius and nodded. At this prompting, Honorius spoke to the Belgic knight, his tone defiant. "Rome is not in the habit of negotiating with an enemy so disposed. Therefore, General Cicero makes your king a counter-offer. If you wish your lands to be barred from the legions, then lay down your arms and depart these grounds at once. The general will then happily convey Ambiorix, and any ambassadors he desires, to Caesar where he might plead his case through deliberation instead of blood, as might be expected of any civilized king. Do this before the sun sets this day, and General Cicero will be your lord's most fervent advocate before Caesar, for it is well known that the proconsul can be merciful when given the proper incentive. Do it not, and Ambiorix will find the general to be a most terrible antagonist. When your siege fails, and fail it will, the general will lay bare all your lord's transgressions before Caesar, in their plain, brutish form. No embellishment will be needed. Your lord is well acquainted with the proconsul, and surely must know how terrible his wrath can be when kindled. I leave it to you to reckon at the outcome."

The warrior eyed Honorius skeptically, and then Cicero, and then, for the briefest moment, once again, Lucius saw him glance at the woman. Was it Lucius's imagination, or did she nod ever so slightly, as if surreptitiously communicating something to this man?

"Shall I then tell my master, you answer no?" the Belgic knight said.

"I believe our response was clear enough," said Honorius.

"Very well." The knight raised his voice such that the ranks of legionaries could hear it clearly. "Be warned, General. You will receive no further propositions. When you see my lord again, it will be on your knees in supplication, with your entire legion lying slain around you."

"Be off!" Cicero shouted before Honorius could reply. "Before I send your master an answer of a different sort, but equally as clear."

Without another word, the warrior bowed his head slightly, wheeled his mount, and departed, the silence ominous as the hoofs of his horse clopped and echoed within the confines of the walls, diminishing as they passed through the gate, as if the last glimmers of hope faded with them.

The gates clanged shut, as if to seal all their fates, but before the cohorts were dismissed, Honorius faced them.

"Take heart!" He shouted, stirringly. "Be true sons of Rome and defend your posts with courage! Hope is not lost!" He then looked at Cicero. "The general wishes to share something with you all."

Wearing the same grim expression, Cicero walked his horse out to the center of the formations. He held a paper in one hand. "I am pleased to inform you, that I have received this message, thrown over the wall by one of our agents only last night."

You lying sack of mule dung, Lucius thought, recognizing the cut and color of the papyrus. *It wasn't last night. It was nearly a week ago.*

"It is addressed to the commander of the Seventh Legion," Cicero announced. "And it reads. *Do not surrender! Fight like true Romans! Expect succor.* And it is signed, *Gaius Julius Caesar, proconsul of the provinces of Cisalpine Gaul, Transalpine Gaul, and Illyricum.*"

The words were hardly out of his mouth before the crowd of legionaries erupted into a rousing cheer. It was welcome news to men who had received very little of late. Lucius detected the amendment to the letter, but it had served its purpose. The formations dissolved and streamed back to their barracks, nearly every face wearing a smile.

Before leaving the plaza, Lucius caught sight of Erminhilt across the crowded space. His eyes were naturally drawn to her feminine form, and his mind drifted wistfully to how she had looked in her purest form, lolling amongst the furs on the general's bed. Perhaps the odd glances by the enemy ambassador had been nothing more than that of a man admiring beauty. Still, there had seemed a familiarity between them.

Now, Erminhilt discoursed quietly with a large Belgic knight in mail wearing a white armband to signify he was an ally. It was quite normal for nobles from prominent families to be accompanied by bodyguards, and apparently Erminhilt was no exception.

"Ah, there you are, Legionary Domitius!" A voice broke Lucius from his thoughts, and he turned to see it was Honorius. The tribune still wore the polished cuirass and plumed helmet, but he was dismounted now and greeted Lucius with a welcoming smile. "I told you the general would come around, didn't I? What did you think? Quite the unexpected, eh?"

"Yes, sir."

Drawing a cautious expression, Honorius continued in a lower voice. "Incidentally, I made a few minor edits to the proconsul's message, to give it the proper effect, you understand. I would prefer no one was the wiser. You haven't told anyone about the message's true contents, have you? Not even your tent mates?"

"No, sir."

"Good!" The tribune appeared somewhat relieved. "It's for the best, you know. Best to keep their spirits up."

"Yes, sir."

Honorius then cast him a sidelong glance. "I was just on my way to talk to your centurion, Legionary Domitius."

"You were, sir?"

"Yes. The general requires a few soldiers – soldiers who can think as well as they fight – for a mission of the utmost importance. I believe you are the precise man for the task."

"Are you sure the general wants me, sir?" Lucius asked guardedly.

"I told you, the general holds no grudge against you. His tirade can be attributed to the drink, and those infernal herbs the wench keeps feeding him." Honorius regarded him encouragingly. "Have no fear, Lucius. The general still listens to me on some matters."

VIII

The Belgic knight trotted his horse across the icy field back to his own lines. Once past the earthworks, he tossed the banner away, the poised smile of complacency he had worn to dishearten the Romans now absent from his blue-bearded face.

Men toiled all around him, deepening the trench and raising the embankment, their frozen breaths rising from the dark earth like the steaming jets of a hot spring. The works stretched off in both directions, weaving through the woods in an imperfect yet imposing arc that would soon hem in the Roman garrison. With so many thousands working day and night, it would not take long.

As the knight weaved his horse through their construction, he marveled at the seemingly innumerable horde - surely, more warriors than he had ever seen

75

assembled in one place. But he had to remind himself it was not enough. The tens of thousands amassed here would never be able to hold back the might of the legions once word of the rebellion reached Caesar's ears. There were hardly enough to properly ring the Roman fort, let alone breach its walls, as it now appeared they must do.

A few of the warriors looked up from their labors to hail him, and he returned each salute with a raised fist and heartening grin. He must not let them see his own despondency. They must remain steadfast and confident.

The knight reined in his horse before a crude hut beneath leafless trees, where banners ornamented with the images of various creatures of earth and sky snapped in the stiff breeze. From the crossbars of several standards hung an assortment of severed heads, rotting and blackened, grisly trophies of the victory over Sabinus and his legion.

A crackling campfire struggled to survive in the wind, and around it stood three grim-faced nobles. They were older men, bedecked in ornamental woven cloaks, fine mail, and crowned helmets fashioned to look like the heads of lions, bears, and wolves. They did not greet the mounted warrior with the same unswerving adoration he had received from the rank and file. The age-lined brows of the three nobles regarded the knight with something between cynicism and contempt.

A band of younger, sword-wielding nobles stood nearby, not in a threatening manner. One of them was bare-headed and held out a helmet with both hands. It was a decorative helmet affixed with a bronze falcon head and topped with feathers. The man grinned widely at the knight's approach.

"Your head is too big, Lambert!" the knight said merrily as he dismounted. He removed the plain, dented helmet from his own head and handed it to Lambert. "I must borrow Judoc's next time."

"The Romans quiver with fear at my approach, my king," Lambert said deferentially, returning the ornate helmet for his own.

"You must have the smithy beat out that dent, my friend."

"I keep it, my king, to remind me of the time it stopped a German axe."

The man whom Lambert had called king laughed out loud. He did not bother donning the helmet, instead throwing it to the same servant who had taken the reins of his horse. He then exchanged the plain cloak on his back for one richly adorned with embroidery that had been draped over Lambert's arm. The king now looked much more like the three nobles by the fire.

"Greetings, my lords," he said heartily as he joined them, ignoring their scornful expressions.

"Need we ask, Ambiorix?" the oldest of the nobles said irreverently, after it became evident the newcomer intended to do little more than warm his hands. "Are we to assume your deliberations with the Romans produced nothing, that you have failed?"

"Not failed, Cativolcus," Ambiorix, King of the Eburones, replied without taking his eyes from the flames. "Our plans are simply delayed."

Cativolcus eyed Ambiorix with misgivings. Cativolcus was also king of the Eburones. Like the two consuls of Rome, he and his younger colleague shared a dual kingship. He had never enjoyed the idea of ruling side-by-side with this upstart, whose ambition knew no bounds and whose impetuousness he believed would someday lead the tribe to ruin, but he had little choice. Ambiorix told the warriors what they wanted to hear. He spoke of taking back their kingdom, of throwing off the yoke of Rome and pushing the Latins out of Gaul forever. This resonated not only with the knights, but also the farmers who did not relish yielding any of their harvest or their women to the invaders.

In the three years since the defeat of Boduognatus of the Nervii, the last Belgic chieftain to challenge Rome, Ambiorix's star had been on the rise. He had stirred the embers of revenge in the breast of every man shamed by that defeat, and had called the other tribes to join him. Now, like a boulder tipped over the crest of a hill, the revolt was gathering momentum, impossible to stop. Whether he agreed with it or not, Cativolcus had little choice but to throw his support behind the young king. There were times, before the attack on the Roman legion of Sabinus, when Cativolcus had considered attempting a flat-out coup, in the interest of saving his people from certain destruction. But, there were reasons he did not act – reasons for which he was ashamed.

While Ambiorix warmed his backside in silence, Cativolcus glanced at the other two nobles, chiefs of the Aduatuci and the Nervii, the leaders of the two ten thousand-man armies that had recently joined the siege. The irritated expressions on their faces told Cativolcus that they shared his exact thoughts.

Cativolcus spoke with forced politeness. "Perhaps, Ambiorix, you would consider sharing with our two brothers, here, and with me, the outcome of your dialog with Cicero."

The young king turned around to face the fire, warming his hands and staring into the flames as if in deep consideration. He had an arrogant air about him, as if Cativolcus's request could be addressed after he had finished his thought, when he was good and ready.

"They will keep to their walls, I think," Ambiorix said finally. "Cicero is not the fool Sabinus was. But it is of little consequence. Our works will be completed in a matter of days, and then they will be cut off from any aid."

"The Roman camps are well supplied." Fridwald, the chieftain of the Aduatuci spoke with a measure of aggravation in his tone. "They can hold out for weeks before they even begin to starve. By that time, other legions will arrive, and the balance will tip in their favor."

"Patience, my lord." Ambiorix sighed.

"Patience? My men did not endure a one hundred mile forced march through ice and mud only to dig ditches like some sordid Latin. They came to plant their spears in Roman bellies. You promised us a fight!"

"Our numbers are too few to carry their walls without great loss," Ambiorix replied. "Until more tribes arrive, we must content ourselves with a siege. Have no fear, the other tribes will come."

"Bah!" the chieftain spat. "Another of your empty promises. You told us the other tribes had assembled, and that ours were the only two yet to arrive, and that we must hurry to take a share of the glory and the spoils. In no way did you imply that we would comprise the bulk of your force." When Ambiorix did not respond, he added, "You also told us the fight against Sabinus's legion was an overwhelming victory."

"It was a great victory!" Ambiorix snapped, looking irritated for the first time since joining the group. "Nothing less than total and complete victory."

Fridwald shook his head incredulously and then turned to the old king. "Lord Cativolcus, do the Eburones no longer teach their children their numbers? I suggest you implore your young colleague here to learn his, before another such victory deprives you of the few warriors you have left. I count less than three thousand Eburones capable of standing in the shield wall. Where are the rest of your warriors, my lord? I'll tell you. They lie dead on the same field with Sabinus's legion. Victory indeed! You have but a paltry force left with which to take on the might of Rome!"

Cativolcus glanced grimly at Ambiorix, hoping he might say something to pacify Fridwald's concerns, but the young king acted as though he had not heard any of the tirade, as if he were busy considering greater matters. It was shameful to treat fellow chieftains so.

"You owe our brothers an explanation," Cativolcus prompted. "You owe me one as well. Against my better judgement, I allowed you to bring our people into conflict with the Romans. I allowed you to deceive and attack Sabinus, and now – Fridwald is right – half our army lies slain. An entire generation of Eburones warriors lost to destroy one Roman legion. Your actions were costly, and they have not produced the desired results. The Aduatuci and the Nervii have come here in good faith, at your request. Can you blame them now, if they cast a wary eye on your judgement?"

"Sacrifices must be made, my lords." Ambiorix glanced from Cativolcus to the other chieftains. "If we are to achieve what we all desire, then we must stop thinking of ourselves as Eburones, Nervii, Aduatuci, or any of the dozen other tribes of our race. We must consider ourselves Belgae, nothing more. You squabble over trifles, when so much more is within our grasp. We are the Belgae, blessed by the gods, the fiercest warriors these lands have ever seen. Combined, we are unstoppable. Can you not see this? Our losses were heavy, yes, but an entire Roman legion was destroyed. Such has not happened in living memory. News of this victory spreads throughout the land, and it will bring the other tribes here. You must have faith."

"It is difficult," Fridwald replied, "when he who appointed himself our leader tells half-truths."

"I do not lie!" Ambiorix snarled, looking at him with blazing eyes and placing one hand on the hilt of his sheathed sword. "You would do well not to say that again, my lord. I have welcomed you here with open arms, as my brother, but if you care to settle this the old way, we can. It is well-known, that I am your better at swordcraft,"

Fridwald stewed in silence, cutting a glance at the Nervii chieftain who appeared equally unnerved.

"The other tribes will come. You will see," Ambiorix said in a more amicable tone, ever aware that he needed these two chieftains and their twenty thousand warriors more than he needed to prove his dominance around this campfire. "They will come, as will our German allies."

"Allies?" Fridwald said with raised eyebrows. "Do you not mean mercenaries?"

"They come as our friends."

"I have never known the Germans to cross the Rhenus unless conquest and plunder awaited them. How do you propose to pay them? It will take more gold and silver than Cicero has within those walls."

"Leave the Germans to me, my lord," Ambiorix replied after a long pause. "You need only concern yourself with your own men. Encourage them to work faster. Whip the slackers if you must, but we must complete the siege wall quickly."

The Aduatuci chieftain appeared somewhat miffed by this attempt to divert the conversation and drew a sinister expression. "Word has reached me that your warriors recovered scarcely a single libra of gold or silver from the camp of Sabinus. Is this true?" He said it in a challenging fashion, as if to test the young king to see if he would try to wriggle his way free of this rumor.

"Yes. Very little was recovered." After a long pause, during which Fridwald brandished a smug look, Ambiorix continued. "As I said before, leave the Germans in my capable hands. Now, my lords, it has been a long morning, and I am tired. So, if you will excuse me, I will retire to my quarters for a while."

In the privacy of his hut, when he could finally enjoy a few moments free of the encumbrances of both his mail coat and the nagging tribal chieftains, Ambiorix sat on a stool and relaxed as best he could, though the weight of responsibility that rested solely upon his shoulders was still there. He sighed and caught sight of his helmet on the other side of the hut. It had been placed atop an armor crossbar by his servant such that it faced him, the empty eye sockets looking directly at him. They seemed to stare back at him accusingly, like the eyes of the dozen kings that had worn the helmet before him.

The chieftains were right. There were not enough men to fend off the might of Rome. Caesar would certainly attempt to muster his Gallic allies to his side, presenting Ambiorix's part in the revolt as the ultimate betrayal. While it was true, Caesar had called in favors to secure the release of several of Ambiorix's kin from a rival tribe, Ambiorix felt certain the Gauls would see it for what it really was. They would understand the complexity of the matter, that those freed hostages, while family, were the troublemakers of his house, and he had not wanted them back. They were his unrequited kinsmen – the would-be usurpers that plagued every ruler, imbued with a dangerous combination of noble blood, cleverness, and ambition. Indeed, in the year since the hostages' release, he had already been forced to arrange the murder of two of them. They were much more of a headache as free men, and Ambiorix suspected Caesar well knew it. The cunning proconsul had pretended to be so magnanimous, interceding with great fanfare between the two tribes, when, in reality, the move had been nothing more than a political power play, a means of disrupting a kingdom he knew would be trouble for him someday.

Once word reached Caesar that the tribes had rebelled, he would muster his scattered legions into a massive army that would sweep through the land, just as he had three years ago, when the Belgic army under Boduognatus was defeated. Boduognatus had mustered far greater numbers and, still, he had not been able to stop Caesar. The nobility of Belgica and most of the warrior class had been killed in that great battle.

The Eburones had not participated in that alliance, and perhaps the shame of their absence is why they had fought with such valor against Sabinus's legion. Although Ambiorix would never admit it before Fridwald and the others, the fight against Sabinus had been a close-run thing. The legion had been caught stretched out over a two-mile forest path, perfect for the plucking, yet the Romans had still fought with fierceness and remarkable order. He had lost far more men than expected, and the number of dead would have been even higher had the few hundred Romans who had managed to fight their way back to the fort held out longer. By the grace of the Odin, they had committed suicide to a man, evidently convinced that they faced a much larger army.

Yes, he had defeated an entire Roman legion. It was a stirring victory, a landmark moment in Belgic history, and would surely populate the war songs for generations to come, but those songs would mention nothing about the thousands of Eburones that lie slain upon the field, nor that the enemy had been taken on disadvantageous ground marching under a flag of truce, nor that the enemy commander had been a gullible fool.

This time, it would not be so easy. Cicero would never

put himself at a disadvantage as Sabinus had. He would stay behind his walls and defend to the last man. And those legionaries were formidable, if the perfectly dressed ranks and stolid expressions he had just observed were any indication of their resolve. Cicero had not flinched, even when he had told him the lie about Labienus's legion, sixty miles to the south. While it was true that legion had been attacked by the allies of the Eburones, the Treveri, it was not true that they had been defeated. Just as Cicero had done here, Labienus had pulled his legion inside the walls of his winter camp, and were defending it just as vigorously. Ambiorix had also lied about the Germans. They were not two days' march away, nor had they even crossed the Rhenus.

The revolt was in danger of losing its momentum. He was in a race against time. Ultimate victory depended on him mustering enough tribes to overwhelm whatever Caesar eventually threw at him, and the tribes would not come without more victories. He must score another to keep the revolt alive. He must either breach Cicero's walls or crush him in open battle.

Ambiorix sighed heavily. He had shown bravado in front of the chieftains, but he was not sure the thirty thousand inexperienced warriors he now led were up to the task. He needed the Germans. The Germans were the key. They were the counter-weight that would tip the balance in his favor. They were why he would succeed where Boduognatus had failed. Where Boduognatus had led an army of warrior-farmers, he would lead an army of screaming, warmongering Germans, who lived for battle, and who were unstoppable once they had a taste of Roman blood and plunder. With the Germans supplementing his force, he would easily overcome Cicero, and then take his army south to help the Treveri destroy Labienus. Once he had the eagles of three legions under his belt, he would not have to worry about Caesar. All of Gaul would rise to serve under his banner. His army would number in the hundreds of thousands. If the Roman Senate had any sense, they would intervene and sue for peace. The tyrant Caesar would be shipped back to Rome, where he would meet the fate of a failure and a criminal.

But none of that would happen if the German army did not cross the Rhenus, and they would not cross the Rhenus unless he paid their chieftain, a scroungy barbarian by the name of Raganhar, a hefty sum in gold and silver. Ambiorix had hoped to find that sum of money in the camp of Sabinus. It was one of the reasons he had chosen to attack Sabinus's legion first. His own spies had reported a great quantity of it, the winter payment, due to be distributed to the legionaries. It amounted to roughly 50 denarii per soldier, or, in other words, enough silver to get Raganhar's hairy arse across the river. But, the fates had played their devilish tricks once again. The money had not been found.

The spies were executed, of course, as traitors and liars. But, after his wrath had abated, Ambiorix had convinced himself that the money had to be there. Perhaps Sabinus had been cleverer than he had given him credit for. Perhaps it was hidden somewhere, and he needed only to rake the area in search of it. Such a search would require an army, and his was otherwise disposed at the moment.

Ambiorix mused about his moments in the Roman fort, seeing Erminhilt's enchanting face in the crowd, and the small smile that had formed on her lips when their eyes had met.

There were other possibilities, other pokers in the fire. Perhaps the fortune in Roman silver was not lost after all.

He heard the flap over the doorway open behind him and turned to see Cativolcus duck inside. Behind the old king's yellow-white eyebrows and beard, was a diffident expression, as if he dreaded coming here, but was compelled to.

"Did you see her?" Cativolcus finally asked. The question had obviously been on the old king's lips since the moment Ambiorix had returned from the fort, but he had waited until now, when the other chieftains were not around, to ask it.

"Yes. I saw her."

"Was she…was she…?"

"She was well," Ambiorix said brusquely. "I have no reason to believe anything has changed since her last message reached us."

"Then perhaps, there is a chance," the old king said tiredly. "But at what a cost? You demand such a thing from an innocent child, the poor child with her precious emerald eyes."

"She is no child, my lord," Ambiorix eyed him. "And she is not as delicate as you like to believe."

For an instant, Cativolcus's eyes flashed anger, but he quickly regained his even bearing. "I advise you to be cautious, Ambiorix. I have not changed my mind. I still disapprove of your actions against the Romans. I have allowed you to lead our people down this path, because –"

"Because you have little choice!" Ambiorix interjected.

Cativolcus gave an unfeeling smile. "Do you remember the story of the eagle who flew too high? He rose higher and higher, gaining more confidence with each sweep of his powerful wings, until the gods, angered by his arrogance, withdrew the wind. The brazen eagle fell from the sky. Only then, as he tumbled helplessly to his fate, did he realize he had overestimated his own abilities. He had not given proper credit to the wind, without which he could not fly at all."

"Did you come here to tell me children's stories, old man?"

"No. Only this. You pursue that which cannot be obtained. While it is true, you have gained renown for your victory over the Romans, it is a fleeting fame. You see an old man before you, but when I was your age, it was I who led our people into battle, and I have seen more slaughter than you could ever imagine. We always knew the Romans would come. The great city beyond the great mountains was just a whisper in the wind when I was but a youth. Now, it is a great voice that cannot be drowned out. I see the Roman boot encroaching on our land, the Roman merchants extorting our craftsmen and farmers, our resources. They have come, and we cannot send them back."

"Says the meek and the impotent!" Ambiorix sneered.

"It is the inevitable way of things. Old traditions must change or die. The tree must bend in the wind, or be uprooted and swept away entirely." Cativolcus then looked at him searchingly. "Listen to me, Ambiorix. I care nothing for my own fate. You know this. But I do care for Erminhilt, and I can only hope that you do, too. I tell you, you are leading her on a path that can only end in pain and sorrow. If not for me, if not for our people, if only for her sake, stop this madness. Send ambassadors of peace to Caesar. Tell him the exiled warlords were responsible. Tell him the other tribes started it. Give him any excuse you can think of, but make peace now, while there is still time."

"We are the Belgae!" Ambiorix replied firmly. "We bow to no one. In a hundred generations, we have never bent our knee to an invader. Not the Britons! Not the Germans! Not the Latins! And I vow to purge every one of those skirted whelps from Gaul. Those we capture, will be sent back to Rome as a mob of castrated, blinded ghouls, so hideous to look upon, their countrymen will never encroach on our lands again." The young king faced Cativolcus and narrowed his eyes. "And if I hear of you making such talk among the warriors, among the nobles, among the other chieftains, I will personally see that your wrinkled skin is stretched and made into a grip for my sword."

Cativolcus said nothing. He simply gazed upon Ambiorix despondently, as one might watch the house he had built with his own two hands go up in flames. Eventually, the old king left, and Ambiorix once again was alone, staring into the hollow, accusing eyes of the helmet of kings.

IX

The forest was too quiet for Lucius's liking. The chill wind rustling through the bare boughs above him, and the incessant rattling of a red-crowned woodpecker did little to assuage his unease. The others felt it, too.

"I don't like it, Lucius," Honorius said, squinting beneath his helmet as he stared out into the snowy wood ahead, thick enough that one could not view fifty paces in one direction.

Lucius knelt beside Honorius, both concealing themselves behind a large tree, both wearing full armor and cloaks. Behind them, the seven men of Lucius's squad were spread out at wide intervals, also using trees for cover, waiting for the signal to resume the march.

"How long have they been gone now?" Honorius asked.

"I'd say half an hour, sir."

Lucius saw that the tribune was unconsciously fingering the hilt of his sheathed sword, and Lucius fully understood why. The squad had left the protection of the walls in the dark hours of the morning and had spent several terrifying hours passing through the enemy lines, through the mile-wide gap not yet enclosed by the wall of circumvallation. Though devoid of siege works, this gap was, however, filled with enemy campfires and sentries, and skirting around these had been a hair-raising experience, to say the least. The gray dawn had found them trudging through a blanket of snow undisturbed by man or beast. They moved quickly, having left their trenching tools and standard cooking utensils behind, and, before the full light of day, they had opened the distance to the enemy camp considerably. The forest in the winter often seemed like a barren, lifeless landscape, devoid of leaf or green, but the silence had been unusual and forbidding, as if they walked through a sacred grotto of the druids. Every crunch of their boots had seemed to reverberate off the trees like clanging bells.

Now, as they waited for their companions, it felt quieter still.

"Perhaps they have encountered the enemy?" Diogenes said impatiently, shivering within his cloak, as he came up behind Lucius and Honorius.

"Conversing with them, more likely," Honorius said bitingly. "I trust that Gallic whore no more than I do Hannibal's ghost." He glanced up at the clerk impatiently. "You must get down, Diogenes. There are enemy patrols about. How you ever managed to survive three days in the forest alone is beyond me."

The clerk looked somewhat put out but then hunkered behind the same tree.

"I told the general bringing the woman along was a

risk," Honorius vented to Lucius. "But he insisted we bring her at the last moment. He is too swayed by the tits of that Gallic whore, the fool." The tribune smiled at the expression on Lucius's face, for it was uncommon for a senior officer to speak thus of a legate in front of a common soldier. "You should not have to hear this, Lucius. I am sorry. It's just that this mission is of the utmost importance, and I believe our good general has jeopardized its success."

"It's alright with me, sir."

It was alright with Lucius because he did not know what the mission was, where they were going, or why. Early on the previous evening, when Lucius had accompanied Honorius to the praetorium, he had been directed to assemble his squad at the decumana gate at the changing of the watch, fully armed and carrying only one week's rations. Honorius had informed him that he needed only one squad as an escort and that the small numbers would have the best chance of slipping through the enemy lines. Jovinus had been displeased to be losing eight of his best men.

"What in Pluto's name is this, Lucius?" he had said, as he looked over the ambiguous orders. "This have something to do with that damned message?"

"I do not know."

"I'll wager you're going to contact Caesar." Jovinus then had added jovially. "If I'm right, you tell that bastard of a proconsul to march at the double-quick. We cannot hold out here forever." He had extended a hand and grinned. "Mars protect you, comrade."

Lucius had concluded the same thing, for where else would they be going. But in the dark hours of the morning, when he had quietly assembled his squad at the gate, and saw that Diogenes was coming along, his thoughts immediately returned to the silver. The master clerk had not been the only unexpected addition to the party. The general's woman, Erminhilt and her large bodyguard were there, too. Fuming, Honorius had informed Lucius that Cicero had given new instructions. The woman and her guard were to accompany the squad as guides. The general was convinced their knowledge of the local surroundings would be invaluable.

Now, as he and Honorius crouched in the woods miles away from the fort, Lucius still did not know where they were going, but he did have some theories, which he would keep to himself, just as he would keep his earlier acquaintance with Diogenes to himself, a decision the clerk seemed to agree with, the two only acknowledging each other with formal courtesies.

Honorius continued to fidget as the squad waited for the woman and her guard to return. They had, supposedly, gone ahead to find the path.

"Cicero ignores my counsel, as if this were my first bloody campaign. You'd think that woman was the queen of the Amazons The way he listens to her. I don't care whose daughter she is, I don't bloody trust her!"

"Whose daughter is she, sir?"

"Oh, some insignificant chieftain who claims to be Caesar's ally. This Erminhilt is very likely his least significant daughter. No doubt, he sent her to Cicero as an insurance should the revolt fail."

"If she's the least significant," Lucius said vivaciously, "I'd like to see what his other daughters look like."

"That is one she-wolf you do not wish to suckle, believe you me." Honorius then looked at Lucius and smiled. "But you do not lie, Lucius. I have some sympathy for the general. The old man has reached his unpleasant years, and he's not much to look at. When a young, vibrant woman like Erminhilt tells him what he wants to hear – does what he wants her to do – who can blame him?"

"Maybe his wife, sir?"

"Ever been captivated by a woman, Lucius? A woman that was no good for you?"

"A few times, sir."

"If Quintus Cicero has one weakness, it is the allure of exotic young females. The more exotic the better. There have been many such women in the general's life, and, every time they have led him to folly. Whether to gain a favor, money, or some other motive, eventually, the seductress's true intentions are exposed, and he falls into a brooding anger. He is unapproachable at such times. Try to warn him about a woman's affections, and he will come at you with the vehemence of a lion in the arena. Is it, perhaps, the reason he never attained the eminence of his brother."

"You've been with the general long then, sir?"

"Longer than I care to remember," Honorius replied emptily. "You have probably guessed, I am not his greatest admirer, but I am a devoted friend of the general's brother, Marcus Tullius. I accompanied Quintus to Gaul at Marcus's bidding, to ensure Quintus did not embarrass himself – and the family."

"So, the general's brother sent you to wet-nurse him, eh, sir?"

Honorius chuckled. "I suppose that's one way of looking at it. I know it is difficult to imagine, but our good general was once propraetor of Asia. It was not the most successful posting. There were…troubles, to put it mildly."

"Troubles, sir?"

Honorius gave an embittered smile. "They say the soul is the master, Lucius, the body the slate. I would it was so with our general. Let's just say that, due to a few ill-advised and ill-fated affairs with noble women of the east, he quickly developed a reputation for heavy-handedness. He dealt with the locals most severely. A quick temper and a liberal use of the lash were his methods of maintaining order – or his perception of it, anyway. Sometimes he resorted to harsher punishments. It has been said that he nearly provoked the province to rebellion. Several of the leading nobles and merchants petitioned his brother back in Rome to do something about his brother before it was too late, and my gracious friend, Marcus, did just that. A brother often has influence where others cannot, and so it is with Marcus over Quintus. Quintus does not hold many in esteem, but he does admire Marcus, even idolizes him. Marcus has a way with words, you know, both written and spoken, and seems to know how to restrain his brother. Unfortunately, he cannot accompany his brother everywhere he goes. He certainly could not come to Gaul, so he sent me in his place, to keep Quintus in line. Gently, of course." Honorius's face scrunched beneath his helmet as he observed the blank expression on Lucius's face. "You do know who the general's brother is, do you not?"

Lucius shook his head.

"Have you not heard of Senator Marcus Tullius Cicero, the great orator, writer, and statesman, the former consul, the great man who saved our republic from the Catiline debacle?" Honorius looked at him in astonishment.

"I'm just a soldier, sir. I march where I'm told to march, fight who I'm told to fight. I don't know much about what goes on in Rome. Don't care to. I've never even been there."

"But I detect some refinement in your Latin," Honorius eyed him curiously. "Surely, there is more to Legionary Lucius Domitius than boots, javelin and shield."

"Not much more, sir." Lucius shrugged. "I come from Spain. There were times, in my youth, when I fought the scraggliest street dog for a few scraps of bread, and then times when I lived more comfortably than most in the province. In the fairer times, my father made sure I got a proper education, with a Greek tutor who made me read my letters and count my numbers every day. My father never wanted me to have to march in the legions as he did. He wished me to become the proper son of an eques – and I would have been, too, had my family not met with tragedy."

"Tragedy?"

Lucius paused before saying succinctly. "They died, sir. After that, there wasn't much left for me in Spain. I joined the Seventh, and have been marching with the legions ever since." Realizing he had already said too much about his past, Lucius decided to withhold the whole facts – that his family was murdered, that the man responsible for their deaths was now a member of the Roman senate, and that the devious senator had already tried to have Lucius killed here in Gaul. Nor did Lucius mention that he would not rest until he buried his gladius deep within the two-faced senator's gullet, just after cutting out the bastard's lying tongue. It was improbable that Honorius, whom Lucius judged to be of good character, would socialize with the likes of Senator Marcus Valens, but Lucius had run across a tribune before who later turned out to be an ally of his nemesis.

"I am sorry for your loss, Lucius," Honorius said, apparently detecting that Lucius did not wish to discuss it further. "But I am glad you are here. Marcus has often said a man of courage is a man of faith. You are a man of courage. Soldiers like you make victories happen. We need soldiers like you, and these good men of yours." He gestured to other legionaries behind them. "Good, loyal soldiers. Soldiers with a sense of honor."

Lucius laughed inwardly but maintained a respectful outward nature. Leave it to an officer, who had never slept a wink in the common legionaries' barracks, who had never dug a latrine, planted a palisade, or carried a forty-pound kit on the march, or stood in the front of the battle line with spear points as thick as brambles and the ground soaked with blood and entrails. Lucius liked Honorius, but he was like most equites, who applied their own reasons for being a soldier to their men, perhaps realizing but not fully comprehending that they were from two separate worlds. If this noble fool could guess what truly motivated the men who made up this squad, he might swallow his garum.

Of course, Lucius knew them. He knew them like he knew his own shadow. A few of them, he had known for years. They had seen officers come and go, and together they had endured brutal campaigns. From the warm plains of Spain, to the frozen forests of Germania, to the hill forts of Britannia across the angry northern sea, they had marched together. As their decanus, his life depended on knowing their every strength and weakness. There were many words he might use to describe the men in his squad, but good and honorable were not among them. That the civilized and pampered may dwell in blissful ignorance, harsh men must face their enemies. These were harsh men, oftentimes callous and cruel, but Lucius would rather have them by his side in a fight than a hundred Ciceros.

There was Geta the one-eyed, an ox of a man, and one of the few in the legion taller than Lucius. Geta lost his right eye not in battle but in a tavern brawl. The loss of the eye had done little to handicap him in battle. If anything, it made him more intimidating. The strip of leather covering the empty socket, along with a rough scar running from forehead to jaw, made him look sinister, like something infernal. Lucius himself was enormously strong, but Geta was built like a brick fortress had beaten Lucius every time when wagers from their other tent mates set them to arm-wrestling. In battle, Geta was like an immovable rock embroiled in the rushing surf, and had been known to stop the press of an advancing shield wall.

There was Maximus, the son of a fisherman of Carthago Nova. A solid warrior in the battle line, and one who believed the gods had ordained him indestructible, so long as he served Rome. He followed every command of the officers like they were mandates from the deities, and the precision and speed of his jab had no equal in the century. His weakness manifested itself when the battle was over, when he descended on the spoils like a half-starved carrion. As much as he was devoted to the gods, he was more so to his father back in Spain, who bad him keep nothing for himself and send it all home to help his alleged starving family. Maximus obeyed this order faithfully, as if it had come from Caesar himself. He always gathered a more than ample share of the spoils, sometimes even before the battle was won. Any slaves or booty were immediately sold in the markets of the camp followers, and the money placed on the first caravan back to Spain. His father always wrote back to him after each delivery, providing a detailed accounting of every last sesterces, to make certain the traders had not made off with any of it. Boasting that he took his own plunder with a clear mind, since the entire balance went to a noble cause, the devoted legionary often scoffed at others for keeping theirs. Several in the legion who came from the same village and knew Maximus's father to be a lazy cheat, sniggered that the father was likely spending every denarius his son sent him frivolously, and that someday Maximus would return to find his father a drunk and buried under a mountain of debt. Such rumors had certainly reached Maximus's ears, but they did not dissuade him. Lucius had seen the dedicated legionary pry a gold tooth from a dead Britain's mouth and then consider taking the real teeth as well, knowing they could fetch something from the right trader.

And then there was Sergius, a wiry legionary and the comedian of the squad, always wearing a grin that bespoke of some hidden jest, as if he had just bedded the legate's daughter, and no forced march or punishment could stop him from laughing about it. Sergius did not have a family, at least none that Lucius knew of. He had joined the army more out of curiosity than anything else, and had soon discovered that he was a natural soldier. He was extremely agile, could duck or sidestep nearly any sword stroke, and ran with almost supernatural swiftness. Like Lucius, he was deadly accurate with the javelin, and could put a pilum through the eye of an axe-head at twenty paces.

The other four legionaries in the squad were newer men, but Lucius had marched with them long enough to know their mettle. They were perhaps not as reliable as the veterans, but they would obey his word with little prodding, and hold their own in a fight.

"I think I see them!" Diogenes pointed ahead. "I saw movement. Over there!"

"Keep your voice down!" Honorius scolded. "The enemy works are not yet five miles behind us."

The crunch of footfalls in the snow became clearly audible above the echoing hammer of the woodpecker. They grew louder, until Erminhilt finally emerged from the trees to their front, followed by the long-bearded guardsman.

"We have found the path," the woman announced neutrally, her Latin heavily accented. "It has not been travelled in some time, but that does not mean the enemy are not nearby. We must hurry."

Honorius looked at her disapprovingly. "Where in Juno's name were you all this time? Had I known you and your brute would be gone for nearly an hour, I would have insisted on accompanying you."

"That would have been unwise," she said dismissively. "Belfric and I know how to move unheard and unseen. You Romans tread heavily, like so many bulls in a potter's barn."

"You have not answered my question." Honorius demanded.

"Do you doubt me, Roman?" she said challengingly, then looked amused. "Remember, Roman, this is our country. Belfric knows it like the curve of his wife's hips. He is a skilled pathfinder. He can find a trail after the deepest snow, but even he cannot perform miracles. Do you wish your dirty Roman boots to muddle his search?"

She smiled at the large, grim-faced, blonde-bearded guard who wore a conical helmet, a long sword sheathed at his waist, and a large round shield slung across his back. The warrior acknowledged her with a single nod.

In the hours since they had left the fort, Lucius had seldom heard Belfric speak, and when the knight did manage to utter something, it was only to Erminhilt, and only in the Belgic tongue. Both wore the deerskin cloaks common among their kind, but Lucius could not help pondering how they might appear wearing the cloaks of legionaries in a dark alley in the dead of night.

"I wish to be on our way," Honorius said to Erminhilt. "Enough of these delays! From this point onward, we stay together. Is that understood?"

Erminhilt looked at him harshly. "A typical Roman. You see an enemy where there is only a friend. We are loyal, tribune. If I meant you harm, you would already be in the hands of Ambiorix. But, have it as you wish. It will only take us longer to traverse these perilous woods. There is a secluded vale a little more than ten miles from here. We should rest there tonight. Tomorrow's march will be even farther."

Honorius nodded. "Your man Belfric will lead, but you will remain in the center with me." He then added sardonically. "I would not wish for anything to happen to such a devoted ally of Rome." Her eyes narrowed at this, but Honorius ignored the resentful look. "Lucius, take two men and stay close to Belfric. Never let him out of your sight. The rest of us will follow you."

"Aye, sir," Lucius said. "Maximus! Sergius! With me. The rest of you, keep wide intervals and stay sharp."

As Lucius drew near to Belfric, the Belgic warrior gave him a patronizing glance as a master regards a slave. It was clear from the quality of Belfric's weapons and armor that he was no common household warrior. He was a most likely a noble who had lands in his own right. Belfric shot a pitiable glance at the gladius hanging from Lucius's belt, and his eyes filled with amusement, as if the short sword were a mere child's toy. Lucius had known many a Gaul to eye the Spanish sword with the same apathy, often only moments before it disemboweled or castrated them. Where Belfric's heavy long sword was made to smash into shields and helmets, the leaf-shaped, twenty-five-inch gladius was made for rapid thrusts and pin point precision, to strike at the narrow gaps between shields and under armor.

Smiling back at the arrogant Belgic knight, Lucius gestured for him to lead the way.

X

The squad made camp that night in a secluded depression where their fire would be hidden from distant eyes. Their guides had led them east, deeper into Belgic lands, and in the exact opposite direction from that which Caesar or any legions coming to the Seventh's aid might approach. But Honorius did not seem alarmed by this, and put off Lucius every time he questioned him about it.

"We are indeed travelling in the right direction, Lucius," the tribune had said. "I'm afraid I cannot share any more with you. Rest assured, I am keeping a wary eye on our guides. If I have the notion they are leading us astray, I will let you know."

Lucius had not pressed the matter. He was, after all, just a soldier, and was expected to follow orders without question or hesitation. Clearly, Diogenes knew the destination, too, and Lucius thought the clerk might feel compelled to share it with him, given their recent past. But all Lucius's attempts at conversation were met with a stone wall. Not only did the clerk treat Lucius as though he had just made his acquaintance, he was downright discourteous, any vestiges of gratitude for saving his life all but vanished.

As if this were not insulting enough, Erminhilt and her guardsman seemed wise to the destination as well, leaving Lucius and his men the only ones in the dark. The frustration of this was only slightly tempered by the many clues Lucius had managed to accumulate within his head. He had, he believed, pieced together enough to generally deduce where they were going, and the mission's ultimate objective. The details, however, remained vague.

Now, as the squad sat around the fire supping on a few scraps of hard bread, Lucius noticed Erminhilt conversing with Honorius and Diogenes. The three sat together reviewing a map by the light of the fire. Lucius was too far away to hear what they discussed, tomorrow's march perhaps. On several occasions, Erminhilt appeared to petition the tribune over some matter on which he was not inclined to bend. She spoke in a pleasant, almost playful manner, as if to break through Honorius's misgivings with her natural charm, but it was clear she was getting nowhere. The tribune was unflappable, all business. The clerk, on the other hand, seemed completely enamored with her, though her appeals were not directed at him.

Lucius, too, found himself captivated by Erminhilt's assertive, yet lovely, manner. She spoke to Honorius as a peer, indifferent to his military rank. It brought to mind a time when he encountered a troop of auxiliary archers from Bithynia comprised entirely of women. Perhaps Erminhilt was of a similar warrior cast, though she was attractive, unlike those uncomely Bithynian huntresses, many of whom could have passed for men in most armies. Erminhilt was woman in its finest form. Her waist-length, black hair was coiled in an intricate braid adorned with a scattering of tiny rubies, but not too many to be extravagant. The tattoos accentuating her pale skin and perfect features somehow made her more fascinating. The markings had meaning to her people, no doubt, but were indecipherable to Lucius. He found her strangely appealing, almost hypnotic. Perhaps it was this harsh land so devoid of warmth, in which any glimmer of beauty could shine like the sun, or perhaps it was simply that he had not seen a Latin woman in many months. In either event, he wondered if he himself would be as strong as Honorius were he under the gaze of those alluring eyes.

Eventually, the meeting ended. Erminhilt appeared somewhat disappointed as she rose and retired to the shelter her guardsman had prepared for her. Whatever she had wanted from the tribune, she had apparently not obtained. Honorius continued to study the map in silence, late into the night, sipping from his wineskin, clearly deep in thought. The tribune was still there when Lucius himself finally bedded down.

Nights spent in the severe cold often consisting of a series of painful naps, the intervals between which one struggled to get warm enough to fall back to sleep. Lucius had only just managed to drift off when he was abruptly awakened by a gargling sound. He bolted upright, his breath fogging the night air, and saw a figure writhing in a bedroll on the far side of the smoldering campfire. Within moments, Lucius was hovering over the choking man whose veins bulged from his temples as he spewed foam and blood from his mouth.

It was Honorius. He was in enormous pain, perspiring despite the cold. The tribune clutched his belly, curling into the fetal position between spasms. He looked up at Lucius with wide, desperate eyes, as one who stood on death's door, unable to speak.

Most of the squad was awake now, watching with curiosity from their bedrolls.

"Fetch the tonic, Geta!" Lucius said. "Hurry!"

Geta kept the squad's medical supplies – a collection herbal remedies and bandages – in his kit. The big legionary rummaged through his knapsack, produced a small vial, and tossed it to Lucius. Grasping Honorius's head to hold it steady, Lucius poured the vial's contents into the tribune's mouth. The aroma of the tonic alone was enough to turn a man's stomach, and it had the desired effect on the tribune almost immediately. He began vomiting, in long heaving movements that contorted his body in unnatural ways, each lurch discharging a noxious flood of bile. When it finally subsided, the contents of Honorius's stomach lay in a crimson pool in the mud beside him. The spasms had stopped, leaving the tribune in a depleted, withered state. Even by the light of the fire, his skin had the pallor of death.

A trembling, bloody hand reached up and clenched Lucius's tunic to pull him closer. He turned his ear to the tribune's mouth, at first hearing only guttural sounds. Finally, Honorius managed to speak just above a whisper.

"It was the woman," he rasped.

"Sir?" Lucius looked at him quizzically, then across the camp to Erminhilt's shelter, where he saw no movement, nothing to indicate she was even awake.

"The woman!" Honorius continued, breathing heavily as if it pained him to speak. "The witch poisoned my wine when I wasn't looking. I am sure of it. And now I realize, Lucius, this was all a mistake, that we've played right into their hands. This woman has deceived us, just as I knew she would." He paused again, catching his breath. "No matter. Send the others away, Lucius. Call Diogenes. I must speak with you and the clerk, alone."

After Lucius had dismissed the squad and summoned the groggy-eyed clerk, Honorius continued, under great strain. "Listen, both of you. I am dying. Diogenes, you will bear witness to this. I appoint Legionary Domitius to take my place. He is now in command, and your safety I entrust to him."

"Me, sir?" Lucius replied uncertainly.

"I do not know how long I can resist this poison. Charon waits to convey across the river of death. I go to Elysium." Honorius grabbed the clerk's arm with a trembling hand. "Diogenes, you will swear to me now, on the gods of your ancestors, that you will obey Lucius's commands, that you will trust his judgement, and his alone."

The master clerk drew a grim expression, hardly making eye contact with Lucius, as if being placed under the command of a common soldier was somehow an embarrassment to him. But he finally nodded. "I swear, tribune. I will trust him as I have trusted you."

"Good. Good, Diogenes. Now, you must tell him the information you carry in your head, and may he safeguard it better than I have."

Again, Diogenes hesitated, eyeing Lucius with misgiving, as if he had not just sworn to the contrary. Eventually, he acquiesced, speaking quietly that his voice might not carry.

"I have told you, legionary, how I escaped the massacre."

"Yes."

"But I did not tell you the whole tale. It was not by fate alone that I survived." He paused, glancing once at the shivering tribune. "I told you my general, General Cotta, and his five cohorts were there to bolster the strength of the Fourteenth Legion since it was so deep in barbarian territory. That was not entirely true. You see, the Fourteenth had not been paid for many months."

"Neither has the Seventh," Lucius said grudgingly.

"No one expected the Eburones to welcome our legions in their lands. The proconsul and everyone else knew our demand for a measure of their winter grain supplies would stir anger and discontent among the firebrands. Caesar believed this anger could be tempered, and good sentiments engendered among the barbarians, if the legionaries were given money to spend in the local markets. It was to be back pay, so to speak, delved out in regular intervals all winter. The money would also be used to buy provisions from the Eburones kings to get the legion through the winter. As you can imagine, it would take an enormous sum to do this – three hundred thousand silver denarii to be precise. Thus, payments were stopped to the other legions, and all funds were diverted to the Fourteenth. This vast fortune accompanied the legion into the Eburones lands, loaded in plain chests aboard plain oxcarts, all under great secrecy."

"Not too secret," Lucius said casually. "We all knew about it in the Seventh. We were fairly upset about it, too."

Diogenes's mouth dropped open as if Lucius had just told him the last two weeks had been nothing but a bad dream. "But, how could you…?"

"The teamsters talk, from one camp to another, and they like to gamble and drink and play games of chance. How else do you think we in the ranks find out what's going on?"

"But I don't understand how…" Diogenes was dumbfounded. "We went to great lengths to –"

"Never mind, Diogenes," Honorius gasped. "Get on

with it."

"Well, yes. Anyway, when the Eburones attacked the fort, I was commissioned by Cotta to convey the chests outside the walls under cover of darkness, with the help of a half dozen slaves, and to bury it deep under the mud and snow. I did this, thinking it only a precaution, for no one at that time expected Sabinus to quit the fort. I am sorry to say, when that decision was made, Cotta had the slaves who had helped me quietly put to death, in the event they were captured and tempted to buy their lives with the information. Cotta bad me keep the treasure's location a secret. I was not even to tell him where it was." He paused. "You know the rest – how we were attacked on the march. You asked me before, if Cotta had said anything to me before he died. I answered no. That, too, was untrue. With his dying breath, Cotta instructed me to flee, to forget my personal honor and escape the battle any way I could. He told me to head west, to reach friendly lands and to find Caesar. I was to tell Caesar, and Caesar alone, the location of the chests, and he impressed upon me the calamities that would befall Rome should the enemy get their hands on it. I gave him my word, but when I arrived at Cicero's camp…when I told Cicero –"

"I convinced Diogenes to tell us his secret!" Honorius interrupted, his face contorted with pain and frustration. "Like a fool, I convinced him to impart to us what Cotta had so wisely told him to keep to himself. And to further my idiocy, I convinced Cicero that we should try to recover the chests ourselves. That was our objective – to go to Aduatuca, where Sabinus had his winter camp, and find the silver. And, now, look what has happened. Our good general, no doubt, shared the information with his Belgic whore, which is why she insisted on coming with us. She wants what's in your head, Diogenes. She wants the location of the chests. Now, she's gotten me out of her way. She's one step closer."

"She is a traitor then?" Diogenes appeared aghast.

"Whether she plans on using the fortune for her own gain or that of her people, I do not know, but she will try to take over. She is not to be trusted, Lucius! No matter what she says, no matter what wild claims she lays on you, do not trust her. Do you hear?" Honorius had spoken too much, and was momentarily overcome by dry heaves.

"Aye, sir." Lucius answered. The words had hardly left his mouth before he heard the woman's voice calling from the other side of the camp.

"What has happened? Is Honorius alright?"

Erminhilt sounded surprised to see Lucius and Diogenes hovering over the retching tribune. Her tone was one of concern, but its innocence sent shivers up Lucius's spine. It was a bit too rehearsed, a bit too compassionate. Honorius grabbed Lucius's hand and looked fervently into his eyes.

"She thinks she's beaten me," he whispered. "She thinks the money is as good as hers. But we'll show her, Lucius. We'll show that witch yet! Listen to me. You must do as I say. Forget the pay chests. You must head west."

"Back to the fort, sir?"

"No. It's no doubt encircled by now. There's little chance you'd get through. You must head west, to find Caesar's army. That is the safest place for Diogenes now." A shudder passed through the tribune's body. "I'm cold, so very cold. I must set right what I have nearly led to ruin...to remove this dishonor from me. Diogenes must reach Caesar. Swear that, no matter what happens to me, Lucius, you will see it done."

Lucius was not sure how he would do that, or if he even wanted to. He was more interested in recovering the money for himself. With such a fortune, he could set himself up comfortably for the rest of his life, not to mention settle a few scores with those responsible for his family's murder. There was little sense in risking his neck just to make sure Caesar got it. But then, how could he deny the last wish of a dying man? Especially this man. As far as officers went, Honorius was one of the better ones. He wasn't a pompous snob, like so many others. Like most tribunes, he had a skewed view of the army, and the driving force behind the legionaries, but, still, he was a far cry from the likes of Cicero.

"You have my word, sir." Lucius finally agreed.

A smile crossed Honorius's face, but then faded into a delirious expression. He looked beyond Lucius at the heavens above. "I feel my soul slipping away, Lucius. I long to fly to the glittering stars." The tribune's speech began to slur as he recited dazedly, *"Now spring brings back balmy warmth. Now Zephyr's sweet gales hush the rages of the equinoctial sky. The fields of Phrygia are forsaken...My trembling soul yearns to roam..."* He drifted to unconsciousness, still breathing, but for how much longer, there was no way of knowing.

As Erminhilt and Belfric approached, Lucius shot Diogenes an urgent look. "Say nothing. She's after what's in your head, not mine, so just let me do the talking. Understand? Not a word. Your life may depend on it!"

The clerk seemed reluctant to accept that arrangement, but he eventually nodded.

"What has happened to him?" Erminhilt cried, now looking over Lucius's shoulder. "The gods preserve us! Not Honorius!"

It was all too innocent, made to play on the minds of simple, dull-witted soldiers. But Lucius was not a simple soldier.

"He's taken ill, ma'am," Lucius replied. "The camp fever, I suspect. Nothing to worry about."

"Is he not dead then?" she asked tentatively, a trace of expectancy in her voice.

"Not yet, ma'am. He may yet recover. Only time will tell."

"He looks so deathly pale. Can nothing be done for him?"

"Each must go in his time, ma'am, as the fates decide. That's the way of the world. It's not the tribune's time just yet. Maybe hours, maybe days, maybe years from now."

"Surely, we cannot leave him like this."

"I don't plan on leaving him, ma'am." Lucius then called to the cluster of legionaries who had remained a respectable distance away. "Geta, bear a hand. You too, Maximus. Let's get the tribune back in his bedroll. The rest of you get to work on a stretcher. We'll likely have to carry the bastard on the march with us tomorrow."

The woman gritted her teeth, barely perceptible in the firelight. "And now you, a common soldier, have assumed command?"

"Nothing to assume, ma'am. The army makes it easy for us. Legate comes above tribune, tribune above centurion, centurion above optima, optima above signifer, signifer above decanus, decanus above the soldiers. Since I'm a decanus, and I don't see any of those other ranks around here, that leaves me in charge of these mates. But not to worry, ma'am, they're used to it. Besides, with your man Belfric there guiding us, we should get to wherever we're going without any problem."

She eyed him warily now, as if she had discovered a new obstacle in her path. Perhaps she was finally suspicious that he was playing games with her.

"You were the one who delivered the message to the general." She said it more as a statement than a question.

"That's right, ma'am. Legionary Lucius Domitius, at

your service."

"You seem a buoyant fellow, legionary."

"First rule in the army, ma'am. Take what the gods and the blessed officers hurl at you, and make do the best you can. No sense in despairing. Never did anyone any good."

Erminhilt stood there for a long moment, as if considering her options, exchanging glances with Belfric that Lucius pretended not to notice. Clearly not amused or deceived by Lucius's jauntiness, Belfric glowered with baleful eyes, his hand resting on the hilt of his sheathed sword. Lucius felt certain the Belgic knight would have tried to kill him right then and there had the woman not waved him off.

"That's it, lads, lift him gently. Put your backs into it!" Lucius said with forced enthusiasm, acting the part of the simple soldier concerned only with the well-being of his ill officer. This drew annoyed glances from the other legionaries, but they kept quiet and played along. "All together, now – and, lift!"

Eventually, Erminhilt and Belfric returned to their shelter, conversing amongst themselves and casting glances at Diogenes who had already bedded down again, seemingly unaware of their attentions. No doubt, they had expected the elimination of Honorius to create confusion amongst the legionaries, either to lead them into a trap, or to spirit away the clerk in the dead of night.

Like an over-sized sack of grain, Lucius now felt the weight of command rest heavily upon his shoulders. It was up to him to protect Diogenes and see that the location of the hidden chests was safely delivered to Caesar. But where in Pluto's realm was Caesar? Was the proconsul even coming to relieve the Seventh, or had the message on the javelin been a forgery, as Cicero had asserted? Perhaps it made more sense to continue with the original mission, recover the fortune, and then decide whether to rejoin the legions or divide it amongst themselves. Of course, Erminhilt and her brute would have their own plans.

Tomorrow, Lucius thought as he discreetly observed the woman whispering to Belfric on the other side of the camp. Whatever they had planned, they would make their move tomorrow.

And he would be ready for them.

XI

The squad awoke the next morning to a mist-shrouded camp. The air was crisp and cold, the woods more silent than ever. Lucius oversaw the preparations for the day's march, fully aware of Erminhilt's eyes following his every move. Mumbling and incoherent, Honorius still lived, but his condition had deteriorated considerably overnight. At one point that morning, Lucius saw Diogenes standing over the tribune's shivering form, staring at the dying man and wearing a forlorn expression, likely still not thrilled to have been placed in the charge of a legionary.

Yawning and stretching, Lucius looked out to the east, where the land formed a narrow depression and the mist settled amongst the sunken woods like a blanket of milk. The forest there was much thicker than the one they had traversed the day before, and it was where their Belgic guides intended to lead them today.

More out of habit than practice, Lucius had always looked beyond the trail on which he marched, to spy out a hidden enemy, or to identify an advantageous spot for defense should its use become expedient. Yesterday afternoon, when there had been no mist to obstruct his view, he had gotten a much better look at the country ahead. From the summit of a low hill, he had seen how the path ahead sank away into a deep ravine, bounded by steep hills on both sides. It did not take a veteran soldier to perceived how suitable the place was for an ambush. With that in mind, he had woken in the dark hours of the morning, venturing away from the warmth of the campfire while the others slept. Creeping quietly through the moonlit valley ahead, he had found a suitable spot to perch, and there he had waited, watched, and listened. He had sat there for the better part of an hour, and had not liked what he had heard.

Now, with the sun about to break over the horizon, the squad prepared to march through that same defile. Wearing a sympathetic smile, Erminhilt approached Lucius, as he had surmised she would. He had not yet informed her of the change of plans.

"Good morning, ma'am." He greeted her cordially. "You seem to be missing your guardsman. Is he off relieving himself? you'd best fetch him. We won't wait much longer."

She seemed slightly taken aback by his assertiveness. "Belfric is scouting the path ahead. He will be back shortly." She was defensive. Clearly Belfric's absence was not what she had come to discuss. But the momentary pause passed quickly, and she once again assumed her former manner, looking down her nose at him, as if to establish her supremacy. "Legionary Domitius, I have come to a difficult decision, after much contemplation."

"And what is that, ma'am?"

"The unfortunate events of last night were an ill omen, one that I have decided we should heed." When Lucius responded with only a skeptical look, she added, "I am, of course, referring to Honorius's sudden illness. It is clearly a message from the spirits."

"Not sure I follow you, ma'am."

"I would not expect a common Roman to understand such things. The spirits of wood and fire speak only to those endowed with, shall we say, special gifts. Last night, they spoke to me."

At that moment, Belfric returned. He crossed the clearing to Erminhilt. A few words were exchanged between them in their language before she turned back to Lucius.

"Excellent," she said propitiously. "Belfric reports, the way ahead is clear."

"Does he now? Good for him, ma'am."

At this caustic, blatantly sardonic reply, Belfric eyed Lucius bitterly. He may not have understood the full meaning of Lucius's words, but he certainly understood the tone. With a baleful, contemptuous expression, the big, golden-haired warrior squinted his blue eyes at Lucius, as one might regard a grotesque forest beetle before crushing it underfoot.

Erminhilt obviously detected the anger rising in her consort, and interjected. "Belfric says the way is clear, for now, but he did see signs of enemy patrols, not two days old. As I said before, Legionary Domitius, the spirits spoke to me last night."

"I thought I heard the spirits, too, ma'am," Lucius replied jovially, "but then realized it was just your man here, farting."

She placed a pale hand on Belfric's bulging, mailed forearm to restrain the infuriated warrior.

"This mission is of the utmost importance, legionary," she said evenly. "Last night, the spirits told me it was doomed from the start, that Cicero never should have sent Roman soldiers into the forest. It has offended them. The spirits, however, do not find the Belgic peoples offensive. They welcome us and help us on our journey. Therefore, it is only sensible that Belfric and I escort the clerk the rest of the way. We can move much faster without you and your men hindering us, especially now that the tribune must be carried." She paused as if to see if any of her words were resonating, but Lucius met her with only a blank expression. "Do you understand me, Legionary Domitius? I have decided that you and your men are no longer needed on this quest. You will return to the fort at once. You are much more valuable there. Cicero will need every man to hold out until Caesar arrives."

"I can't do that, ma'am. I have my orders. A soldier must obey orders."

"I am giving you new orders."

"Begging your pardon, ma'am, but I don't take orders from you."

"I am the daughter of a chieftain. A noble of the Menapi, a friend of Rome."

"You could be queen of bloody Atlantis, it makes no difference, ma'am. No Roman soldier takes direction from a foreigner. Apologies, but that's the way it is. My lads and I are coming along."

She sighed, looking Lucius up and down. "There is no surmounting Roman stubbornness. Very well. Since you insist on defying the warnings of the spirits, I will not argue with you further. But, understand, Roman, you are making a grave mistake."

The fire was covered with snow and all traces of the camp obliterated. The shivering Honorius was firmly secured to the newly constructed stretcher, a great cloak secured between two stout oak poles, and Geta and another legionary bore him between them. They were ready to depart.

Upon a nod from Erminhilt, Belfric gestured for the tiny column to follow him into the defile ahead, but before they began moving, Lucius suddenly called them to a halt.

"A change of plans," he announced. "We'll head west from here. Sergius will take the lead."

"West?" Erminhilt looked at him incredulously. "What is the meaning of this? Aduatuca is to the east."

"We're not going to Aduatuca, ma'am. We're going to find Caesar."

"But your general Cicero expects us to – "

"We've got new orders now, ma'am."

Brief confusion crossed her face, but then she glanced once at the unconscious Honorius and seemed to comprehend the source of the new orders. She smiled patronizingly. "You do not know your way through this wilderness."

"Maybe not, ma'am, but something tells me we don't want to go that way."

"Belfric scouted the path not an hour ago," she protested. "The way is clear."

"Call it an old soldier's intuition, ma'am. We will head west. Belfric can march with you in the center."

"You are being irrational, legionary. These woods are full of the enemy. Your man does not know what to look for?"

"You never know where the enemy's going to turn up, ma'am," Lucius replied shrewdly. "Always good to be cautious. Don't worry. Sergius there has the eyes of a hawk.

I've seen him spot a Britain in a tree a half mile away. If they're out there, he'll see them."

Erminhilt and Belfric exchanged anxious glances, but there was little they could do. As previously directed by Lucius, the squad had casually moved to positions surrounding the two Belgae. Each legionary held his javelin in both hands, not threateningly, but clearly ready for use. With evident reluctance, Erminhilt gestured for Belfric to follow Lucius's instructions, her only alternative to be run through by eight pila.

"And please try not to make any loud noises, ma'am." Lucius eyed her coolly, knowing he was reading her thoughts. "This country of yours gives my lads jitters. I'd hate for one of them to skewer you by accident."

The ominous insinuation left Erminhilt speechless. She nodded in unwilling obedience, again waving off Belfric whose hand had moved to the hilt of his sword. The rest of the squad seemed amused at their discomfort – all but Diogenes, who seemed quite disturbed by their treatment.

He pulled Lucius aside and spoke lowly that the others might not hear.

"Might I have a word with you, Legionary Domitius?" His tone indicated he was already having doubts about Lucius's leadership. "It might be wise to tread lightly with these people. They are our allies, after all. Any doubts about their loyalty must be sequestered until we have clear proof."

Lucius motioned toward Honorius on the stretcher. "Tell that to the tribune."

"Yes, well, since you bring it up…I've been contemplating what our unfortunate tribune told us last night, and I must tell you I have been having second thoughts. I know the tribune seemed to have his wits about him, but it is quite probable we were listening to the hopeless delusions of a dying man, whose sickness had already taken hold of his mind. I ask you, legionary, do we even know for certain that he was struck down by poison? Might it not have been the same plague that has already claimed so many others?"

Lucius looked at him skeptically.

"Hear me out, Legionary Domitius. Before you go off on some invective about the soldier code, and how you must follow every order without question, give ear to my thoughts. There are times, I'm sure you will agree, when exceptions should be made, when orders should be ignored. I'm sure we have nothing to fear from that woman or her guardsman. Consider this. If they were disloyal, then why did they not betray us when we passed within a stone's throw of the enemy camp? It would have been the perfect opportunity. I have seen nothing that makes me question their devotion to our mission – which brings me to another point." The clerk grew more confident, each word from his mouth more patronizing than the last. "It was, in fact, General Cicero who dispatched us on this mission. With all due respect to poor Honorius, it is not a tribune's place – nor yours, legionary - to countermand the general's orders. Instead of hacking our way through this forest, trying to find Caesar – Jupiter knows how long that will take, or if we will ever find him – we should proceed with the original plan. We are here for the pay chests." He paused and attempted an appreciative expression. "Believe me, I understand the difficult position you're in. Such responsibility is too much to ask a common soldier to bear. Therefore, I suggest – in fact, I insist – that I make all the decisions from here on out." He said it flippantly, as if he had just told Lucius the price urine pots were fetching in Rome. "You may, of course, see to the ordering of the squad, but you are to leave all major decisions to me. Is that understood? We will return to the original mission, as planned and – "

Taking Diogenes by the arm, Lucius squeezed it to the point that the clerk's face turned red, his audacity replaced by agony and fear. "You listen to me, you whelp of an Illyrian whore! The tribune placed me in command, you swore to accept it, and you're going to keep your word! Is that understood?" After the clerk's contorted face gave a nod of consent, Lucius eased his grip slightly. "And consider this, while you grovel back to your place in the line. You were attacked by two rogues in the alley that night. You were damn near insensible, but I got a good look at them. One of them was a woman. The other was a big fellow who left with a wrist nearly shattered. You are good with numbers, are you not? Does two not equal two? Have you not noticed how that bastard Belfric favors his sword arm?"

Diogenes stared back at him clearly stunned by the revelation, as a man who had walked all night along a precipice, only to discover by the light of the dawn how deep was the chasm he skirted. With anxious eyes, he looked beyond Lucius at the two Belgae, a visible chill creeping over him as the truth of Lucius's words registered. He glanced at Lucius with something like regret, nodded compliantly, and made no further petitions. But Lucius was still angry with the bastard for trying to usurp his authority, and wanted to make sure it never happened again.

"I want to cover a dozen miles before the sun sets," Lucius announced to the group in general. "It'll be hard going, but we must keep moving." He glanced at Diogenes, and then looked at his veterans. "Maximus, you will stay with Master Diogenes. I'll have your hide if I catch you more than an arm's length from him. Is that clear? If we encounter the enemy, if we are attacked and it appears we are overwhelmed, you will drive your pilum through the clerk's heart."

"What?" Diogenes replied in shock.

"Do it without hesitation," Lucius said to Maximus, ignoring the clerk. "Make it a clean blow, such that he dies swiftly."

"Aye," Maximus said, eyeing the clerk sinisterly and smiling as he rubbed two fingers along the talon-sharp iron point of his javelin.

"What?" Diogenes said again, glancing from Maximus to Lucius. "Kill me? In Juno's name, why?"

"Not unless we're jumped by the Belgae," Lucius finally replied with a shrug. "It is only a precaution. That message you carry in your head might be of some use to the enemy. We can't let them get it, can we?"

"But I would never talk!" Diogenes shook his head desperately. "No. Not I. Never. Not if they throw me into the darkest pit."

"The Belgae are capable of much worse than that. They've ways of torturing a man, ways that would turn the stomach of a Numantian cannibal after a fortnight's fast." A look of panic crossed the clerk's face as Maximus moved over to stand next to him, then Lucius added reassuringly, "Most likely, Maximus will not have to slay you. But if he does, believe me, you could not have a better executioner. A quick death is far preferable."

"No," Diogenes said, nearly as white now as the patches of snow on the ground, glancing disconcertingly at the all too smug Maximus.

Several of the other legionaries chuckled, while Erminhilt and Belfric appeared impatiently annoyed.

Soon, the party set out with the wiry Sergius carefully leading the way. Lucius marched behind the two Belgae, determined to keep an eye on them at all times. He had reluctantly chosen not to disarm them, for the simple reason that Diogenes might be right. They may indeed be loyal allies, and Belfric's long sword might come in handy should they run into an enemy patrol. Still, he did not intend on letting them approach the clerk within ten paces without feeling the point of his gladius in their spines.

Lucius glanced behind him at the stretcher-bound Honorius. The tribune seemed oblivious to the jostling movements as his two bearers negotiated hedge and snow. At times, Lucius thought he heard the tribune mutter his name, and then wheeled around only to see him completely unconscious. The episodes were as unsettling as the prospect of finding Caesar, or even the bloody road on which the proconsul and his army should be marching.

If that Belgic woman was as attuned to the spirit world as she claimed to be, it was more likely they would find themselves surrounded by Eburones spear warriors. Perhaps they would meet their ends in this unforgiving wilderness, their mutilated bodies frozen in the snow, destined to become the spring banquet of some beast of the forest when the sun's warmth once again brought green and vivacity to this dismal land.

Perhaps, Lucius mused, they would become spirits themselves.

XII

Against bare trees and frozen fields, a column of horse trotted east through the Belgic countryside, riding along a muddy road that snaked in and out of the ominous woods. Conveying travelers and traders in times of peace, armies and engines in times of war, the ancient path had slowly sunk under a hundred years of wear. It was now a time of war, and the four hundred horses that deepened it further on this day carried men weighted down with armor and weapons. Half of these were Roman cavalry, the equites of the army, gleaming bronze cuirasses flashing beneath their cloaks, close-fitting helmets adorning their heads, iron-tipped lances resting across the necks of their beasts. The other half were Gallic horsemen, knights and nobles from the tribes of western Gaul, wearing long beards, cloaks of various color, mail shirts and conical helmets. Ever the opportunists, they rode with their Roman allies to suppress the Belgic revolt and, at the same time, settle age-old disputes with their long-standing enemies in the east. Like a clumsy slave new to his master's kitchen, the din of this mass of men and metal nearly drowned out the clop of the war steeds' hoofs.

At the head of this orderly horde, rode a band of Roman officers. Two were much older than the rest. One, a balding, hawk-faced man in his fifties, wore no helmet, abandoning the heavy encumbrance that he might easier peruse the correspondence fed to him by an orderly. Some letters he would read thoroughly, others he would hand back for the orderly to disposition.

"This one comes from Haerviu of the Lexovii, Proconsul," said the orderly. "In it, he swears allegiance to Rome and pledges his five hundred spears once the spring thaws come."

"The spring thaws?" the proconsul said chuckling. "Meaning the wily old rascal plans to wait and see if this rebellion is successful, and then choose sides. And what of Commius and the Atrebates?"

"He, too, claims it will take some time to assemble an army. A fortnight, at least, my lord."

"That's some improvement, I suppose," the proconsul quipped.

Gaius Julius Caesar, Proconsul of Gaul and commander of all Roman legions and auxiliaries therein, may have displayed an air of indifference on the outside, but inwardly he cursed. The damn chieftains were trying him, even those who owed him favors, even those who had felt his mercy and who owed him their very lives. They were hesitating, waiting to see if this rebellion in the east took hold and spread throughout Gaul.

"Our worst fears have come true, Caesar," commented a

middle-aged legate who rode beside him.

"Not entirely, Trebonius," Caesar replied, not missing the bitter frown on the general's face. Trebonius was just one of the many legates who had counselled Caesar against dispersing the legions to the far corners of Gaul, arguing that the shortage of rations should be addressed by sending half the army back across the Alps to winter in Cisalpine Gaul. That made perfect sense to legates and adjutants who had the luxury of looking at things from a purely military perspective, but, in Caesar's mind, such a move was out of the question. While it was tactically foolish to separate his outnumbered forces across a hostile land, the decision had been more for strategic purposes – and perhaps personal ones. Had he sent the legions back to Italy, he would have likely never seen them again. Come spring, his enemies in the senate would have found a way to keep them in Italy, by instigating a slave revolt, or fabricating some other national crisis. In any event, he had chosen to take the risk of keeping his legions in Gaul, quartering them where they could draw from the winter stores of the barbarian tribes – and Fortuna had chosen to frown on that decision.

It had always been there, like a black feline lingering on the doorstep, the terrifying prospect of the Gallic tribes uniting, rebelling, an innumerable force of spear-wielding, ferocious barbarians bent on one purpose – to drive out the Latin invaders. And now, Gaul seemed on the brink of such an event. Every revolt began with a spark, an incendiary incident to set flame the dry wood of discontent. And some spark this had been. An entire legion destroyed, another under siege in its winter camp. If ever his so-called allies wished to stab him in the back, this would be the opportune time to do it. Even if he assembled all his legions and auxiliaries into one giant army, it would scarcely equal a tenth of the number the Gauls could field. That simple fact had dictated his strategy during his first years in Gaul, when he had won battles by allying with the enemies of his enemies. Now, he had foolishly abandoned those earlier doctrines and had placed too much faith in the oaths of the chieftains, their promises of cooperation. Many of those now in revolt had even sent him nobles to be his hostages – or guests – for the duration of the winter, as a sign of their good will. Those same nobles now sweated it out at his headquarters in Samarobriva, no doubt believing their executions imminent, but Caesar had no intention of killing them. Though his hostages came from prominent families, he knew they were mostly comprised of the bastard children of the noble elites or political rivals of the ruling chieftains. Their deaths would serve little purpose other than to inflame their countrymen further and solidify their chieftain's hold on power. One does not kill a snake by attacking its discarded skin. Caesar intended to kill this snake by cutting off its head.

Ambiorix was the head. He was at the heart of this revolt, and he must be quashed before others rallied to him.

Caesar had dealt with the younger Eburones king before, in more peaceful times, and knew him to be an impetuous man with unbounded ambition and little patience. From their first meeting, he had known Ambiorix would someday give him trouble. The resentment behind the smile, the impassive gestures of friendship, the hollow expressions of gratitude, all exhibitions Caesar would have expected to encounter in the forum in Rome, he was surprised to discover in the young Eburones king. Now, he lamented not having arranged Ambiorix's murder. If he had, seven thousand Romans might still live.

"Perhaps we should reconsider this hasty movement, Caesar, until we have further clarification of the situation." Trebonius ventured. "Every mile puts us deeper into

Belgica and further from our allies. We are essentially blind, with no information on the enemy army, its size, its disposition – nothing. We do not even know if Cicero and the Seventh Legion still exist."

"They are there, general. We march to their aid. We would go, were you and I the only ones left to do it." Though Caesar's curt reply had been admonishing in nature, he knew there was some justification to Trebonius's bleak outlook. Several days ago, Caesar had dispatched a Gallic horseman, a man good with the javelin, to infiltrate the Eburones camp and deliver a message to Cicero promising relief. The Gaul had been instructed to return and report his success and the state of the siege, but there had been no sign of him.

The message itself had been insignificant. Caesar had sent it more as a safeguard than anything else – a glimmer of hope to encourage Cicero and inspire him to hold out to the last. That was, of course, expected of all Romans, but Caesar had wanted to ensure the idiocy that had provoked Sabinus to leave the protection of his own walls and allow his legion to be slaughtered in the open, did not manifest itself in Cicero. Caesar knew there was little chance the Seventh would give up, even if commanded to do so by their legate. They were one of the stoutest legions in Gaul, filled with veteran tribunes and centurions that would never consent to such a blunder.

"We may find ourselves the ones in need of succor," Trebonius spoke again. "Would it not be wise, Caesar, to wait until the allied tribes have sent us more troops before going any further?" The legate was cordial and polite, but his tone clearly communicated he thought the proconsul mad for taking such a risk.

"Have you forgotten, general, that Fabius and Labienus are coming?" Caesar said it with confidence for the benefit of the nearby Gallic horsemen, who were sure to be eavesdropping on the conversation. "We do not require any more troops. Your legion, Trebonius, and the other two will be sufficient."

The legate uttered something like a guffaw, but said nothing. Turning in the saddle, Caesar looked several miles behind the cavalry to see a rippling snake of gleaming spear points stretching off into the distance – four thousand legionaries, marching with shields slung on their backs, cross-tees and javelins resting on their shoulders. Trebonius's legion had been hastily assembled from its winter camp and put to the forced march. So far, it and the few hundred horsemen from the allied tribes comprised Caesar's entire army. It was indeed a small force to take into a hostile Belgic land, but it would soon grow substantially.

Caesar had chosen three legions for this impromptu winter expedition. The Ninth Legion, under Trebonius, now marching on the road behind him. The Twelfth Legion, under Fabius, quartered near the northern coast among the friendly Morini. And the Tenth Legion, under Labienus, his own right-hand, wintering to the south in the land of the Treveri. If all went as planned, the three legions would converge on the march, and move as one body to Cicero's relief. All three were well below full strength, but together they would number nearly twelve thousand spears, more than enough to deal with the amateur Ambiorix.

Speed was the key. Every day the risk of a general revolt grew. Caesar knew, should that happen, should all of Gaul combine against him, his little army would surely be annihilated, and every one of his remaining legions would be isolated in their winter camps and destroyed.

The thought was enough to make Caesar sick to his stomach – not so much at the euphoria that would be felt by his enemies here in Gaul, but at that with which his enemies in Rome would surely greet the news of his fall. Outwardly, they would condemn the massacre, demand vengeance and the head of every chieftain responsible, but inwardly they would rejoice. After thoroughly dragging his honor through the mud, they would suggest a more skilled general, such as the magnanimous Pompey, come out of retirement to clean up what the bumbling Caesar had muddled.

The idea of it troubled Caesar. It troubled him more than the thought of his bleached skull serving as a sloshing goblet passed around some Belgic victory feast. His auctoritas he valued more than life itself. For what else was there to live for in this world other than honor and achievement, to leave an indelible mark on the column of time, that some essence of the mortal might pass into legend to linger long after the soul had flown. The great Alexander, unfettered by the size of the Persian army at Gaugamela, had boldly met his foe in battle and had prevailed, and, though the Macedonian king died at the young age of thirty-two, the magnificence of his name echoed through the centuries, and would for millennia to come. Fortuna had smiled upon Alexander. If she did indeed favor the bold, Caesar mused, then she must certainly laugh at the imprudent.

"Riders approach, my lord!" one of the adjutants announced.

Caesar looked up to see two horsemen emerge from a file of trees across a muddy field. Both kicked their mounts into a full gallop, throwing up clots of earth as they sped toward the column. It was clear that one was a Roman officer, from his plumed helmet and flowing purple cloak. The other was a Gaul, wearing the tell-tale white band on his exposed right shoulder to indicate his allegiance to

Rome. The horses blew out great jets of steam, their nostrils expanded from great exertion. They had obviously been pushed to their limits.

"Hail, Caesar!" the officer proclaimed as both men reined in their heaving mounts.

"What news do you have?" Caesar asked.

"General Labienus sends you greeting, sir." The officer paused to remove a splatter of mud that had found its way beneath the dangling cheek-piece of his helmet. "He acknowledges your summons, but regrets he is unable to comply."

"Unable to comply?"

"The Treveri are under arms, sir. They have pavilioned within three miles of his camp, clamoring for war. Labienus believes an attack is imminent. He will need every last man to defend his walls. He therefore begs you to call on a different legion for the expedition against the Eburones."

With incredulity, Caesar stared at the letter thrust into his hands. It bore the written form of the same message, signed with the mark of Labienus. As the reality of it sank in, Caesar exercised great restraint to hide his consternation.

Damn the Treveri! Always a shifty-eyed people. He had never fully trusted them, but neither had he expected them to rebel. He had critically misjudged their loyalty, it seemed, as he had so many other things.

"That leaves us with just two legions, Caesar," Trebonius needlessly voiced his thoughts. "Assuming Fabius can make the rendezvous."

"He will make it." Caesar answered with a confident smile, ever aware of the Gallic ears all around him.

"Perhaps we are in the Tiber over our heads, sir. May I suggest, we go no further until we are certain Fabius's legion is on the march?"

Caesar regarded the legate harshly. Like many of the others, Trebonius had been growing brasher of late, more forthcoming with his own personal opinions and commentary.

"Shall I order a general halt, Caesar?" Trebonius persisted.

"No!" Caesar snapped, but then caught himself and softened his tone. "One legion or two, it matters not, Trebonius. We march on."

From his expression, it was clear Trebonius wished to protest further, but his better judgement prevailed. As the legate stewed in silence, Caesar considered how Alexander's generals must have similarly petitioned their king to reconsider his push into distant India, to be satisfied with his immense conquests, and not press his luck. Caesar wondered how much longer before his own generals mutinied as Alexander's had.

In four years, he had subdued Gaul and Britannia, and had secured the loyalty of dozens of tribes. To the Senate, to the people, to his men, he had done it in the name of Rome, but, in truth, it had all been done to satisfy an insatiable hunger burning within him – a ravenous yearning for a mere thimble-full of the great Alexander's fame. Had it been boldness or imprudence that had led him to it? Either way, there was no turning back now.

He must be bold.

XIII

"You will get us lost, Legionary," Erminhilt said as she climbed over a fallen tree as wide as a man. It was just another of the innumerable obstructions the squad had surmounted in the last several hours of marching. "There are secret paths, unknown to the Romans, but well known to Belfric. They would allow us to move much faster."

"Our aim is to reach Caesar, ma'am," Lucius said with barely veiled sarcasm. "I'd rather move slowly, than walk into an ambush."

Erminhilt cast him a jaded look over her shoulder, appearing to grow weary of his mistrust. Lucius suspected most of the squad felt the same way, though they did not voice their feelings. He had pushed them hard all morning, groping farther and farther into the tangled wilderness, directing Sergius to choose the more rugged terrain and to avoid any fields or clearings. The legionaries had taken turns carrying Honorius, slowing their progress considerably, and prompting them to curse under their breaths at Lucius's choice of routes. Lucius knew about the secret paths that allowed the Belgic tribes to move entire armies with ease through their densest forests and tallest hedgerows, but those were precisely the paths he wished to avoid.

Earlier that morning, as the squad had rested briefly beneath a high hill, Lucius had climbed to the summit for a look around. He had gone alone, and had found an escarpment affording a clear view of the forested valley below. It was the same valley through which Belfric had intended to lead them, and it was not long before Lucius spied what he was looking for. Far across the valley floor, in a small clearing where a long-forgotten forest fire had reduced the trees to saplings, two score horses stood bivouacked together. All of them were saddled, and all were war steeds. They were being watched by a handful of black-cloaked men in mail, hard to discern from the distance, but very likely the same Eburones cavalry Lucius had observed riding amongst the enemy siege works. The rest of the horsemen were nowhere to be seen, but Lucius suspected they were somewhere in the trees beyond, waiting along the forest trail.

Their presence here did not surprise Lucius. In fact, he had expected them. During his secret vigil in the dark hours of the morning, he had heard the distant neighing of those horses. Had he and his men unwittingly followed Belfric into those woods, they would have strolled right into an ambush. Lucius suspected Belfric had been in communication with the enemy horsemen during his long absences from the squad, and had arranged the whole thing, hoping to eliminate Lucius and his men with overwhelming numbers and surprise, allowing Diogenes to be taken alive.

After returning from his hilltop reconnaissance, Lucius had considered disarming Erminhilt and her brute, but decided against casting his dice just yet. Any attempt to seize them would likely result in a fight in which the two Belgae, and perhaps one or two of his own men, would end up badly wounded or dead.

Throughout the march that morning, he had instructed the squad to take care to minimize their tracks as best they could, avoiding the patches of snow whenever possible. Belfric had ignored this direction, and had on several occasions pretended to lose his footing, each time grabbing hold of a low-hanging branch to stop his fall, snapping the limb in the process. He was obviously attempting to leave clear signs for someone to track, which led Lucius to believe they were perhaps being shadowed by another band of horsemen. If that was indeed the case, he wanted to keep their two Belgic companions alive. Hostages could be useful in a standoff, and he had an inkling Erminhilt was a person of some importance.

Belfric was a typical Belgic noble – a knight, born and bred for fighting his chieftain's enemies and bullying the commoners beneath him. Lucius did not expect an attacking enemy to pause to save Belfric's head. But Erminhilt was something else. She was altogether too devious, too skilled in the murderous ways of the elite, to be the insignificant daughter of an inconsequential chieftain as she claimed to be. From his own observations, she had full power over Belfric, and he treated her like a queen. Lucius suspected any shadowing enemy might think twice about attacking as long as she was within the reach of his javelin.

Whenever the squad stopped to rest, he did not miss the conspiratorial glances between Erminhilt and her grim-faced guardsman. Lucius surmised they now viewed him as their chief obstacle, something they had not counted on, but which they would now have to eliminate, as they had Honorius. They would have to make their move soon. The farther west the squad traveled, the more likely they would encounter Caesar's column, and then Diogenes and the secret he carried would be safely out of their reach.

At the setting of the sun, the wind picked up, blowing freezing air and snow in their faces. The squad stopped for the night, to hunker beneath shelters and cloaks in a protected hollow carpeted with the icy forest mulch. Lucius insisted on no fire lest it bring the black-cloaked riders down on them.

"We will rotate through the watch," he announced. "I will take the first watch."

"I won't argue with you," Sergius replied, staking his javelin and wrapping himself in his cloak. "It's cold enough to freeze a fart. My bloody balls have shriveled to the size of pebbles."

"Don't get too comfortable. You have the second watch. I'll wake you before long."

"If it's still this infernally cold, I just might not get up." Sergius said jovially.

Lucius looked at him coarsely. "You will, when you feel my grimy boot planted firmly in your arse."

The other legionaries, including Sergius, cackled between blue lips. Lucius laughed with them, pretending to be caught up in the jovial moment, but his eyes cut to Erminhilt and Belfric. They conversed in whispers, obviously planning something. Of course, there was still a small chance they were innocent, and were not conspiring, but discussing trivial things. Lucius intended to find out once and for all tonight.

The only way to know if a crocodile lurked beneath the

surface of a murky pond was to throw in a large piece of bait. And so, he would be the bait, and he would wait for the crocodiles to stir.

XIV

The winter moon soared across the glittering night sky, it's full face bathing the earth in an azure light that made the patches of snow glow distinctly across the dark landscape. Lucius sat on his shield, leaning against the trunk of a centuries-old oak which stood alone upon an otherwise barren hilltop. The wind buffeted against his ears, the leafless tree affording little protection from the biting gusts that penetrated his cloak and helmet. But Lucius had not chosen the spot for comfort, nor for the good view it offered of the surrounding countryside. He had chosen it because it was the highest point within a hundred paces of the camp, and that he might be easily observed by anyone wishing to find him.

In the springtime, one might lie among fields of daisies, basking in the warmth of the sun, feeling blessed by the gods, as if the deities cultivated life and wished fruitfulness upon the world. But this chill night felt cold and uncaring, harsh and lifeless, like the world in its infancy, pitilessly indifferent to the existence or nonexistence of man.

An old comrade once told Lucius that the gods favored these remote untouched lands over the cities of the civilized world. In the great cities like Rome, reverence for the gods was procedural and fashionable. Here, where man fought against element each day, it was fundamental to survival. Here, the gods were feared and, here, they preferred to make their presence known. But, whatever gods cast their all-seeing eyes over Belgica in the warmth of summer, Lucius was certain even they chose to leave during the cruel winter. Perhaps they spent their winters far to the south, meddling in the affairs of men who lived around the great sea.

The blood-curdling cry of some beast of the forest echoed over the dark voids below, stirring Lucius from his reflection. Whatever it was, it was four-legged, and too far away to be of concern. Propping his javelin against the tree, he took off his helmet, sat it on the earth beside him and sank further into the hood of his cloak, attempting in every way to exhibit a weary and unsuspecting watchman. He bobbed his head as if struggling to stay awake, and finally rested his head against the gnarled trunk, pretending to fall asleep. But beneath the fluttering folds of the cloak, his gladius was free of the sheath, its cold steel ready to drink the blood of his enemies. He was, in fact, more vigilant than ever this night, for he expected to be visited by one intending his murder, and it was not long before the expected guest arrived.

Barely audible against the beating wind, he heard careful steps in the snow and mud behind him. The footfalls were close, only a few paces by Lucius's estimation, and he briefly marveled at the intruder's nimbleness, since Lucius had always considered his own sense of hearing exceptional. Though startled by this, Lucius did not move. He continued feigning sleep, hoping to lure the would-be assassin closer, waiting for the moment that he knew would come.

A slight change in the wind wafted a putrid body odor past his nostrils, and it took every bit of self-control to keep from turning to see the approaching danger. He had carefully laid a trap, one that would only be successful if he drew his attacker closer, but now the footfalls were getting too close for comfort, and Lucius was beginning to think the intruder had somehow managed to avoid it. Just when Lucius concluded the assassin's blade must be inches from his throat, and that he must make a break for it, a man winced behind him and then cried out in a great wail of agony.

Lucius sprung to his feet, bolting away from the tree and wheeling around at the same time. Bathed in the moonlight a mere spear's thrust away from where he had been lounging, lay Belfric writhing on the ground. The big knight clutched his foot, his face twisted in rage and pain. Even in the dim light of the moon, Lucius could see the dark stain spreading across the leather boot, and the twinkling barbs that protruded from the sole. The soft leather boots worn by most Belgic knights were ideal for moving silently through mulch and snow, but less than ideal when the wearer traipsed upon a sharp pointed object – such as the dozen tribulae Lucius had carefully planted in the ground around the tree at the start of his vigil. The palm-sized tribulus was defensive in nature. Each one contained four dagger-like spikes, pointing outward in different directions, such that, no matter how the device came to rest on the ground, one spike would always point up, supported by the other three – like a large, three-legged insect. The devilish devices were designed to be deployed by the thousand around the works of a fortified camp with the intent of breaking or slowing the momentum of an enemy charge. Lucius had ordered every other man in the squad to carry a sack full of the sinister snares in their kit, in the event they were needed to slow a pursuing enemy, but he had found a more adequate use for them this night.

Belfric had taken the bait. Seeing Lucius as easy prey, he had snuck up on him, intending to open his throat with a quick thrust of his dagger. In his salivating haste to dispatch Lucius, the Belgic knight had paid less attention to his footing than he should have.

The big man gasped heavily, holding his pierced foot with both hands, groaning pathetically as if the pain was too great for him to do anything else. Lucius advanced, intending to finish the job with the point of his gladius, but now it was his turn to be taken by surprise. Carelessly closing to within a sword's length of the writhing warrior, Lucius made the near fatal discovery that Belfric was only playing a ruse. A sudden flash of moonlight was Lucius's only warning that the long sword was now in the knight's hand. A heartbeat later, the band of steel sung past Lucius's head. Had he not ducked an instant earlier, the whistling blade would have decapitated him. Belfric could handle the three-foot-long sword with astonishing ease, despite the wound his arm had received from Lucius's gladius in the alley. The second stroke came quickly after the first, so quickly that Lucius lost his balance avoiding it and fell to the ground. Instinctively, Lucius used his sword-fisted hand to keep from tumbling down the slope and inadvertently left himself wide open to his opponent's next strike. It would have been nothing for Belfric to stab the blade down hard into Lucius's side, punching through mail, tunic, and skin to slice into his internals, and this surely would have happened, had fortune not intervened. Belfric's second stroke had been haphazard, and in stopping the impetus of his heavy blade, with the barb still piercing his foot, he, too, lost his footing in the mud. Lucius had a momentary reprieve in which to act, and he did. With his opponent standing over him, and his own sword arm trapped beneath him, Lucius used his other hand to snatch the pugio dagger from his belt. In one fluid motion, the blade went straight from its sheath to Belfric's exposed groin, all of Lucius's strength driving the blade directly upward as far as it would go. A torrent of warm blood sluiced down the blade and over Lucius's forearm, and then more of the red spray splashed his face when he finally wrenched and ripped the blade free.

Belfric stood dazed, grunting from the blow, his legs shaking, while Lucius scrambled out from under him, easily avoiding a final feeble swing of the gelded warrior's blade. The two stared at each other for a long moment, Lucius still wary but satisfied he need not strike again, Belfric struggling to stand up straight and clearly comprehending the lethality of his wound. With his lifeblood streaming down the legs of his trousers, the bearded warrior's eyes measured Lucius with a visage that spoke curses, anger, hatred, and regret for having failed his mistress. After teetering for a few steps, Belfric dropped his heavy blade into the soft mud. Moments later, he followed it, his limp form sliding facedown down the slope for a short interval before finally coming to rest.

The Belgic knight did not move again, and the howl of a distant wolf sailed amidst the icy wind as if to beckon the warrior's soul to the afterlife.

XV

In the cold gray of the early dawn the travelers rolled out of their blankets and prepared for the march. Erminhilt looked worried. She glanced at the Romans skeptically, an obvious question on her mind, but Lucius ignored her, chewing on a strand of dried beef.

"We are ready then?" Lucius announced. "Sergius, you take the lead, as before."

"A moment, Roman," Erminhilt said before they could set out. "Belfric is missing. I have not seen him this morning."

"Probably off somewhere emptying his bowels, ma'am. Or perhaps he's caught the scent of an enemy patrol and is off investigating. Whatever his reason, we'd best be off. Every mile we put behind us puts us that much farther from those sullied, double-crossing Belgae." Lucius said indifferently, then eyed her audaciously. "Apologies, ma'am. Anyway, a stout warrior like Belfric can take care of himself. I'm sure he'll catch up. Lead on, Sergius."

" We must not abandon him, legionary!" She demanded ardently, after some hesitation.

"Looks to me like he did the abandoning, ma'am. Either way, we must march now."

"He would never leave without my permission!" She was clearly growing more irritated by Lucius's nonchalance.

After a long, awkward moment of silence, in which Lucius regarded Erminhilt smugly, he nodded at Maximus. The legionary smiled at the distraught woman, then sauntered over to a fallen tree. As Erminhilt watched, Maximus reached behind the log, lifted a muddy, blood-covered object off the ground, and then held it up for Erminhilt to see it.

"Here he is, ma'am," Maximus said proudly. "I found the bastard."

He tossed the slick object and it thumped into the mud at Erminhilt's feet. She gasped loudly, one hand going to her bosom, as she stared into the face of Belfric, the eyelids half-shut, the bearded, chiseled features locked in an open-mouthed stare. She started to scream, but Lucius instantly grabbed her by the hair and placed his pugio to her throat.

"Hold that lying tongue, Lass," he said, firmly but quietly. "The games are over. You're all alone now. I know you poisoned Honorius, just like I know you sent that bastard to kill me last night."

"No – " she started but was cut short by the increased pressure of the blade.

"What in Hades?" Diogenes interceded, crossing from the other side of the camp, a look of shock on his face as he stared at the severed head. "What have you done, Legionary Domitius?"

"Shut up!" Lucius snapped at the aghast clerk, then looked into Erminhilt's eyes. "You've got friends out there. I don't know how close, or how many, but I know we're being followed. I expect answers from you, or you're going to end up like your guardsman there. You're going to tell me what I want to know, and you're going to tell me nice and quiet. Cry out, and it'll be the last thing you ever utter in this life. Is that understood?"

She nodded, a frightened look replacing the contemptuous one she had worn only moments before.

"Good." Lucius smiled, and eased up on the blade. "Those men out there. how many are there? And do not lie to me!"

"Six, perhaps. Possibly more," she replied with a tone in which Lucius detected no deception.

"Eburones?"

"Yes. But you do not understand –"

"Keep your voice down!" he applied the point of the dagger again. "You must understand, if one of those bastards even shows himself, I'll drive this blade through your witch's throat. Your man Belfric was leaving them signs to follow, wasn't he?"

She nodded.

"And they are either waiting for a sign from him to attack, or they are waiting for more men. Otherwise, they'd have attacked us by now. Which is it?"

"They wait for more men," she said, then expounded at a prompting of Lucius's dagger. "They want the clerk. When their numbers are strong enough, they will kill you, and take him."

"For the pay chests?" Diogenes exasperated, a look of shock and horror on his face.

Lucius nodded as he kept hold of Erminhilt. "Men do not plot such ruses to discover military secrets. Where an intricate subversion is involved, there is always gold or silver at the end of it. It only perplexes me, why they did not try to take us when we passed through their lines." Lucius thought for a moment, and then a thought suddenly came to him. "Unless someone amongst our enemy wants to recover the fortune for themselves, and keep it a secret from the rest of the Belgic army." He looked at Erminhilt, and saw he had come close to the truth. He spoke lowly to her. "Your friends out there – the ones watching us – will not allow us to reach Caesar's column. And they won't attack until they have the advantage."

"Surrender to them," she said suddenly, with resolve in her voice. "Surrender, and you have my word, you and your men will not be harmed. We only want the clerk. The rest of you may go free."

Diogenes turned white at the proposal, but Lucius ignored it.

"Your friends will not attack us until their mates arrive," Lucius said. "So, we will just have to entice them into action."

"Surrender to them…," she said again, but her voice trailed off when she saw Lucius smile craftily.

"And I know just how to entice them." His eyes cut to the bulge of her bosom beneath her woolen dress.

As Lucius began to pull at the strings holding the dress in place, Erminhilt's hitherto defiant eyes grew wide with terror and full comprehension of what he intended.

XVI

The Belgae had finished circumvallating the Roman fort. The ditches had deepened, the earthworks had risen, and the nearby woods stripped bare to top the crest with a palisade in many places, like rows of uneven teeth. The works ran off in both directions disappearing into the smoky haze hanging about the fields, and now nothing could reach the Roman fort or escape from it. The construction was certainly not up to Roman standards, but most of the thirty thousand men who had strained to erect it could not help but gaze upon their achievement with a sense of awe.

Ambiorix walked along the crown of the earthen berm with an entourage of kings and chieftains, surveying the completed works. The mud-caked warriors and slaves looked up at the passing dignitaries, but few smiled.

Ambiorix offered words of encouragement wherever he thought it appropriate, but he knew the grumblings were reaching a breaking point. The men were restive, and who could blame them? They dwelt in a dismal world of ice, mud, and felled trees shrouded by a low hazy cloud that grew thicker each day, as the chimneys of a thousand makeshift huts belched out more smoke. Visibility was reduced to only a few hundred paces, such that the druid priests who stood beyond the works, incessantly chanting curses in the direction of the Roman fort, looked like shadowy phantoms in their hooded robes.

A foul aroma hung in the air, a repulsive swirl of vapors from the dung of both man and beast and from the thin stews being prepared for the afternoon meal. The noxious concoction made one wish the smoke was thicker. The pestilence often spawned by such great concentrations had begun to take hold. Nearly six hundred warriors and slaves had already fallen victim to the camp fever. Three thousand more lingered on death's door, coughing and shivering in their huts.

The protesting bay of an unseen cow was cut short as it was slaughtered. Horses whinnied in the distance. The axes and hammers never ceased.

Ambiorix gazed at the dark shape of the Roman fort in the mist. He could just make out the faint music of a cithara, accompanied by the hearty laughter of a deep-voiced man. Even facing certain death, the Romans found ways to amuse themselves. How different from his own men – grim, weary, and dismal.

"You fight like Romans, now, Ambiorix," the man walking beside him snarled in disapproval as he gazed upon the fresh earthworks. He was a tall man with sandy-hair and blue eyes. His harsh, scar-ridden face was hidden by a beard speckled with gray. "I never thought I would see the Belgae cower behind walls. The great Boduognatus never sat behind a wall when an enemy was afoot in his country."

"Lord Boduognatus is dead, Raganhar," Ambiorix replied succinctly. "Certainly, you have heard how he met his end. Or have those songs not yet reached Germania?"

Raganhar grinned. "They have. I emptied many a cask reveling at his defeat. He slew many of my people over the years."

"Those he slew were raiders and outlaws!" The old king Cativolcus retorted testily. He walked one pace behind, leaning on a staff and struggling to keep up with the younger men as they surmounted each work. "Your own men invaded our lands, burned our farms, befouled our women. The great Boduognatus did nothing more than reciprocate the dastardly acts of the deceitful German."

Raganhar's grin faded. "Ambiorix, I hear the buzzing of a fly – an old fly who should go back to licking turds, before I stove in his careless gray head."

Ambiorix glanced over his shoulder at the old king. "Lord Raganhar is our guest, Cativolcus. The age-old quarrels between our people are in the past. We face a mutual enemy now."

Cativolcus did not respond, but the disapproval was evident on his face. He wore the same expression he had worn earlier that morning when Raganhar rode into camp at the head of three hundred German horse warriors. The Germans had contemptuously returned the curious gazes of the mud-covered Belgic troops. Raganhar was hated by most Belgae, and many of the nobles, like Cativolcus, had kept their hands close to the hilts of their swords, but Ambiorix had greeted the German chieftain with open arms. The timing of the visit was something of a surprise to Ambiorix, though he knew the reason for it.

"This is a time for unity between German and Belgian,"

Ambiorix continued genially, more for the benefit of the other nobles than for Cativolcus. "Once enemies, German and Belgian are now friends and allies, bent on a common purpose, to drive the Romans from our lands."

Raganhar gave him a circumspect look. "Enough of that nonsense! I care not what you wish to do with the Romans. I am here for one purpose, and you well know it. You promised me gold and silver, Ambiorix. Where is it? I have twenty thousand spears waiting to cross the Rhenus – twenty thousand killers eager to drink the blood of any enemy you choose – but they will remain where they are until your end of the bargain is fulfilled."

"I swore an oath to you, my brother," Ambiorix gave him a conciliatory smile. "I shall keep it."

"Good thing for you, *brother*," Raganhar said sardonically. "Because if I do not have real silver streaming between my fingers very soon – my men may go looking for it elsewhere. I will not be able to control them. Perhaps they will search for it on your side of the Rhenus – perhaps, in your own oppida."

"Is that a threat, dog?" Cativolcus snapped, nearly stumbling as he took one step toward the German chieftain. "You dare come to this land with threats on your vile lips!"

Raganhar scowled at the old king before turning to Ambiorix. "Your old dog is in need of a muzzle!"

Ambiorix raised a hand between them. "Your concerns are understandable, Lord Raganhar. We will see that the payment is delivered to you at your camp beyond the Rhenus. Until then, I implore you to keep your army intact and prepared to fight. Have no fear. You will be paid."

The German chieftain looked around him at the nearby Belgic nobles, seemingly amused by their discomfort. After glancing disgustedly at the simmering Cativolcus, he turned back to Ambiorix.

"Since I have ridden all this way," Raganhar looked searchingly into Ambiorix's eyes, "perhaps I might take it now. That is, if you have it."

"Unfortunately, it is not here." Ambiorix forced a smile, struggling not to display his own frustration.

"Where is it then?" Raganhar said playfully, then gestured to the Roman fort in the mist. "In there, perhaps?"

When Ambiorix did not respond, and the other nobles averted their gazes elsewhere, Raganhar laughed out loud. "The Belgae are as poor at lying as they are at fighting! You do not have it! You never had it!"

"Watch your tongue, my friend," Ambiorix said, remaining cordial. "We value this alliance, but will not suffer your insults unanswered. Must I remind you that it was this army that defeated the legion of Sabinus. An entire Roman legion, destroyed. A feat no German army has ever managed, I might add."

"Aye, I've heard of your glorious victory," the German said mockingly. "At the cost of half your fighting men, no less. I've also heard you did not find the Roman pay chests as you had intended. No doubt, it was with this that you intended to pay me."

Ambiorix's mouth went suddenly dry, but he remained composed. He had not expected this German fool to know about the pay chests. He had taken great pains to keep the existence of the money a closely guarded secret, not even sharing it with the chieftains of the other tribes. Suspicious looks now crossed their faces. He would have to come up with a suitable explanation to placate them.

Waving them all away, Ambiorix pulled Raganhar aside. "I'm sure you can appreciate, Lord Raganhar, there are things a king must withhold from his own people. How come you to know about the pay chests?

Raganhar shrugged. "You have spies in my army. I have spies in yours. Like all true allies, there are no secrets between us, *my friend.*"

"The Roman fortune has eluded us temporarily. But we will have it, soon. I have tasked my own personal guard with recovering it."

"Whom we have not heard from for quite some time," Cativolcus added grudgingly. The old king considered himself immune from the earlier dismissal and had joined the two in their private council.

"These are matters best handled amongst ourselves, Lord Cativolcus. Lord Raganhar has no desire to hear of our own bothersome problems."

"Nor have we heard from Erminhilt," Cativolcus continued, ignoring the mild admonition entirely. "Had she been at the rendezvous, had she been where you said she would be, the guard would have returned by now. Where are they, Ambiorix? Are they truly seeking out the Roman fortune, or are they off securing alliances with more of our ancient enemies?"

Ambiorix seethed silently. Cativolcus's presence here was becoming more than a mere nuisance. It was bordering on intolerable. Ambiorix knew, one day, he would have to get rid of the old bastard, but, for now, he needed the third of the Belgic nobles who still swore fealty to the old king.

"My guard will leave no stone unturned," Ambiorix assured Raganhar. "They will find it."

"I do not give a swine's snot in muck who finds it, how you get it, or where it comes from. I care only that you pay me. Pay me, and then you will have the army you so desperately need." As if to emphasize the point, he cut his eyes to the frail old king Cativolcus, and then to the trenches filled with the unimpressive-looking soldiers and slaves of the Belgic army. "Do not pay me, and my men will do as they please. Some may wish to return home. Others may first wish to make their long journey to the Rhenus worthwhile. You understand my meaning?"

"I propose a grace period of five days." Ambiorix kept his composure under the lightly veiled threat. "If you can keep your army together and under control for five days, Lord Raganhar, the payment will be delivered to you."

Raganhar grinned with cynicism, and then bowed extravagantly. "So be it then, my lord. Five days. After that,…" He did not finish, the consequences of failure quite apparent. Before storming off to rejoin his waiting horsemen, the German chieftain cast a final menacing glance at the cluster of Belgic nobles. Moments later, the three hundred German riders thundered away, their horses' hooves tossing mud into the air to splatter on any careless bystander.

No sooner had they left than Ambiorix was confronted by Cativolcus and the other chieftains.

"Are you mad, Ambiorix?" Fridwald of the Aduatuci said. "Why did you ever bring the Germans into this? They will loot our lands at the first opportunity. You know well their manner. There is not enough loot in all of Gaul to placate them."

"I agree!" the Nervii chieftain added. "The Germans must not be allowed to cross the Rhenus. I say we forget this hopeless digging and take the fort by assault. I have never understood the reason for this siege, anyway. We should move on the fort immediately, while there is still food within its walls for us to plunder. The sting of battle will silence the grumblings and breathe life into our soldiers again."

This met with approval from the others.

"No!" Ambiorix snapped, looking from one chieftain to

the other. "Do you not understand? We lay siege to the Roman fort, not to take it, but to draw Caesar to us, to spur him into rash, reckless decisions. If we take the fort, there will be no reason for Caesar to hurry. Thus, he will have time to assemble a great force, perhaps six legions. Do you truly think our army will be able to stand up to six legions in a pitched battle?" Ambiorix glanced around the group. They were all attentively listening now, for as much as they hated to admit it, his words rang true. Ambiorix walked over to the Aduatuci chieftain and laid a hand on his shoulder in friendship. "Is the meaning of this siege not clear to you now, Fridwald? As long as there is a legion to rescue, Caesar will try to do it, even if he can muster only a minute force. He will not have time, nor the resources, to summon most of his legions from their winter quarters. If he comes swiftly, his army will be weak, and we will crush him. As you say, our men are ready for battle, and I intend to give them one. How much surer our victory will be if Raganhar and the Germans stand shoulder-to-shoulder with us. I have made peace with Raganhar with this in mind."

"Is it true what the German said about the Roman treasure?" another chieftain asked. "You kept this from us?"

Ambiorix pretended to be unfazed. "The silver he referred to is that of my personal estate, which I have promised Raganhar if he helps us." He caught the dubious look from Cativolcus, the only one who knew he was flat out lying, and pleaded with his eyes for the old king to keep silent. "Have no fear, my lords. The silver will soon be in Raganhar's hands and his Germans will be our steadfast allies."

Later, after the chieftains had dispersed to their tribes, and the two Eburones kings were once again among their own pavilions, Cativolcus voiced his displeasure.

"You put too much trust in that girl," he said. "And you place her in great peril."

"She is not the pubescent child you seem to think she is, o king. She is a Belgic woman, cunning and brave. She knows exactly what is at stake, and is prepared to do whatever is necessary." Ambiorix paused, looking the old king in the eyes. "Are you, my lord?"

At that moment, Ambiorix's attention was drawn away by three riders galloping into the camp. Their distinct black cloaks and mail identified them as his own royal guardsmen. They appeared to bear news of some importance, judging from the way they pushed their mounts, leaping some of the camp obstructions, skirting others, while foot soldiers scrambled out of the way.

"My lords!" the leader said hurriedly, after dismounting before the two Eburones kings.

"Report," Ambiorix commanded, somewhat startled at their disheveled appearance. They had undoubtedly spent many long hours in the saddle without rest. "Where is Belfric? Where is Erminhilt?"

"We did not find either of them, my lord. Nor the Romans."

"Did not find them?"

"We waited at the eagle's stone along the old smuggler's trail, just as we were commanded to do. We waited in ambush amongst the trees — waited for nearly two days — but no one came."

"The Romans got wise to their treachery and slew them!" Cativolcus said, his face suddenly filled with anguish. "That has to be it! A fine end to your grand plan, my young colleague! You have killed her! Your overconfidence has killed her!"

"What else?" Ambiorix prompted the guardsman,

leaving the old king to his blathering. "What of Torvald's band who were ordered to shadow the Romans?"

"No sign of them either, my king. Whether he follows them still, or lies dead in some hidden grave, we cannot know."

"And the rest of the guard?"

"Split up into groups, my king, combing the countryside. If they live, we will find them."

Ambiorix's thoughts ran wild as the guardsman waited and Cativolcus silently lost all composure. Had he interpreted Erminhilt's messages properly? Yes, they had been clear enough. In them, she claimed to have discovered a Roman clerk from the Fourteenth Legion who knew the location of the legion's hidden pay chests. She planned to convince Cicero to dispatch a squad to recover the chests, and she and Belfric would accompany the expedition under the pretense of serving as trail guides. She had planned to lead the Romans into a trap at an agreed upon location along the old smuggler's trail. There could be no other interpretation of her intent. Something had gone wrong. As much as the old king was consumed with whimpering, Ambiorix refused to believe Erminhilt was dead. The idea that she had betrayed him was out of the question, for Ambiorix knew for certain he had complete control over her. There had to be another reason for her disappearance, and it did not take long before another possibility entered his thoughts. What if Erminhilt had been fed false information about the destination of the expedition?

"Have any of the search parties gone west?" he asked the guardsman.

"No, my king. They all search along the path to Aduatuca."

Ambiorix cursed inwardly. The Romans might be halfway to Samarobriva by now, and with them, the knowledge that was his only hope of finding the hidden pay chests – his only hope of paying off Raganhar.

"How long have you been in the saddle?" Ambiorix demanded fervently.

"Nearly half the day, my lord."

"Rest yourselves. Get something to eat. Then fetch fresh mounts for your return. I will accompany you."

The guardsmen bowed and retired, leaving the two kings alone.

"What of Erminhilt?" Cativolcus said, a glimmer of hope in his voice.

"I will join up with the royal guard, and I will find her, if I have to scour the countryside and upturn every stone." He decided not to mention he was more concerned with finding the Roman clerk.

The old king regarded him meekly. "Then may Odin go with you."

Ambiorix returned a scowl. "And you had best not try anything while I'm gone, old man. I have the chieftains doing my bidding, and they had better be just as loyal when I return. Is that clear? They must not know where I have gone nor why."

"They will, of course, inquire of your absence."

"Tell them anything. Tell them I've gone on a reconnaissance. Tell them I will return directly. Just keep them together. This army must stay together! Understand? I will rejoin you once I have found Erminhilt and the money."

Cativolcus nodded thoughtfully and then limped away to his tent. As Ambiorix watched him go, he considered that, eventually, the old king would have to be killed, too. Their shared kingship was an archaic tradition, and old custom that had outlived its time. It was one of the first things Ambiorix planned to do away with when he was high king.

He could not have that codger hovering about him, muddling his affairs. He would think up a particularly painful manner of death for Cativolcus, an appropriate remuneration for all the trouble the old bastard had caused him. Erminhilt would not be pleased with that, but she would accept it. She would accept it, or she would be done away with, too.

Ambiorix sighed, as he strode to his tent and summoned his attendants to saddle his horse.

Perhaps, in the end, doing away with Erminhilt would be for the better. For it was not wise for a great king to become too attached to anyone. Especially, when a whole campaign of conquest lay before him.

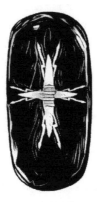

XVII

Torvald had been watching the group of Romans for the better part of two days. It had not been difficult to follow the signs left by Belfric – a collection of stones, a jumble of sticks, faint carvings in the trees, and a dozen other secret methods that would have been unnoticeable and meaningless to all but their own tribesmen. Like Belfric, Torvald was an Eburones sword warrior, a member of the tribe's nobility.

Two days ago, Torvald and his patrol of horsemen had come across the signs. After dispatching a galloper to fetch the rest of the royal guard, he and his seven men had shadowed the Romans, remaining at a safe distance. Though many times, Torvald had been tempted to rush the enemy, he had abstained. He doubted the insignificant band of Roman foot soldiers could put up much of a fight against his horse guards who excelled at sword melee, but he also knew that nothing but an overwhelming attack could ensure that the Roman clerk was taken alive – not to mention Belfric and Erminhilt. And King Ambiorix had made it abundantly clear, in the most threatening terms, that Erminhilt and the clerk were to remain unharmed at all costs.

There had been no sign of the royal guard. They could not be far off, and would probably arrive any hour now. Torvald had fully intended to wait for them, but now he faced a dilemma.

"Still no sign of the others?" Torvald asked the warrior next to him, as he and six of his dismounted horsemen now crouched in the brush. "No sign of Belfric?"

"None," the warrior replied. "Nothing. Just her."

The man gestured ahead to the object of their attention. Nearly a hundred paces distant, through a natural cut in the trees, a pale, naked form writhed and twisted up against the trunk of a tree. It was the woman Erminhilt. With arms drawn back and hands bound together behind the trunk, she grunted and struggled vainly to free herself. A gleaming amulet dangled from around her neck, glancing from one undulating breast to the other as she thrashed about. It was her only adornment, and did little to prevent her extremities from turning blue in the frigid air. Her hair was disheveled, her face twisted in both ire and fear.

As Torvald watched the struggling woman, knowing well her safety was of the utmost importance to his king, the worst fears entered his thoughts. As if to confirm them, he now saw a helmetless Roman stroll into view. Torvald recognized him as the same rugged legionary he had often observed giving orders to the others. A devilish grin appeared on the Roman's face as he approached the bound woman. He began to taunt her with words, and they seemed to have great effect, because she jerked and whipped in her bonds in an apparent effort to get away from him. Torvald heard the laughter of unseen men, and imagined the other Romans lounging nearby, watching the spectacle with great amusement.

"What are we to do?" the warrior next to Torvald asked expectantly, the anxiety on his face reflecting Torvald's own thoughts.

"The king will have us flayed alive if we do nothing but sit and watch while the woman is savaged," Torvald replied.

"Yes, but which king? Ambiorix or Cativolcus?"

"Swords!" Torvald said, ignoring the quip. He was unable to hide his own frustration at the quandary, but he had made his decision. Donning helmet and shield, he gestured for the other guardsmen to join him. "We attack, brothers! We must move quickly, before the foul Roman touches her. Kill the Latins. Take the clerk alive, if you can."

On Torvald's signal, the seven warriors broke from their concealed positions and advanced on the clearing, each man firmly clutching the hilt of a three-foot, double-edged shaft of polished steel. When only thirty paces remained, and the taunting Roman still seemed unaware of their presence, they broke into a sprint. Shouting a great war cry and swinging their swords wildly above their heads, they rushed forward with murder in their eyes, braided beards and mail flapping. Their round, bright-striped cavalry shields were much more conducive to rapid movement than the cumbersome Roman scutum – the oval shield of their enemy, which was nearly the size of a man.

Within moments they had reached the clearing. Torvald expected a brief, savage killing spree, in which the Romans would discharge their bowels at the sight of his charging warriors and either flee or be cut down. But this was not the case with the helmetless legionary who now turned away from the woman to face them. Torvald could clearly see this scar-faced Roman had no intention of running, and there was anything but fear in his eyes. The solitary legionary was also without a shield, but he looked eager to fight, holding a Roman short sword in one hand, and beckoning them closer with his other. The show of bravado in the face of seven charging warriors was almost humorous, and Torvald came near to laughing when he thought of how easily his men would mince this overconfident Latin fool. Torvald would have been further emboldened had he not been suddenly struck with bewilderment. He could see the entire clearing now, including the area that had been hidden from view, and where he had expected to find a squad of lounging Romans – the ones whom he had heard laughing only moments before. Now, he saw only two men – one, the unarmed Roman clerk; the other, a deathly pale man sleeping upon a stretcher. But even this pitiful discovery did not disturb Torvald as much as the sight of the woman, who no longer looked fearful, but rather aggravated as she reproached him from her bonds.

"Go back, you fools!" she shrieked, looking directly at Torvald. "Go back! They lie in ambush!"

Torvald comprehended her meaning a moment too late. Out of the corner of his eye, he caught the glint of steel, then wheeled to see a half dozen javelins erupt from the thicket to his left. The iron-tipped missile flew with deadly speed into the exposed flank of his warriors, whose shields still faced forward. Exposed legs and sides bore the fusillade with devastating results. One warrior beside Torvald went down with a two-foot-long rod of iron protruding from his neck, the gore-covered point having passed completely through after savaging the man's arteries and wind pipe. Another man was transfixed by two missiles, one lancing into his ribs, the other pinned through his calve. He fell to the ground, the wooden shafts thrashing the mud and snow with each convulsion of his body.

The warriors had hardly turned to face the storm of missiles when a half dozen screaming Romans burst from the same thicket. The Romans held their large shields before them, emblazoned with the emblems of the Seventh Legion, hiding all but bronze helmets and blazing eyes. They came on quickly, but not breaking order, each legionary keeping station with those on either side of him, like a moving wall of plywood.

Shocked by the suddenness of the attack and desiring retaliation for the missiles that had felled two of their comrades, the Belgae rushed at the Roman line. Torvald knew this was folly, but he could not stop them. He knew that hunkered behind those giant shields were the unimpressive but exceptionally deadly gladii that had slain countless Belgae in open pitched battles. Torvald's men, while exceptional at single combat, were now playing into the Romans' hands, acting on instinct, employing their heavy swords in overhead sweeps to hack away at the giant Roman shields. Each legionary crouched and waited for the moment when he could either ram his shield's iron boss into the torso of an outstretched, off-balanced attacker, or jab a finger's length of whetted gladius into an exposed abdomen, groin, leg, or foot. Blood sprinkled earth and shield. One by one, Torvald's men winced and cursed, dropped their weapons and crumpled to the ground, until all lay twitching, clutching at spewing arteries. Their battle cries had faded to desperate pleas for mercy, which fell on deaf ears as shield edge and upturned gladii finished the work.

Witnessing the despicable fate of his men, Torvald let out a roar of rage, banging his sword on his shield. He stepped toward the legionaries, expecting to satiate his wrath by plunging his sword into at least one Roman breast before they did the same to him, but he was stopped short by a cry of warning from the woman.

"Look out!" she screamed.

He spun to look in her direction, but not before he felt a powerful steel point part the links of his mail shirt and plunge into his back. The blade was withdrawn and thrust into him again, three times in rapid succession, before he could draw in a single breath. And then, it was over. With his lifeblood ebbing, Torvald released his sword and shield and dropped to his knees.

The blows had been delivered by the helmetless Roman, who had moved behind him in his distraction, and now stepped away from him holding a crimson blade. The Roman clearly understood the wounds were mortal and did not intend to strike again. His face was no longer filled with the lustful joy of a ravager of women, but the stern and cold gaze of a veteran soldier. Torvald knew, at that moment, that the whole scene had been a ruse, staged by the helmetless Roman to lure him into a hasty attack.

Torvald felt his strength rapidly leaving him, his vision starting to blur. The other legionaries approached him warily, their swords dripping with the blood of his men. Erminhilt watched him with a forlorn expression, as one watches a prized jewel fall into a bottomless abyss.

The next moment, the world turned sideways and Torvald felt the cold mud of the earth against his cheek. The Romans were talking to one another, but he could not hear them, nor did he care to hear a single word of their foul Latin language. He simply reached out to clutch the hilt of his sword and wait for his forefathers to welcome him into the drinking halls of Valhalla.

But then, in the distant trees beyond the gaping Romans, Torvald saw a face, and it was a face he recognized. It was Munfred, the youngest man in his band. Lacking battle experience, the lad had been left behind to watch the horses, bivouacked nearly a half-mile away. The commotion of the fight must have drawn the lad from his duties, and now the youth gazed on the carnage-ridden clearing with astonishment. The Romans, examining the dead and jesting over their victory, had not noticed him. Torvald met eyes with the lad, and then managed a slight nod of his head. This was all the instruction Munfred needed, for he was not daft, and knew better than to throw his life away avenging his comrades. The next moment, he was gone.

A smile crept over Torvald's face as he breathed his last, content that the merriment of these Romans would not last long. Munfred would find the royal guard, and the mass of horsemen would scour the hills until the foul Romans were found.

The swords would sing in a great slaughter, and Torvald and his men would be avenged.

XVIII

"But I had no choice!" Erminhilt pleaded for the third time since the last rest interval. "You have to believe me!"

"Believe you?" Lucius replied. "After betraying us? After you left Honorius an invalid and tried to have me killed? No telling what fate you had in store for the rest of these lads."

The squad traveled in single file, strung out in wide intervals as they made their way across the forested countryside. The crisp air of winter turned their breaths to steam and numbed ears and noses, only marginally shielded by damp cloaks twice their normal weight. The squish of cold mud between boots could be heard whenever great formations of fowl were not squawking across the sky on their long journey south. They had spent the day traversing the wooded hills, and had seen few signs of life, and, thankfully, no enemy horsemen.

They had come to a small river where an acrid odor had alerted them to the presence of a tanner's hut beside the water. The Belgic occupants had scattered on their approach, leaving them a simmering stew to fill their bellies, a warm place in which to dry their cloaks, and a small boat which they had used to crossover to the west bank.

A few paces behind Lucius, Honorius groaned upon his stretcher. Though clearly uncomfortable, he no longer trembled and his coloring was improving. He was, perhaps, on the mend. Lucius noticed Erminhilt studying the tribune, and thought he detected a trace of sympathy in her expression. Indeed, her entire demeanor had changed, as if a new spirit now inhabited the body.

After the last Belgic warrior had fallen, Lucius had untied her and had returned her clothes. She had seemed surprised by that, and further shocked when Lucius laid flat one of the younger legionaries for suggesting they make the naked and bound woman pay for her betrayal in other ways. The unfortunate soldier would be favoring his jaw for a week, but he would never think of such a thing again, at least not when Lucius was present. The veterans of the squad knew better than to even mention rape when Lucius was around, for they knew he despised any man who would force himself on a woman. None could match him, with or without arms, and so they never challenged him on the issue.

Now, Erminhilt marched a few paces ahead of Lucius, unbound save for a slack rope looped around her neck, its bitter end tied to Lucius's belt.

"I had no choice but to betray you!" Erminhilt repeated desperately. "Ambiorix forced me to do it!"

"The Eburones king?" Lucius said skeptically. "You mean the same mule turd that's behind this revolt? So, you belong to his tribe, do you?"

"He is not my king, and I am not Eburones. You must believe me. I despise Ambiorix. He is a brigand and a tyrant! I am from a small clan far to the north, at the edge of the Eburones lands, along the confluence of the Mosa and the Rhenus. My father is chieftain there. The Eburones have always considered us under their dominion, but we have never accepted that. They are a warlike people, but we are peaceful. We seek nothing but harmony with Rome and all our neighbors.

"Weeks ago, Ambiorix sent messengers to my father demanding our clan join the revolt. When my father refused, Ambiorix had him kidnapped. He took my father to the main oppidum of the Eburones at Aduatuca, and had him thrown into a pit of refuse. There he remains to this day, a hostage to compel my people's obedience. I, like my people, was forced to do Ambiorix's bidding. He swore my father would suffer unspeakable torture and death if I did not."

She hesitated, as if it was difficult for her to go on.

"I love my father, so I did as Ambiorix commanded. He bad me go to Cicero's camp and claim that I came from a tribe allied to the Romans. He even gave me credentials to substantiate such a claim. My task was to get close to Cicero, to penetrate his inner circle in the days leading up to the revolt, and learn anything I could about the dispositions of the legions across Gaul. I was commanded to do this through any means possible." She paused, closing her eyes, and shuddering visibly. "So, I became Cicero's woman, his willing *whore*, whispering pleasantries into his ear while eavesdropping on every one of his war councils. He told me much more when he was drunk, which was most of the time, and I prayed to the gods that talk was all he wanted from me. But, it was not. You Romans have exceptionally twisted minds, and Cicero is no exception. I bore the most abhorrent and unnatural things a woman can endure. Day after day, night after night, I was subjected to every humiliation, every depraved act conceived by that corpulent degenerate's perverse imagination. I fear I will never purge it all from my memory. He is the most repulsive man one could ever envisage – an oily, blubbery whale of the land – a slobbering, beady-eyed, three-chinned troll." She whimpered slightly, but then faced him, the cold wind carrying the tears away from her reddened but resolved eyes. "But I did it. I did it all for my father. I would do anything to save my father! Please, Legionary Domitius! Is there any compassion in your Roman veins? Do you not have a father? Do you not love him? My father is more dear to me than life itself."

Lucius said nothing, still unsure whether this soft-tongued woman was telling the truth or simply attempting to save her own neck. If the latter, then it was indeed a good attempt, for it had piqued his interest.

"Cicero's advisors were not happy about my presence." She continued. "They saw that I was distracting their general from his duties, and they pleaded with him to send me away. But when news of the revolt reached the camp, Cicero ordered the gates sealed, and insisted they pester him no more about it, claiming he was concerned for my safety. By that time, he was too enamored with me to ever consider sending me away, and I soon had his advisors eating out of my hand, as well. Men are so easily lured to their dooms by lust." Her eyes skimmed up and down Lucius's muscular frame, as if he stood there for all men. "All but Honorius. He never trusted me. He never stopped watching me with a wary eye."

"Is that why you tried to murder him?"

She looked at him stoically. "I was desperate, Legionary

Domitius. I had to deliver Master Diogenes to Ambiorix or my father would die. He still might. He may already have. What would you have done were you in my situation?"

Lucius shrugged. "I'd have not let my father get kidnapped in the first place. Perhaps had your clan been less peaceful, warlords like Ambiorix would not be able to subdue you so easily."

"You do not understand. It is not as simple as that."

"I understand that one faces a choice in life, to be defiant or submissive, to be strong or weak. No matter what anyone tells you, there are no other options. Whichever path is chosen, one must accept the consequences. *Woe to the conquered.*"

"What?" she said confusedly.

"It was something an old centurion of mine used to go around saying whenever we sacked a Gallic town. *Woe to the conquered.* I think he took delight in it, since it was Brennus who first said it – the Gaul bastard who sacked Rome centuries ago. But it is true, isn't it, lass? The conquered are entitled to nothing. It's a cruel world, aye, but that's the way it is."

She stared at him as if he had grown ears out of his forehead, but then turned away and said nothing. Lucius smiled inwardly, for he had seen the same look on the faces of many officers upon realizing their suppositions about Legionary Lucius Domitius were all wrong. While Lucius's speech was often rife with the slang of the army camp, it also carried detectable strains of a cultured past, the vestiges of the Greek tutor of his youth. Lucius could scarcely remember a day of his adolescence when the aging grammaticus did not summon him to the estate's vine-laced veranda and subject him to lesson after lesson. Under the warm sun of southern Spain, with the azure sea spanning a gap between two yellow hills in the distance, Lucius had studied writing, poetry, philosophy, Latin, and Greek, never suspecting he would someday march with the legions to the far reaches of the empire. He had hated every moment of those lessons, but they had served him well in later years, allowing him to quickly learn several of the Celtic languages spoken in Gaul, knowledge that had saved his life on at least two occasions.

"And Belfric?" Lucius asked in a more amicable tone. "Was he also of your clan?"

She shook her head. "Ambiorix's man. Not mine. He accompanied me to ensure I carried out my instructions, and kept his king informed of my discoveries. Everything I did was directed by Ambiorix."

"You speak as though you were in regular contact with him."

"I was," she replied succinctly, then explained further when Lucius shot her an inquisitive look. "You see, Ambiorix knew there might be a siege, long before the revolt began. He worked out a way for me to communicate with him from within the fort. It was simple, really. Every other night, I was to stroll along a dark portion of the northern rampart, pretending to observe the stars for favorable omens. At a certain time, one of Ambiorix's agents would approach the wall unseen, and pass a message up to me affixed to the end of a long staff. In this way, I received my instructions. The next night, I would write a coded reply. Belfric would attach my message to a black-feathered arrow and shoot it into a nearby field, where Ambiorix's men waited to receive it."

"Clever," Lucius remarked, thinking of the message from Caesar that had been delivered by similar means. He then chuckled to himself.

"You find something humorous?" she said, clearly annoyed.

"I was just thinking. Perhaps Ambiorix used the same trick when he laid siege to Sabinus's fort. Perhaps there was another lass like yourself within the walls. A whore to warm Sabinus's bed and convince him to lead his legion to disaster."

Lucius had said it flippantly, but he had meant to be insulting. He was testing Erminhilt, watching for her reaction, and what he saw was far from what he had expected. Her repentant face suddenly twisted into a look of revulsion, as if the thought of another woman fulfilling an identical role in Sabinus's camp had never occurred to her. Now that it had, she was clearly vexed by the idea. For the briefest moment, her face flushed, and she appeared to be stewing with anger. Not the anger of a woman who had just been likened to a whore – for Lucius knew well that look – but the anger of a jilted lover, one whose soul burned with jealousy, and who was exerting great effort to contain it. The episode passed just as soon as it had begun, and she continued with her story offering no explanation for the momentary lapse.

"At first, Ambiorix wanted only simple things from me," she said. "How many Romans were inside the fort? How many slaves? Which wall had Cicero reinforced? How many engines? That kind of thing. I was present in Cicero's chamber the day Master Diogenes gave him a full report on the fate of the Fourteenth Legion, and the secret he carried – the location of the pay chests. The night after I reported all of this in my regular message, I received much more specific instructions. I was to either discover the location of the chests or devise a means of spiriting the clerk out of the fort. I tried every means I could to get close to Diogenes, even tried apprehending him, that I might convince him to tell me what I wanted to know. For I did not wish to deliver the poor man to Ambiorix, knowing well what means the Eburones use to extract information. But all my attempts met with failure. When Honorius finally convinced Cicero to try recovering the hidden fortune, I saw an opportunity and took it."

"You asked Cicero to send you and that bastard Belfric along as guides," Lucius concluded, then smirked. "And our fool of a general agreed to it."

"What choice did I have?" she said hotly. "I have told you, legionary, I am no friend of the Eburones. I would much sooner spit in Ambiorix's eye." Erminhilt glanced back at Diogenes, huffing through the mud, three intervals behind, well out of earshot. "I did not wish any harm to come to him. I would have offered him a portion of the silver in exchange for the location of the pay chests, and I would have kept my word. I only wanted to save my father."

"Generous of you," Lucius said derisively. "Especially since the money does not belong to you."

She gave him an apathetic look. "Do not pretend to be above reproach, legionary. In your years as a soldier, how many settlements and villages have you ransacked? I'll wager if you knew the location of the chests, you would retrieve them for yourself and never tell a soul."

Though Lucius did not reply, he admitted to himself that she did indeed have a point.

Erminhilt began to sob once again, presumably besought with grief and worry over her father's unknown fate. Lucius was almost inclined to believe her story. But whether she was lying to win sympathy, or her father truly did sit at the bottom of a pit awaiting a grisly death, it did not matter. There was nothing Lucius could do about it. His task was to safely deliver Diogenes to Caesar. It was for someone higher in the ranks to determine Erminhilt's fate, and so he asked her no more.

The squad continued marching well into the night, beneath the glittering heavens, amidst the howl of the wolf and the hoot of the owl. Since they were staying off the well-known trails, Lucius was not exactly sure of their route. He only knew they headed west, where Caesar was assumed to be, and, if not Caesar, then at least friendlier Gauls and perhaps other Roman legions.

Near midnight, Lucius finally ordered them to stop. The weary legionaries thankfully bedded down in damp blankets on the cold ground, and two men were posted to the vigil. Lucius bound Erminhilt's hands and feet firmly, but not harshly, and rolled into his own bedroll beside the woman prisoner, his gladius held firmly in one hand in the event of treachery.

As Lucius drifted off to sleep, his eyes settled on Erminhilt. She stared wistfully at the night sky, no doubt still pondering the fate of her father. Her figure formed pleasant curves beneath the blanket, and Lucius felt desires deep within him not satiated for far too long. Yes, she had betrayed them. Yes, she had tried to kill them all. But there was something enchanting about her, even when helpless. His mind lingered on how she had looked naked and bound to the tree, and it stirred the fires of lust within him. He was, after all, as mortal as the next man.

It would be easy for him to take her now, to quench those flames in a few breathless moments of warmth and passion, in exchange for her freedom. But a wave of guilt suddenly flooded over him at the possibility she might be telling the truth. His thoughts strayed to another time and another place, far away from this cold land, when a mob of escaped slaves attacked his family's estate, raping and murdering his mother and sister, then torturing his father and leaving him to die slowly. His father had died shortly after the eighteen-year-old Lucius had found him, his final breaths taken in Lucius's arms.

Lucius turned his head away from Erminhilt's tempting form, any desires for her squelched by the pain of his past. He knew he should not trust her, nor should he let himself be consumed by her troubles, but her story had touched a chord deep within him.

It was near the eighth hour when Lucius awoke to the sound of snoring, or at least that is what he believed had awoken him. Maximus slept nearby, snoring like the dying gasps of a horse run into the ground, and loud enough to stir Scipio from the crypt. Lucius got up and used his booted foot to brusquely roll the legionary onto his other side, and the dissonant noise soon ceased. When he returned to his bedroll, he noticed Erminhilt was still awake, still staring at the twinkling sky, no doubt still pondering her father. There was something odd about the lay of her hands, something unnatural, but Lucius dismissed it as a consequence of the rope that bound them together.

"You had best rest," he said. "We have a long march tomorrow."

"Release me," she pleaded, holding him in her gaze, as if she somehow knew he had been contemplating her predicament. "I must save my father!"

"That is impossible. I doubt my officers would be pleased if I let an attempted murderess go free. Besides, lass, where will you go? The Eburones king won't appreciate you showing up empty-handed."

"Release me!" she said again, desperately. "You must release me. You must!"

Sighing heavily, Lucius gave her a sympathetic look, but said nothing. He pulled his blanket over him, closed his eyes, and did his best to purge any thoughts of the woman or her father from his mind. As sleep quickly overcame him, he heard a faint sound floating on the wind – a frail, wispy voice. Was it his imagination or was it a mere trick of the night air? It sounded like the voice of Honorius, wheezing and shivering upon his stretcher only a few feet away.

"Do not trust her, Lucius. Do not trust her."

XIX

The next morning, Lucius climbed to the crest of a nearby hill to survey the land ahead. Far off to the west, a smudge of smoke lingered above the rolling hills. It could be Caesar's column. It could also be marauding Belgic cavalry torching the farmsteads of those who had refused to join the revolt. Whatever its source, the smoke was in their path, and they would reach it this day.

As Lucius strode back to the camp, expecting to find his legionaries in kit and ready to march, he sensed more than heard an unnatural stillness that made his warrior instincts suddenly bristle. Where he had expected to hear voices and the rustle of arms and equipment, he heard nothing. No sooner had he drawn his gladius from his scabbard than he was suddenly surrounded by sword warriors on all sides, wearing black cloaks like those of the horsemen he and his squad had slain. They were ready for battle, holding shields and weapons as though they had been waiting for him, their jaws set in anticipation of his resistance. Though without his own shield, Lucius considered making a dash at them, for he had taken on as many enemies before, but a glance beyond them into the camp clearing told him any such action would have fatal results for the rest of his men. He saw the bloody, stretched-out corpses of two of them, obviously killed while they stood the morning vigil and then dragged into the camp. Sergius, Maximus, Geta and the others were kneeling, helmetless and disarmed. Around them stood no less than a score of the Belgic horsemen, all on foot, all brandishing longswords and clearly ready to strike off the heads of their prisoners. Diogenes knelt there, too, white with shock and fear. The woman, however, stood with the swordsmen, her bonds now cut, her eyes glaring back at Lucius with venom.

In the few moments it took Lucius to register all of this, one of the men in front of him suddenly advanced with a lunge. Lucius parried it easily enough, but it allowed another man to rush at him from behind and strike him across the head with the flat side of a sword, sending Lucius's helmet flying and knocking him momentarily senseless. The next instant, his attackers were on top of him, pummeling him with the hilts of their swords while others pried the sword and dagger from his hands. Once disarmed, he was pushed into the circle of prisoners to join his men.

Diogenes gave Lucius a regretful look, as did the others, as if they were ashamed at having been taken so easily. But Lucius surmised there was little they could have done. They were vastly outnumbered. He guessed the enemy warriors had left their horses some distance away, and had crept up on the camp in the night, for he had not heard the whinny of any beasts. For a moment, he wondered how they had managed to find the camp in the dark, when he and his men had been careful to light no fires, but a glance at Erminhilt told him she was responsible. She brandished a small iron object the size of two fingers, holding it up for him to see and smiling at him victoriously. Lucius instantly recognized the object as his own fire starter, and he suddenly realized it had not been Maximus's snoring that had awoken him the night before. It had been the sound of the woman rummaging through his kit, where she had no doubt found his stone of flint and the iron fire starter. Like a fool, he had been inclined to believe her story, and his sympathy had led him to deviate from the normal method of dealing with prisoners. He should have bound her hands tightly around a tree, no matter her discomfort, but he had instead used the iron shackles they had found on one of the dead Belgae. The shackles had allowed her arms a good foot of movement, just enough to strike the fire starter against the flint and produce a brilliant flash of sparks in the darkness. Knowing her countrymen were likely searching for her, she had probably struck the flint continuously throughout the night, ensuring the men on watch were facing away whenever she did it. In his own exhausted state, Lucius had not woken to the light tapping of the stone. The Eburones horsemen would have had their eagle-eyed scouts in the tallest trees, scanning the hills for any such sign, and had spent the night converging on her signal.

Now, the men of his squad were on their knees, helpless. Any resistance on their part would result in little more than their own deaths. Their shields had been tossed into a pile and were being hacked to pieces by several enemy knights who laughed as they laid into the painted plywood with giant axes. Honorius lay on the ground amongst the prisoners, roiling in pain, obviously having been dragged there from his litter with no regard for his already wretched condition. The tribune's face grimaced and blood trickled from his lips. Lucius made one move towards him but was instantly cudgeled on the head by a sword hilt.

By the time Lucius had collected his senses again, he heard hoofs approaching and looked up to see a troop of mounted horsemen enter the camp. A large-framed, bearded rider was at their head, a warlord of some sort, wearing an ornate, feather-topped helmet and a polished bronze breastplate. Ignoring the deferential greetings from the other knights, the warlord dismounted, doffed his helmet, and quickly strode over to Erminhilt who met him with a warm embrace. He held Erminhilt's face in his hands and spoke to her gingerly, as if to confirm she was unharmed. As Lucius observed this, he got the notion he had seen this man before, though he could not quite place him.

"That's him," Diogenes whispered beside Lucius.

"What?" Lucius muttered.

"The Eburones king!" Diogenes replied exasperatedly. "I remember the helmet, the cloak, the face. That's Ambiorix!"

At this revelation, a fog suddenly lifted in Lucius's mind, and he remembered where he had seen the warlord before. It was the same Belgic knight who had ridden into the fort under the banner of truce – the envoy from the Eburones. He had not been an envoy at all, but the Eburones king himself. And now the stolen glances Lucius had witnessed on that day between the pretend envoy and the woman made perfect sense, and he began to realize that he had been played for a complete fool. He could not make out every word the two exchanged now, but it was clear that

Ambiorix spoke to Erminhilt tenderly, as a man speaks to his wife, and that she regarded him with an adoration bordering on infatuation. Erminhilt was not the victim of the Eburones king, as she had claimed. By all observations, she was his wife or mistress, and everything she had done – infiltrating the fort, attempting to kidnap Diogenes, betraying the mission – had all been willful acts to please her lover and king.

Ambiorix listened carefully as she spoke, and Lucius surmised she was filling him in on all that had transpired since leaving the fort. At one point, she said something that appeared to anger him immensely. She then pointed to Lucius, and Ambiorix directed a menacing glare at him.

After Erminhilt finished telling her story, Ambiorix approached the group of kneeling Romans, glancing them over as a trader eyes a flock of disease-ridden cattle. His eyes then settled on Diogenes, and he motioned to the guards. "Separate him from the rest. Guard him closely, for we need what is in his head."

"I will give you nothing!" the terrified clerk said as boldly as he could, but instantly received a savage blow from one of the guards and was dragged away, favoring a swelling jaw.

Ambiorix turned his attention to Lucius.

"You! Stand up!" he said in heavily accented Latin.

Lucius was abruptly pulled to his feet by two guards who cursed him in the Belgic tongue. The Eburones king appeared momentarily taken aback by Lucius's large stature, but his eyes quickly narrowed again.

"You are the leader of these scum?" the king demanded.

When Lucius did not respond, a look of amusement crossed Ambiorix's face.

"I have found most Roman dogs to be obstinate at first," he said with a mirthless smile. "That changes when the torture begins. Yes, you can be assured of that. You will be screaming to your gods, begging them for mercy, Roman, but they will not hear you. They did not hear the others."

"These men are soldiers!" Lucius snapped. "A man of honor would grant them a quick death!"

The words had hardly escaped Lucius's mouth before the guards struck him. They pummeled his face and abdomen with their fists in rapid succession, knocking a tooth loose and drawing blood from his nose. Lucius reeled from the blows and then received a solid kick to his groin that put him down. But before the guards could do any more damage, a raised hand from their king stopped them, and they pulled Lucius back to his feet.

"So, the tall one does have a tongue," Ambiorix said. "My nobles are offended, Roman, when you do not address me properly. It is well known the Romans despise the idea of a king, but you are not in Rome. You are in my land."

"My lord," Lucius said as respectfully as he could manage. "I ask mercy for these men. They showed great restraint in not harming your woman. Is that not deserving of a soldier's death?"

"When a dirty Latin crosses into Belgic lands," Ambiorix snarled. "He deserves nothing but pain and death. I assure you, had you harmed her, your manner of death would have been particularly severe."

Beyond Ambiorix's shoulder, Lucius could see Erminhilt smiling, taking great pleasure in the spectacle.

A grunt came from Honorius. The ailing tribune lay cringing from the pain in his abdomen, coughing now more violently than ever. The Eburones king looked down at Honorius and then back at Lucius, and then smiled as one might after gaining the upper hand. "I understand it was you who slew Belfric."

Lucius stared back at him but said nothing.

"An impressive feat." Ambiorix continued. "Belfric was a powerful warrior. I have seen him slay a dozen men in a single battle. You, then, must also be a great warrior."

"I am a simple soldier," Lucius replied. "Like any other."

"A simple soldier could not have killed Belfric." Ambiorix's smile quickly faded as he spoke. "A simple Roman could not have slain my comrade and champion, my confidant and friend, my companion since childhood. The man you slew, Roman, was all of these things!"

As Lucius watched, Ambiorix's face suddenly transformed into a vengeful scowl. He began to shake as if brimming with rage. Then, with a loud cry of anger, he drew out his longsword, took two steps, and brought the weapon down hard onto Honorius's exposed neck. In two savage, hacking strokes the tribune's head was severed from his shoulders and rolled down the slope to stop at Lucius's feet.

Lucius gazed upon Honorius's frozen features, calm, as if posing for a portrait. He had only come to know Honorius in the past few days. Like all tribunes, he had been somewhat naïve at times, a bit too tied to ideals and honor, but Honorius had been a fair man, and that was rare among the officer caste. Lucius had even come to like him, and perhaps that was why he now felt anger boiling within him. That Honorius should be killed in such a manner, unarmed, sick in his bed, after suffering for days from the woman's poison, enraged him. Lucius looked up at the Eburones king with malice in his eyes.

"You Belgic son of a bitch!" Lucius roared.

This was instantly answered by more blows from the guards, and they did not stop with Lucius. Their comrades began thrashing the other prisoners, kicking them on the ground and striking them with their sword hilts, while the outnumbered and unarmed Romans could only answer their captors with curses.

After the beatings stopped, Lucius was pulled back to his feet to stand before Ambiorix. The Eburones king casually wiped Honorius's blood from his sword using the slack in the dead tribune's cloak. He looked oddly contented, as if the grisly execution had satiated his anger over Belfric's death.

"You hate me, Roman, as I hate you." Ambiorix returned Lucius's baleful stare. "You wish to kill me? You wish for your sword?"

"I need no sword to wrench the life out of a rat." Lucius spat. "Fight me hand-to-hand. Tell your men to back off and not to interfere, and I swear I'll send you to Odin's halls to empty piss-pots alongside those whore-spawn halfwits you call your forefathers!"

The guards moved to strike the Roman but Ambiorix stopped them. He was amused by the challenge. He kicked the headless corpse at his feet. "You asked for mercy, Roman. Have I not given it? This wretch was obviously dying. I have granted him a swift death, as you desired. Consider it my gratitude for sparing the woman. As for you and the others, your fates will not be so painless. Perhaps you witnessed the fate of the others we intercepted?" He paused long enough for the prisoners to recollect the gruesome executions of Cicero's couriers, impaled within clear view of the fort's walls. "You shall suffer as few men have suffered, Roman. You shall know pain conceived only in the darkest nightmares of the shadow druids. You will beg for death, but it will only come when you have been divested of every last quality that identifies you as a man. You will die less than a beast of the field, a grotesque monster whom your own mother would revile and forsake."

Even after these threats, Ambiorix saw no fear in the eyes of the big legionary. Ambiorix had always scoffed at the individual fighting ability of the Romans. Without their formations, and their comrades around them, they were weak. But this Roman with the scar on the side of his face, whose spirit seemed indomitable, appeared he could hold his own in the battle line, or alone and surrounded by his enemies. He seemed a determined fellow. It would be vain and foolish to risk single combat with this Roman.

A hail drew Ambiorix's attention away. Several riders had galloped into the camp. He recognized them as one of the patrols he had sent scouting for any Roman legions marching to the relief of Cicero. The knight at the head of this patrol shared his mount with a boy who wore the modest garb of a peasant.

"Ho, Lambert," Ambiorix greeted the knight.

"We came across this lad in the forest, my lord," Lambert said, letting the boy slide down from his horse. "He drove his own mount into the ground getting here. He claims to have some news of great value which he will share with only you."

Ambiorix examined the boy. The lad could have been no more than twelve years of age. He looked pale and exhausted, as if he had not slept for days.

"Who are you, boy?"

"My name is Iudocus. My father is Isa, elderman of Brosella."

"I know his father, my lord," Lambert interposed, seeing the skeptical look on his king's face. "This lad is who he claims to be."

"Well, speak up boy. What news do you have?"

"I come to tell my king of a Roman column heading this way. It is led by the Roman proconsul himself."

Ambiorix studied the boy's eyes carefully. "Did you see

Caesar, boy, or did someone tell you this?"

"He was this close to me, sire," the boy replied confidently. "And though I have never seen him before, there is no doubt it was Caesar. All in his party addressed him thus, and my father knew his face." The boy gladly accepted a waterskin offered him, and took a long drink before continuing. "My father sent me to tell you, Caesar marches quickly. He means to raise your siege."

"And how did your father come by this information, boy?"

"Two days ago, he was forced to open our village to Caesar's troops and allow them to draw grain from our winter stores."

"He was forced to, was he?" Ambiorix regarded him icily.

The boy looked confused, but then spoke proudly. "I assure you my father is loyal, my king. When he heard you were leading the tribes in revolt, he immediately apprehended all Roman sympathizers in our village and had them put to death."

Ambiorix mused, more than likely, the boy's father used the revolt as an excuse to do away with some of his own political enemies. Whether vying for a vast empire or the poorest scrapheap of a village, some men would do anything to attain total control, unfettered power. It was an attribute, or a curse, that Ambiorix understood well.

"How far away is Caesar now, boy?"

"One day, maybe two. They move swiftly, sire, unimpeded by baggage."

Ambiorix turned to Lambert. "You believe this boy?"

"For his information, I cannot say, my lord. But I can attest he is indeed the third son of Isa. His father did take some risk in sending him here."

"Third son?" Ambiorix raised his eyebrows. "Are your

older brothers dead then, boy?

"No, my king," Iudocus replied modestly. "They remain with my father."

"I see." It was very clear to Ambiorix now just how far the loyalty of Isa of Brosella stretched. Obviously, he was a man with a foot in each camp. The potential loss of his third son was an acceptable risk to remain in the good graces of his king. In the event of Caesar's defeat, the village elderman would have fulfilled his duty as a Belgic magistrate and could expect to reap some reward for the information. Conversely, should Caesar triumph, or happen to capture young Iudocus, the father would have no trouble forsaking this inconsequential son to Caesar's wrath, claiming the boy acted on his own. The proud, yet guileless, Iudocus was not clever enough to understand his father's duplicitous nature. He had simply done what he was told to do.

"Alright then, boy," Ambiorix said, more affably. "Tell us the numbers. How many eagles?"

"One only, sire."

A hush descended on the assembled men, and Ambiorix found himself skipping a breath. He swallowed hard before addressing the boy again.

"You must be mistaken, lad. Not even an arrogant horse's arse like Caesar would dare march into the heart of Belgica with only one legion."

"I may be young, sire, but I know well the Roman order of march. I saw them myself. Four thousand spears, at least. The Furies of Hispania, the Ninth Legion, drawn from their winter quarters in the west."

"And how many auxiliaries?"

"No more than five hundred, my lord. Horsemen and nobles, mostly. Most are Gauls, but there are some Belgae among them."

Ambiorix turned to Lambert. "What say your scouts? Are there any other legions out there, perhaps coming to reinforce Caesar?"

The knight shook his head. "Not all have reported back yet, sire. Those that have report no Romans within several day's march." He then added fervently, expressing the excitement they all felt. "This is truly a gift from the gods, my king! Our penitence has finally roused Odin's favor! Caesar is alone and weak. No one is coming to help him."

Whether the gods had anything to do with it, Ambiorix did not care. This was the turn of fortune he had been waiting for. Though he kept his composure, inwardly he surged with joy, daring to hope it was all true. But how could it be true? How could Caesar have blundered so completely? Rashness and imprudence was not unknown to the great Roman proconsul, but what ill-conceived logic could have persuaded him to march with only one legion? The tinge of an insult fizzled within Ambiorix's breast as he considered what slight regard Caesar must have for the Belgic tribes and their fighting ability. Was that it, or was it simply that Caesar had begun to believe his own legend? The tales had become commonplace around the campfires of Gaul and Belgica, tales of the priest-like Roman proconsul who knew no equal in battle, and who could not be defeated. Had these tales tickled the mortal ears of Caesar, cursing him with that same sense of self-assurance that had presaged the fall of so many great generals of the past? Whatever the reason, Caesar had underestimated him. Like the great Hannibal at Zama, the unconquered Caesar had finally met his match. He had made a foolish mistake, and Ambiorix was intent on making it a fatal one.

All the meticulous planning of the past days – the siege, the Roman silver, the pact with the Germans – none of it mattered now. The grand prize lay within his grasp, and he intended to seize it. Only one thing mattered now – killing Caesar.

"Your father will be well rewarded for his loyalty, lad." Ambiorix clapped a hand on the boy's shoulder, and then turned to Lambert. "Go with this boy. Find Caesar's column and see for yourself if it is true."

"Yes, my lord."

The boy and the knight soon departed on the freshest horses the royal guard had to offer. As Ambiorix watched them go, he glanced up at the position of the sun, and his former exhilaration was quickly replaced by a sense of urgency. If Caesar truly was less than two days away, then there was not much time to act. He must move his vast army from their siege works to intercept Caesar, and he must move them quickly, before Caesar got wind of their change in disposition, before the Roman could withdraw to safer lands. As a man betrothed to a contentious woman faces his wedding day, Ambiorix knew he must act now or this perfect opportunity would be irreparably lost.

"We must rejoin the army at once, Sedgerick," he said to the commander of the horse guards.

"The beasts were ridden very hard last night," Sedgerick replied apologetically. "If we do not rest them, my lord, they will be of little use in battle."

"Rest them, then, and follow when you can. I and my house guards will depart immediately. We will take a dozen of your hardiest and fastest mounts. Do not tarry here long. I wish to have your lances in the coming fight."

"We shall follow in the morning, sire. Have no fear." Sedgerick paused, and then asked. "Your pardon, my lord, but what shall we do with the prisoners?"

Ambiorix glanced at the unimpressive cluster of beaten and bruised Romans. He came very near to telling Sedgerick to kill them, but then a moment's reflection changed his mind. Though the hidden silver was now the furthest from his thoughts, it might prove useful should the battle not go as he planned. He would keep the Roman clerk as an indemnity. As for the others, he might find a use for them, perhaps as sacrifices, perhaps to torture within sight of Cicero's walls once Caesar and his legion were annihilated.

"I have reconsidered, Sedgerick. You and your riders will not join the army. Instead, you will go to Aduatuca. Take the prisoners there and await my orders."

"Yes, my lord," the commander of the guards replied, clearly despondent at the prospect of missing the battle.

Out of the corner of his eye, Ambiorix saw Erminhilt watching him keenly. She would expect to go with him, too, but he could not allow that.

"Erminhilt will also remain with you," he announced. "See that she is well cared for, Sedgerick. Protect her as you would me. You will answer to me if she is treated otherwise."

"Yes, my lord."

"Am I not to come with you?" Erminhilt was suddenly by his side, wrapping her arm around his, studying his face, as if to seek out and discover his true desires.

Turning to embrace her, he stared pensively into her eyes. "No, my beloved." He tried to sound as if the decision had been difficult, but he knew it was the only one that ensured the loyalty of a certain aging king. Back with the army, old Cativolcus anxiously awaited news of his daughter. There was no telling what conspiracies the old king might attempt should his treasured daughter return to the shadow of his protection. For now, her absence kept the old king obedient, and Ambiorix would need that old bastard's help to convince the other tetchy chieftains that a forced march of nearly two dozen miles in the biting, winter wind was essential to their success.

Ambiorix placed a hand on Erminhilt's cold cheek. "I need you to watch over the clerk, my beloved. I am entrusting him, and the secret he carries, to you. Wait for me at Aduatuca. I will join you once I have crushed Caesar."

There was concern in her gaze, but some guardedness as well. Was she, too, now second guessing him, like her father?

"Take heed, my love," he said assuredly. "When next you see me, Caesar will be no more, and there will be a new ruler over all of Belgica." He said this intending to remind her of her station. "My name shall be sung on the lips of every poet from Italy to Britannia. and for generations to come, they will sing of the glorious reign of Ambiorix the Great, King of the Eburones, High King of the Belgae."

A horse was brought to Ambiorix. The armored house guards sat atop their mounts awaiting their king. After an affectionate kiss and one last yearnful look into Erminhilt's tearful eyes, he pulled himself up into the saddle. Without another word, he donned his falcon-crested helmet, wheeled his mount, and thundered away in a stir of mud-clotted hoofs and clanging armor.

XX

Lucius and the other legionaries had been severely treated throughout the day. Stripped of their armor and bound to trees, they were physically tormented at the whims of their captors as the Belgic horsemen pitched their own camp. As night fell, the horses were moved to the natural shelter formed by a thick bank of trees, but no such accommodation was made for the prisoners. They were left to bear the biting wind and elements. The horsemen kept warm by their own fires, too far away to deliver any heat to the bound Romans.

As the chills wracked Lucius's body, he tried to focus on the flames and not his own condition. He picked out Erminhilt among the shadowy figures sitting around one of the fires. She was being attended by Sedgerick and several knights among the group. Diogenes sat uncomfortably a few feet away, obviously of more importance than the other prisoners. Lucius knew the clerk would crack once the Belgae started torturing him for answers. But for now, he was being treated well and was always under the protective eyes of Erminhilt.

Before the horsemen retired to their beds, Erminhilt wrapped herself in a thick deerskin cloak and made her way over to study the shivering prisoners, her gaze finally settling on Lucius. There was little sympathy in her eyes, only triumph and hatred.

"We will travel much slower tomorrow if these men cannot walk or ride," she said to the guardsmen tasked with watching the prisoners. "Build a fire here that they might not freeze to death. Not too large. We do not want them to be comfortable."

As the guards began stacking tinder near the prisoners, Erminhilt drew closer to Lucius.

"You should have released me, Roman," she said bemusedly.

"So, it was all a lie then?" Lucius said. "Your father is not the hostage of Ambiorix?"

She frowned insincerely. "Ambiorix is my king. I would think even a Roman could deduce that."

"He appears to be more than that," Lucius said mockingly, trying not to outwardly display the burning pain he felt in his frozen extremities. "He must have some affection for you, letting you play the part of Cicero's whore to advance his own aims. I'm surprised he still wants you. You said it yourself, lass, Cicero helped himself to every pleasure you had to give."

Her pale hand emerged from the cloak and struck him hard across the face.

"I gladly serve my king, Roman!" She snapped. "It is my pleasure to suffer for him. But that is no concern of yours.

Were I you, I would make peace with my gods, and beg for the mercy of death. For a true terror awaits you." She leaned in close to him and said tauntingly. "One day, your people will bow before my king! They will be his slaves, as will your Gallic allies. Think on that in the few days you have left, Roman."

"Not my people, lass. I am from Spain."

She appeared confused and slightly annoyed at his response, but said nothing more. After gazing upon him exultantly for a long interval, she turned and retired.

XXI

The fires burned brightly late into the night. Whether out of frustration over being left out of the coming battle, or simply because they were out of the purview of their king, the Belgic horsemen chose to employ themselves as ill-disciplined soldiers often do – they drank. A supply of wine was produced and the entire troop proceeded to imbibe liberally, despite Sedgerick's objections. They exhibited a complete disregarded for the prohibition on such spirits normally enforced among their people. Lucius overheard one say the wine had been plundered from a Roman trader whom they had crucified upon a tree with spikes taken from his own merchandise.

They cackled without a care for many hours, pausing only to relieve their bladders onto the bound prisoners with great amusement. Finally, when half had drunk themselves unconsciousness and the rest could hardly stand, the wine ran out, and their jovial mood turned sour. They began to threaten one another. Some brawled physically. Some kicked the abdomens of their unconscious comrades for sport. Some even made a game of a poor, lame horse which each in turn attempted to knock down with a single punch. Sedgerick had lost all control of his horsemen, now a band of violent drunks, and had abandoned any attempt at restraining them. He stood with two of his clearer headed knights, swords drawn, fending off the advances made on Erminhilt by the lecherous mob. Erminhilt stood behind her protectors, Diogenes at her side, a long dagger in her hand held at the ready should any of the thugs manage to reach her.

Deprived of their only possible female entertainment, the frenzied warriors soon turned their attention to the bound prisoners, first contenting themselves with beating them, and then turning to more devious designs. A few began eyeing the Romans as they would the offering of harlots at a bordello, and, after exchanging encouraging whispers among them, decided to act on their depraved notions.

Lucius saw three of them come towards him. Though he was still numb from the earlier beatings and the cold, he feigned the extent of his fatigue. He allowed the three degenerates to draw closer, luring them into underestimating his remaining strength. There was just enough slack in his bindings to deliver a solid blow with his knees should one get close enough. Sinister grins appeared on the grime-streaked faces of the three horsemen as they removed their mail shirts. The one chosen to go first began pulling loose the strings of his trousers, and still Lucius did not move. He waited, fully intending to jerk his body violently enough to knock the reprobate senseless when the right moment came – but he never got the chance.

The drunk had taken only one step towards Lucius, when an arrow flew out of the night and buried itself in the man's exposed belly. The warrior looked at the shaft for a long, confused moment, then emitted a guttural sigh, his eyes rolling back as he crumpled to the ground. The other two sniggered at their fallen comrade, believing he had merely stumbled, but their merriment was cut short when two more feathered shafts streaked out of the dark woods and burrowed into their unarmored torsos. One dying man managed to cry out in alarm, but this did little more than confuse the others, half of whom laughed as if it were a jest.

The next moment, a mass of whooping figures emerged from the shadows. There were dozens of them, all armed with lances and swords which they immediately began thrusting and slashing into every drunk horseman in their path. The faint light of the fires gave the attackers a sinister appearance, but Lucius quickly recognized their armor and accoutrements as that of dismounted Roman cavalry. Gallic knights were amongst them, too, wearing white armbands signifying their allegiance to Rome. They hacked and slew, hacked and slew, felling one confused enemy after another, meeting little resistance. Some of the slumbering Belgae came to their senses in time to see dripping Roman blades before their faces, and to let out horrified shrieks before being butchered where they lay. Those too cataleptic never woke again, pinned to the ground by the iron-tipped lances.

There were few true clashes of steel. The only real challenge came from Sedgerick and the two men with him protecting Erminhilt. They swung their long swords in wild, sweeping arcs that kept the surrounding attackers at bey for a short interval, but they, too, were eventually overcome. Sedgerick was the last to fall, wide-eyed and gasping, his throat sliced open, his mouth opening and closing like that of a landed fish. Splattered with the blood of her slain defenders, Erminhilt saw the futility of further resistance and allowed herself to be disarmed and taken prisoner.

Dawn broke soon after, revealing a field of dead Belgae, the faces of many frozen in the horror of their last moments. Roman knights and Gallic warriors rummaged through the remnants of the camp, impassive to the ghastly exhibit.

"We saw the fires of these whore-spawn, and thought to put an end to their revelry," the tribune in command of the victorious cavalry explained to Lucius after releasing the legionaries from their bonds. "You are Roman, are you not?"

"Yes, sir," Lucius replied, saluting. "Legionary Lucius Domitius, at your service."

"Titus Albinus, at yours." The cordiality of his tone seemed to change when he discovered Lucius was merely a soldier. "And your officers? Where are they?"

"Dead, sir." Lucius pointed to the bloody cloak draped over the rigid body of Honorius.

"The bloody savages!" Albinus exclaimed angrily, but then turned his head abruptly as if annoyed. "Hercules's balls! What is that infernal noise?"

Several coughs came from one of the Belgic bodies lying only a few paces away. The enemy warrior still drew breath, and though he bled from many wounds, he was coming to, his eyes fluttering. Albinus swiftly walked over to the wounded man and, without a word or the slightest trace of emotion, placed his booted foot on the Belgian's neck, slowly increasing the pressure until the flailing and kicking man went limp.

"Am I to assume then, Legionary Domitius," Albinus continued, as if he had done little more than step on an

197

insect. "That you are from Caesar's column?"

"No, sir. We belong to the Seventh. We were trying to reach Caesar's army when we were captured."

"The Seventh? Damn it to Pluto, man! Then we have quite wasted our time with this diversion." After seeing the confusion on Lucius's face, he added. "We are from the Twelfth – under General Fabius. Our legion has been on the forced march for nigh on four days. We, too, seek the elusive proconsul. Fabius has orders to join forces with Caesar, if he can find him in this infernal country. Not the most convenient rendezvous, is it?"

A commotion stirred behind the tribune as several of the Gauls harassed Erminhilt and laughed at her distress. Whether from the tattoos on her face, or her dialect, they had no trouble identifying her as belonging to an enemy tribe.

"And who in Juno's name is she?" Albinus asked.

But before Lucius could answer, Sergius and Maximus were there, mud-covered and adorned in nothing but torn tunics, while carrying a half-conscious man between them. "Begging your pardon, sir. We found Diogenes. He must have taken one devil of a blow. Got a lump on the back of his head as big as my fist, but he's breathing."

"Who in Pluto's Realm is this, Legionary Domitius?" Albinus demanded, clearly irritated by the interruption.

Lucius ignored the tribune, kneeling to examine the dazed clerk.

"Diogenes," Lucius said, lightly slapping the clerk's face. "Can you hear me?"

He looked up at Lucius from beneath half-open eyelids, and coughed out a reply. "You were right, Legionary Domitius. About the woman, about the mission, about everything."

"Don't try to speak. Conserve your strength. We still

have ground to cover."

"I owe you thanks," Diogenes struggled to say. "For saving my life on two occasions…and an apology. I like to think I could have held my tongue, withstood the Belgae's torture, never revealing the location of the money, but I -"

"Say no more!" Lucius interrupted, then turned to Sergius and Maximus. "Stay with him, both of you. Don't let those Gaul bastards mistake him for a Belgian. We'll see him delivered to Caesar yet."

As the two carried their charge away, the tribune Albinus eyed Lucius crossly.

"Sorry, sir." Lucius offered meekly.

"I am not accustomed to being disregarded, legionary. Now, I shall ask you again. What is all of this about? That man spoke of money."

"I made a promise to my late officer, sir," Lucius pointed to the shrouded body. "Tribune Honorius was a good man, and I keep my vows, sir."

"What did you promise?"

"To deliver Master Diogenes there to Caesar. You see, sir, he knows something – something important. He's got information in his head the enemy desperately wants, information meant for Caesar. If you can help me, sir, then I think I can help you."

"Go on," Albinus said guardedly.

"I think I know where we can find Caesar, sir. That is, if I overheard those Belgic bastards correctly yesterday. If Fortuna is with us, we should find Caesar's army by nightfall. Can you spare some horses for me and my mates, sir?"

"I suppose that can be arranged." Albinus appeared disgusted to have to stoop so. "But you still have not answered my question, legionary. What about the money?"

Lucius smiled at the tribune, and said assuredly. "The

rest, with all due respect, sir, is for Caesar's ears alone."

XXII

"The way is clear, great Caesar," the Belgic chieftain said as he feverishly stripped a chicken bone bare and tossed it onto the floor rushes. "Ambiorix remains encamped around the fort. He is completely unaware you are coming, let alone a mere day's march away. If you hurry now, and press on, you can take him by surprise. But only if you hurry, my lord. You must hurry!"

"You have my thanks, Lord Gisilbert," Caesar said, signaling a slave to refill the chieftain's cup. The candles on the table fluttered as a wisp of the icy wind outside made its way past the drawn flaps of the tent. "It is indeed fortunate you found us when you did."

Gisilbert did not make eye contact as he spoke, but continued devouring the roasted chicken and fresh bread set before him. Caesar lounged on a chair opposite the grunting man, while Trebonius, sat off to the side. The legate was beside himself with disgust that Caesar would treat this fork-tongued devil so magnanimously. Could Caesar not see this devious chieftain who now sat before him eating his food and drinking his wine, was playing him for a fool?

In the days of marching through this wretched, frozen country, Trebonius had grown tired of the incessant stream of eldermen and chieftains coming to Caesar to swear their allegiance and their support, insisting they had played no part in the revolt. Conveniently, most had left their warriors back in their oppida, under the pretext that they needed to defend their own lands from Ambiorix's ranging hordes. Gisilbert had given a similar explanation. He led an insignificant Belgic tribe numbering only a few hundred, too weak to be of any consequence. Like the other chieftains, he could be trusted to throw his allegiance behind the victor, whomever that proved to be.

But Caesar appeared completely unaware of Gisilbert's duplicitous nature. In fact, he seemed captivated by the man's wealth of information on the enemy. The proconsul eagerly studied the map laid out on the table between them as Gisilbert's greasy fingers identified the strength and disposition of the Belgic army around Cicero's fort.

"So, you claim Cicero is near capitulation?" Caesar said to Gisilbert. "Can you be certain of that?"

"Yes, Caesar. My men infiltrated the Eburones camp. The things they learned, I hesitate to tell you."

"Speak on, my friend."

"Merciful Toutatis be with them, Caesar, but those poor souls inside the fort are near to starvation. They've barely a horse or a rat left to consume. Corpses are being retrieved from outside the walls, and you know what that means, Caesar. Cicero's men have turned into savages. They now devour human flesh for nourishment." Gisilbert paused to take a generous bite of meat from a leg bone, before tossing the bone over his shoulder. "Indeed, Cicero has made a brave stand, but there are too many arrayed against him. His walls will soon be breached. I would doubt he can hold for another day. Haste is of the utmost importance, my lord, the difference between succor and slaughter."

"And how many fighting men does Ambiorix have?"

"I should hardly call them fighting men, great Caesar," Gisilbert laughed, pausing to belch before continuing. "It is a negligible force, manned by poorly armed farmers and herdsmen. Between the Nervii, the Aduatuci, and the Eburones, I doubt there are scarcely ten thousand spears. That inbred miscreant Ambiorix is as foolhardy as he is disloyal. I tell you again, my lord, I still shudder when I think on his betrayal. To think that he would bear arms against the blessed proconsul of Rome, the one who embraced him, and to whom he owes such a debt of gratitude."

"Yes, yes," Caesar said dismissively, still studying the map as if it were written in the language of the Parthians. "Miscreant or not, he has managed to build a wall of circumvallation around Cicero's camp – an impressive feat for such a small force. Very impressive indeed. Perhaps we should proceed with a measure of caution."

"But, time is of the essence, great Caesar," Gisilbert said, as if to head off the doubts he had carelessly planted in Caesar's mind. "While it is true Ambiorix leads a band of incompetents, there are many of them, and even Cicero cannot withstand such numbers alone. If you join him, Caesar, the dagger will be in the other hand. Your legion can attack the siege-works from without, while Cicero's attacks from within. Ambiorix will be trapped between you."

From his side stool, Trebonius wanted to burst out in

disagreement. It was a foolish plan, the stupidest, most idiotic plan he had ever heard. He would have spoken his mind, had Caesar not previously instructed him to remain silent during the entire meeting. The proconsul, for his part, did not take his eyes from the map, as if heavily weighing Gisilbert's recommendation.

"Yes, my friend. You are right." Caesar finally nodded in acquiescence. "To delay will only work to Ambiorix's advantage. We must move on the enemy with great speed, just as you say."

"You are wise, great Caesar." Gisilbert grinned, visibly relieved as he returned to his feast.

Trebonius shifted uncomfortably in his seat, resisting the urge to draw his sword and run the smug Belgian bastard through.

"Your information is most appreciated, my friend," Caesar said agreeably, then gestured to the map. "It appears our path will cross the Henne. With the rivers swollen as they are, it might take days to find a suitable ford."

"Indeed, it will, great Caesar. That is why you must use the hidden ford at Hunter's Crossing." Wiping his mouth on his sleeve, Gisilbert set the platter to one side and leaned over the map, drawing an invisible line with one pudgy finger. "There is a wagon cut through the forest here. It leads to a shallow valley where the river widens. There, you will find a ford at the base of a barren hill. You will find it suitable to take your army across."

"Are you certain it is shallow enough?"

"I would stake the fate of my tribe on it." Gisilbert chuckled unnaturally, his eyes cutting nervously under the gaze of Trebonius. "Once you are across the river, it is hardly a day's march to the fort.

While the satisfied chieftain buried his face in his cup once again, Trebonius felt his stomach churn. But then he noticed Caesar glancing back at him, a brief trace of amusement in his eyes, like a sly panther perched in the boughs of a tree watching its unsuspecting prey draw closer. When Gisilbert brought the cup down, Caesar was instantly cordial once again.

"Then we shall take your advice," Caesar said, appearing not to notice the gleeful expression on the chieftain's face. "We shall march on the morrow, and place the rest in the hands of Fortuna."

"Excellent, my lord! I am most pleased to have served you in this manner. Now, with your permission, I shall return to my oppidum and tell my people the welcome news – that the great Caesar shall save them from the wrath of that traitor Ambiorix. I will leave at once, my lord!"

He made to rise, but Caesar stopped him with a raised hand.

"Perhaps, Lord Gisilbert, it would be best if you rode with us tomorrow. If we are to face Ambiorix in battle, I would value your faithful sword beside me."

The smile froze on Gisilbert's face. His eyes stared longingly at the doorway as a galley slave might look upon freedom, just beyond the portal. After a long moment, he turned to face Caesar.

"But, of course, I would ride with you, my lord," Gisilbert replied awkwardly. "It would be my honor, and I would certainly do it, never leaving your side, no matter the danger. But, I regret, other pressing matters require me to return to my oppidum. My people, lovers of peace that they are, are sorely unprepared for defense, should the sinister fingers of Ambiorix's ambition reach our lands, we will need every sword, including those of our nobles. I am sorry, Caesar."

"I quite understand, Lord Gisilbert. And I am keeping you." Caesar gestured for an orderly to fetch the chieftain's cloak and helmet. "Go, my friend, with my thanks. Look for news of our victory. Fare you well."

"And you, great Caesar," Gisilbert said, bowing deferentially, and imparting a slight formal nod to Trebonius.

After the clip-clop of the hooves faded in the distance, signaling the departure of Gisilbert and his retinue, Trebonius finally spoke, unable to contain his frustration any longer.

"Why did you let him go, my lord? You know that bastard lies through his teeth. At this very moment, he's probably riding straight to Ambiorix to report on our strength and intentions."

"Yes." Caesar smiled at the legate. Caesar knew Gisilbert had lied about everything, about the size of the Belgic army, about the starvation in Cicero's legion, about the way being clear. He knew this because, earlier that day, while on the march, a haggard, fierce-looking Gaul had approached the column out-of-breath and bearing a message from Cicero. The Gaul's name was Vertico. He was one of the few trustworthy nobles of the Nervii, whom Caesar knew well and whom he knew to have been with Cicero's legion. Had the message not contained Cicero's cipher and his distinct manner of writing, Vertico's word alone would have been sufficient guarantee of its authenticity. The message informed Caesar that the siege had been lifted quite suddenly and that, by all appearances, Ambiorix was moving with his full force to intercept him. The Belgic force numbered thirty thousand, vastly more than Caesar had anticipated, and ten times his own strength.

The bumbling Gisilbert, no doubt, had been dispatched by Ambiorix with the intent of planting false confidence in Caesar and steering his small army toward a carefully chosen river crossing where ambush surely awaited.

"What are we to do, Caesar?" Trebonius said bleakly. "Labienus is not coming. There has been no word from Fabius. We haven't the numbers to defeat Ambiorix alone, and we can't turn back. Should word of our withdrawal reach the ears of the other tribes, Ambiorix would swell his numbers two-fold overnight. Jupiter preserve us."

"We are indeed between the hammer and the anvil, general," Caesar said, returning to the table, and eyeing the plate of leftover meat and bones with something like revulsion. He pushed aside the map and poured a cup of wine, cutting it with less water than usual, then took a long, thoughtful sip as he stared at the flickering candle before him. "The hammer and the anvil," he repeated distantly.

A long, uncomfortable silence passed between them during which the buccina could be heard outside signaling the changing of the vigil.

"Why did you let Gisilbert go?" Trebonius finally said.

"Why give fresh poison to the serpent? That fool is of little value as a hostage. Otherwise, Ambiorix would not have chosen him. Were he not to return, Ambiorix would at least think us suspicious. Better if he believes we are marching straight into his trap, completely unaware."

"What are we to do then?"

"We sleep, general." Caesar smiled bleakly. "We pray. We implore Mars to provide us with an answer."

It rained later that night, a solid steady rain that probed for the holes in the canvas tents and turned the lanes of the camp into mud. Caesar lay on his cot, listening to the pitter-patter above him. He could not sleep, though he knew he must. For if he did not, he might find himself menaced by the falling down sickness that often debilitated him at such times, and he could not afford one of those episodes now. Now, he must have all his wits about him.

Soldiers were a superstitious lot, often losing heart or

gaining courage from the most preposterous omens. Were his own legionaries to witness him in a fit on the eve of battle, they would surely consider themselves doomed to disaster. He might just as well sacrifice a sow to Ceres and walk about the camp with the ferryman's coin in his mouth.

Caesar knew everything hinged on his actions tomorrow – the fate of Gaul, indeed the fate of Rome itself. For the past four years, he had fought numerous battles, forged unholy alliances with more tribes than he liked to count, subdued vast lands and secured abundant resources for Rome on which she could draw for ages to come. True, these conquests had served an ulterior purpose, to put his own financial woes to rest, but that was of little consequence. After all, men were not remembered for paying off their creditors. Money was just a trivial thing, a collection of pressed and cut metals by which small-minded men measured success and failure. It meant nothing to posterity. The great Alexander was not admired for his wealth, nor for his indiscretions, but rather for his conquests, his vision, his divine ability to combine the destinies of many ancient cultures into one grand purpose. For this, his name – his auctoritas – would be revered through the ages. Had the great Macedonian king not met with such a tragic, useless end at such a young age, what else might he have achieved?

The cold, primordial forests of Belgica were far from the sun-bleached columns of Babylon, but Caesar felt some connection with the young Alexander, as he often had in the past. What final thoughts had passed through the ambitious mind of the young king as he lay on his death bed, surrounded by enemies and friends? Caesar was certain he knew. Why now? Why, after all he had achieved, after so many dubious circumstances had resulted in his favor, why had the fates chosen to stop him now? Why now, when all his objectives were finally within his grasp? How forlorn the Macedonian king must have felt pondering the future of his hard-won empire, as his scheming generals bickered over who would succeed him? As the breath of life left the young king's withered form, he must have wondered if his empire would even last beyond his funeral feast.

While Caesar's own meager conquests in Gaul fell short of those of Alexander, they were his crowning achievement, his personal mark on the scroll of time, and the sponge with which to wipe away the tumultuous – some might say lawless, others dung-stained – years of his consulship. Should he be defeated tomorrow, his memory would merge with that of Carbo, Longinus, and a handful of other Roman generals – failures all – who had met their ends in Gaul. There was a senate house full of his enemies, far more sinister than any foe he had faced in battle. Like Alexander's generals, they hovered over his death bed, ready to carve up his conquests the moment he breathed his last. But, unlike Alexander, they would raise no monument to his memory, nor feud over the possession of his corpse. They would label him a war criminal, a failure, and disgrace his family name. Those closest to him, those who had called him patron and friend, could expect ostracism or worse.

Caesar was pulled from these thoughts by a commotion outside, the bellow of the men in the watch towers relaying some bit of news for the general. Within moments, the curtain partition was drawn aside, and the face of his adjutant appeared, heaving with excitement.

"Forgive me, general. But riders have approached the decumana gate."

Caesar first thought this was the return of Gisilbert, the oaf having forgotten some errand dictated by his master, but then realized the chieftain and his horse guards would have left by the praetoria gate, the main gate, on the opposite side of the camp. Perhaps this was another of Ambiorix's deceptions.

By the time Caesar had sat up in bed, the adjutant was beside him, helping him to his feet.

"What is it, Quintus?"

"It's Roman cavalry, sir!" the officer reported excitedly. "They fly the standard of the Twelfth Legion. It's Fabius, general! Juno be praised, they've found us!"

Without donning more than his great cloak, Caesar strode out into the rain just in time to see a column of mud-spattered horsemen streaming out of the darkness from the direction of the gate. In a clamor of armor and hoofs, they reined their hard-ridden mounts in front of the praetorium, forming into two long rows facing him. Their rain-slickened shields bore the four-pronged lightning bolt symbol of the Twelfth. There were auxiliaries, too. The young king Commius of the Atrebates, apparently wishing to prove his loyalty to Rome, had sent lancers and mounted javelin throwers. Many of the legionaries of the camp had stirred and were now crowded around the newcomers, brandishing grins at the welcome sight of allies in this hostile land.

A plumed officer walked his mount out to stand at the forefront. Rain streamed from the officer's helmet as he saluted, but it did little to hide the flash of white teeth as he acknowledged the elation rapidly growing around the formed horsemen. Caesar instantly recognized him as one of Fabius's tribunes.

"Tribune Titus Albinus Of the Twelfth Legion, at the service of the proconsul," he introduced himself.

"Yes, I remember you, Albinus," Caesar said warmly. "You and your men have ridden hard. Do you bring us hope, young man?"

"Not just hope, my lord," Albinus grinned, then, in the true fashion of a man of the forum, he raised his voice that all might hear. "I bear a message from my general. General Fabius begs the proconsul's pardon for his tardiness, but he is here now, and ready for war. He marches at the head of five thousand spears, less than a day behind me. They press hard, anxious that Caesar and the valiant soldiers of the Ninth not take all the glory. Their swords thirst for the blood of the Eburones, and they do not wish to be deprived of their share of the slaughter. They solemnly vow to stand shoulder-to-shoulder with their brothers of the Ninth, and follow Caesar to the fields of Elysium, if needs be!"

Cheers erupted from the legionaries, each man pumping a raised fist or weapon in the air. They had trudged through mud and ice for days on end, penetrating deeper into enemy territory, and the further they had travelled the more anxious they had become. They had expected ambush around every bend, and some had even begun to question Caesar's wisdom, and whether the old man had finally pushed his luck too far. Now, reinforcements were coming, just as Caesar had said they would. The men were pleased by this. They were pleased with the horsemen and the dramatic young officer who led them, but, most of all, they were pleased with their general, blessed of the gods, who always seemed to know the best course of action. Their courage thus bolstered, the whole multitude soon began chanting *"Caesar! Caesar! Caesar!"*

Caesar acknowledged them, as if the news was not a surprise to him, careful not to display any trace of the doubt he had felt lying in his cot only moments ago. There could be no question as to his path forward now. There would be no turning back. With two legions, he would face the enemy no matter the odds. If he was not victorious, then he would at least give the Belgae enough of a thrashing to wipe away the shame of a defeat. But then, of course, to the victors went the historical record as well as the spoils – and so he must win.

As the men continued to chant, raising their voices to the night sky, and more torches were brought to light up the jubilation, Caesar noticed a motley assortment of individuals among the horsemen. Judging from their armor, and the awkward way they sat the saddle, they were foot soldiers. There was a woman among them, too – Belgian, if those tattoos on her face were any indication of her origins. In contrast to the soldiers, she seemed perfectly at home in the saddle – though her wrists were bound to it. A prisoner, no doubt. She bore that same distressed aspect he had seen in a dozen supplicant chieftains over the past days, that of a victim wrongly accused, caught up in a storm over which she had no control. But if the woman was indeed the prisoner, then why did the mounted legionaries look the worse for the wear? Why were they without shields, some without helmets, and their faces bruised as if they had spent the night in a tavern brawl? Then he noticed the slightly built man with them, a cloak lazily draped over one shoulder exposing the tunic of an army clerk. The man appeared on the borderline of unconsciousness and seemed to be struggling to stay in the saddle. He would have fallen many times had it not been for the steadying hand of the large legionary riding next to him. This last was a robust-looking man, with a scar running down one side of his face, a real soldier of the trench. Though swollen, his features looked familiar to Caesar, and prompted him to rake his mind for the time and place where they had crossed paths.

"We are still dreadfully outnumbered, Caesar." Trebonius appeared beside him. "But, this is blessed news, all the same." His tone clearly indicated he thought the news only to be blessed if Caesar intended to employ the Twelfth Legion in covering an immediate withdrawal to friendlier Gaul.

But Caesar knew withdrawal meant defeat – defeat now, and in years to come. He had already decided on his course of action, and there would be no deviation from it. It would be victory or death for them all. He forgot about the exotic woman, the teetering clerk, and the nameless legionary, his mind quickly consumed with all that must be done before the morrow. Fabius's legion would not arrive for another day at least, and he must formulate a plan before it did. To defeat Ambiorix, he would need to be clever, not so much like Alexander, as Aeneas.

Ambiorix was ambitious, a trait only overshadowed by his arrogance. Caesar would use that to his advantage. It was, perhaps, his only chance of pulling victory out of disaster. And so, he would march to the ford on the morrow, as the fool Gisilbert had advised, where the overconfident Eburones king, no doubt, awaited him with a deadly surprise.

Caesar hoped to present a few surprises of his own.

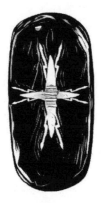

XXIII

The Henne River wound through the shallow valley, a gurgling ribbon laced with ice. Gentle slopes rose on either shoreline to meet ridgelines thick with trees. The ford called Hunter's Crossing afforded a reasonably safe passage across the icy waters. Here, the Henne measured no more than one hundred paces across, rising no higher than a man's waist. On both sides, a wide paddy of mud stretched upon either bank, pock-marked with the tracks of men and beasts, some new, but most weeks old. On the western bank, slightly removed from the river's edge, sat a low hill with a flat top, where Belgae of countless generations oftentimes gathered for great hunts that sometimes lasted for weeks on end. In those peaceful times, weary riders and bowmen would tally and divide their game, separate Odin's share from their own, then drink in celebration of the rich and bountiful forest upon which they depended. Over the centuries, the trees had been cut back considerably to provide fuel for these gatherings, leaving the hilltop quite barren, in stark contrast to the land around it. Though it had been many years since the last great hunt, the remnants of those vast encampments still littered the grounds. Broken tools, chards of vessels, rotting heaps of cut wood along with discarded bones gnawed white by the scavenging creatures of the forest, lay singly and in clusters all about.

It was this hill that dominated the landscape now observed by Ambiorix and the Belgic chieftains as they waited anxiously for Caesar to arrive. From concealed positions along the ridge east of the river ford, they had a good view of the opposite bank, the hill, and the countryside beyond. There was not a single cloud in the sky, no rain or fog to hide the landscape, and thus they had no trouble following the Roman column as it wound its way over the distant hills and valleys like the glistening scales of a snake, sometimes visible, sometimes not, as it slowly but steadily drew closer.

It appeared that the ruse of the previous evening had worked. Ambiorix had sent Gisilbert to fill Caesar's head with false hopes and ill-advice, and it was clear that the impetuous proconsul had taken it. He undoubtedly intended to cross here, at this most convenient of fords, unaware that thirty thousand Belgic warriors lay concealed behind the ridgeline dominating the eastern shore. Added to that was the welcome confirmation that Caesar had indeed brought only one legion with him, a fact that became even more evident as the Roman column drew closer.

At last, the Roman helmets crested the final ridge before the river, and followed the road as it descended toward the ford – straight into the trap. Ambiorix watched the glorious sight, finally content that all the haste, all the effort, all the difficulties of the last two days had been worth it. It had been no small feat getting the grudging chieftains and their spearmen here in time to set the ambush. Through an agonizing round of negotiations, he had finally managed to persuade them that the siege works and towers they had struggled so hard to construct had served their purpose, that the siege had drawn Caesar into a rash decision, and that they must move quickly to capitalize on the Roman's blunder.

The forced march had been grueling, prompting grumbles from spearmen and nobles alike. At least a thousand men deserted. A few were caught and hanged, but Ambiorix let the rest go, not wishing to expend his cavalry chasing them down. Despite the desertions, the bulk of his army had arrived intact, and now waited in their brigades to spring the trap on the unsuspecting Romans.

As Ambiorix watched, a troop of Roman cavalry approached the ford well ahead of the column – advance riders, scouting the area. They trotted their mounts down to the river's edge and reined them in briefly to get a long look at the opposite bank. When the enemy horsemen were finally moving again, they did not cross the ford, but instead remained on their side of the river, riding parallel to the riverbank as they continued to examine the country on the opposite side. Ambiorix concluded that they would not be a problem, providing they did not cross too far ahead of the infantry.

His eyes moved back to the main column. The Roman foot soldiers were discernable now, the horsetail plumes atop their helmets dancing in the wind. The legionaries marched four abreast, the eagle standard at their head surrounded by a cluster of heavily armed centurions, while the lesser standards of cohorts and centuries bobbed behind amongst the glittering line of spear points. Another contingent of mixed Roman and auxiliary cavalry filed through the trees upon either wing, while out in front of the column rode a retinue of officers in scarlet cloaks and plumed helmets. A detachment of lictors were among them, the axe-blades of their fasces visible even from this distance. These attendants accompanied the proconsul on official business, carrying bundled rods and axe heads as a sign of their lord's imperium. That meant Caesar was there.

A murmur ran through the clustered chieftains beside him when they, too, spotted the lictors.

"It is glorious!" Fridwald, the Aduatuci chieftain, said in an exultant tone. "Caesar brings only one legion, and marches blindly into our ambuscade, just as you said."

This was echoed by the appreciative expressions on the faces of the other chieftains, who could not deny the truth of it. They all gazed upon Ambiorix now with a mystical reverence, certain now that he was chosen of the gods to unite the Belgic tribes and propel them to greatness. That is, all but Cativolcus, whose contemptuous manner had not changed, and who had become more defiant since Ambiorix had returned to the army without Erminhilt.

But what did the old fool matter? These other chieftains were sworn to him now. There would be many more. Today, Caesar would brashly cross the ford expecting to meet no resistance, expecting to march unopposed to Cicero's camp to brush aside a few thousand jittery Belgae as one scrapes bath oils from his backside, but the snobbish proconsul was in for a terrifying surprise. Before the sun set on this day, Caesar's army would be destroyed, his aspirations for power and glory shattered, and his own balding head severed from his shoulders and spitted atop a pike.

"The pompous Romans march as calmly as if they were

on triumph," Ambiorix addressed the assembled chieftains. "We will wait until half their number is across the river, then we shall attack. When you hear the signal, advance your men down the slope quickly. Press them hard. Overwhelm the Romans as a frothing sea draws over the shore. We must defeat Caesar before he realizes he is defeated, before he understands the true size of our force and withdraws."

"Then, it's to be an open battle, my lord?" one chieftain asked.

"Not a battle, but a slaughter!" Ambiorix corrected.

They nodded, though several still appeared reluctant.

"Many of these lads have never been in such a battle, my lord," the chieftain of the Nervii spoke up, as if to voice the others' sentiments. "We may prevail, but I fear we will lose too many."

Ambiorix smiled reassuringly, slapping a ringed hand on the chieftain's shoulder. "Take heart, my brother. My victory against Sabinus taught me many things. I know the Roman order of march. I know their vulnerabilities. I have dispositioned our brigades accordingly. Have no fear, our losses will be few."

Even after this assurance, doubt still lingered in the eyes of a few. Most, however, seemed eager to finally face an enemy that was not behind a fortified wall.

The chieftains finally dispersed to their brigades, each saluting Ambiorix and vowing to uphold his portion of the line. As Ambiorix watched them go, a mocking, devilish voice croaked close behind him.

"Our losses will be few, eh, my lord?"

It was Cativolcus. The old king was chuckling as if it gave him great merriment to catch his colleague in such a lie. Ambiorix tore his eyes away from the distant Romans to shoot the old man a long, venomous glare, but this only amused him more.

"Come now," Cativolcus petitioned. "It is not too late to put an end to this madness."

"Speak no more, old man," Ambiorix snapped in a low voice, such that the retainers of both men, who stood nearby, could not hear what was said. "I would keep that withered tongue of yours inside your absentminded head, should you wish to see your daughter's precious emerald eyes again."

All merriment left the old king's face. He eyed Ambiorix with hatred and contempt, but remained obediently silent.

Putting the old fool out of his mind, Ambiorix looked right and left along the ridgeline, examining his own army. The crouching ranks of spearmen stretched off in either direction, waiting for his signal to attack. Many wore mail vests taken off the dead Romans of the Fourteenth Legion. They would have a good half mile of ground to cover before the first blades clashed, a long interval for the Romans to prepare for their charge. It was not ideal, but it would have to do. Had he placed them any closer, the enemy cavalry would surely have sighted them by now.

"Get your head down, dung-brains!" one knight shouted at a lanky, awkward soldier who could have been no more than sixteen – one of many green youths in the ranks.

Further down the line, a pair of slaves struggled to bring an unruly mule to bey. Not far from them, an elderly warrior sat upon a rock using a plundered Roman gladius to scrape the mud from his boots. Another man cradled his spear as if it were his mother's skirt, his lips mumbling in prayer. Some brigades maintained good order, while others acted as though they had come here to watch a horse race. Dozens at a time left to relieve themselves or gather wild winter berries, sauntering back to the lines with little urgency. They expected to have the upper hand today. No doubt, they had been told as much by their nobles.

Old Cativolcus was right, of course, Ambiorix admitted to himself, as he observed these would-be warriors. He had indeed lied to the chieftains. For there was no hope in Midgard the losses would be light. If he had learned anything from the horrific fight against Sabinus, it was that there was no good way to confront a Roman legion. The massive number of casualties suffered by his own tribe were proof of that. This fight would be no less devastating. The young Nervii and Aduatuci warriors would go into battle with fires in their hearts and songs of war on their lips, but, man-for-man, they could not stand up against Roman legionaries. They would be severely mauled, no matter the tactic used. Thus, Ambiorix was placing his trust in overwhelming numbers alone. It was not ideal, and brutally unforgiving on the frontline troops, but effective, nonetheless. For this battle must happen. By the mercy of Odin, it must! Such an opportunity would not come again.

Ambiorix wanted the legion destroyed, but, more than that, he wanted Caesar's head. The proconsul must die. Kill him, and all of Gaul would rally to his vanquisher. And he would kill him, Ambiorix reassured himself, even if it meant sacrificing every man in his army. Even if he himself had to suffer a hundred wounds, he would kill Caesar.

The legion moved closer to the river, still oblivious to the presence of the Belgic army. The flanking cavalry troops fanned out on either side, but still did not cross the ford. Any moment now, Ambiorix considered, nearly breathless with excitement. The Roman foot would cross at any moment, he would give the signal, and set his destiny in motion. A band of men stood nearby with lips pressed to polished elk horns. At one nod from him, they would blow their horns, and the brigades would charge.

But what Ambiorix saw next left him dumbfounded.

The Roman column suddenly turned. Instead of marching down into the ford, the infantry veered right, diverting toward the barren hill beside the river. When the front ranks reached the top, the column came to an abrupt halt. Cohorts were quickly deployed along the river side of the hill, while succeeding units fell out of the line, produced trenching tools and axes from their kits, and immediately began excavation of the muddy ground.

Ambiorix was stunned by all of this. The sun had not yet reached its zenith. There were still many marching hours left in the day, yet clearly, the Romans were raising works atop the hill and intended to go no farther.

"Perhaps Caesar is not quite the fool you have taken him for," Cativolcus said, not derisively this time, simply cautionary.

Ambiorix ignored him, holding out hope that this might be some sort of precautionary measure prior to crossing the river. Perhaps the Romans were merely preparing a fortified position to fall back on should the crossing meet with problems. But as he watched, the construction assumed the unmistakable shape of a Roman marching camp. With remarkable speed and efficiency, the legionaries turned the barren slope into a precise rectangle, following the markers laid out by their engineers. A ditch sank into the earth, and behind it rose an earthen mound. Two dozen or so trees were quickly felled and their boughs hacked into posts to supplement those that had been brought on the march. The posts were planted atop the mound, tightly packed side-by-side, until a palisade encircled the entire camp. At the same time, towers were constructed near each wall. Two thousand legionaries and slaves toiled, while the rest stood in battle-line upon the slope.

"Ambiorix!" Fridwald said hotly, after marching back from his brigades. "Did you bring us here to lay siege to yet another fort? My men are through digging in the mud, I tell you!"

"As are mine!" The Nervii chieftain was suddenly there, too.

Neither man displayed any trace of the idol-like devotion they had exhibited only moments before.

Ambiorix did not turn to face them, his mind scrambling to salvage the battle plan in which he had placed all his hopes.

"If you would care to study those fortifications a little closer, my lords," he said finally. "You would see they are constructing a simple marching camp, not a winter fort such as Cicero's."

"What does that mean?"

"It means Caesar intends to camp for the night and cross the river in the morning." Ambiorix pointed at the distant fortification. "Just look at the expedient manner of their construction. The earthen mound is not as high as it normally is, which means the ditch around it is not nearly as deep. And the camp's dimensions are smaller, too. It is, by far, the least formidable camp I have ever seen the Romans build. No, my lords, Caesar does not intend to tarry here long. One night, at most."

As the chieftain's digested that, Ambiorix prayed his deductions were correct. The camp was indeed smaller, perhaps two thirds the size of the standard Roman marching camp. Perhaps it was simply a representation of how many men Caesar had brought with him. Fewer men called for a smaller camp, and Caesar had only one understrength legion. It would fall in line with the practical logic of the Latins.

"Our plan has not changed, my lords," Ambiorix announced, returning the uncertain expressions with a confident smile. "Caesar will cross tomorrow, at first light, and we will be ready for him. Instruct your men to sleep with their spears tonight."

"Can thirty thousand men can remain hidden here all night without Caesar learning about them?" Fridwald asked. "What of the Roman scouts?"

"Of course, you are right, my lord," Ambiorix replied with compulsory courtesy. "We shall double the watch all down the line. Should any of Caesar's scouts cross the river this night, I want them killed and their bodies hidden. Likewise, we shall call in our own patrols, lest they alert the enemy to our presence. No man is to cross over to the Roman side. Is that understood? See that the word is passed to the others. We hold here tonight, and attack in the morning."

XXIV

The next morning, the Belgic host awoke to discover the Romans had not moved from their camp. The sky transformed from gray to yellow, from yellow to blue, as Ambiorix and the chieftains watched. They were still watching at mid-morning, and still the Roman camp showed no activity.

A few work parties casually repaired sections of the palisade where the mud-packed rampart had sagged in the night. Ribbons of smoke twirled lazily into the sky from the cooking fires within. Just outside one gate, a stick of tethered horses cropped the frozen earth for scant shards of grass. The only turned-out unit was a troop of some fifty horsemen patrolling along the river's edge. It was all routine, the normal activity one might expect for a legion intent on remaining encamped for some time.

"Our scouts report no signs of enemy movement, my lord," Lambert reported to Ambiorix for the seventh time that morning. "Some believe they heard the rustling of weapons and armor during the night, but being restrained to our side of the river, it was impossible to confirm the source of the enemy noise. Our scouts believe the enemy spent the night bolstering the fort's defenses."

"Maybe Caesar intends to march on the morrow," Cativolcus chided Ambiorix in front of the assembled chieftains. "Or, perhaps, the day after that."

Some of the other chieftains were more disconcerted, some expressing doubt, some anger.

"My men would rather assault that puny camp head-on than sit here stroking our pricks for another week," Fridwald said. "Another week of siege and my lads will lose their will to fight. I've already had near two hundred desertions."

"Have faith, my lords," Ambiorix implored. "Caesar will move soon. He must. I swear to it!"

Of course, there was no way Ambiorix could know that for sure, but he said it anyway to head off the disastrous idea of a frontal assault. Such an attack would surely meet with great loss and would likely end with no gain and Caesar still safely where he was.

As Ambiorix and the other chieftains watched, the enemy cavalry patrol stopped at the ford, where they allowed their mounts to drink from the icy river. They were Romans by and large, but there were a few Gauls among them. They conversed unconcernedly, huddled in the warmth of their cloaks, their lances casually crossed over the manes of their beasts. If they had any notion of the Belgic army's presence, they gave no indication of it.

It suddenly dawned on Ambiorix that these enemy horsemen presented him with an opportunity, a way to perhaps force Caesar's hand.

He turned to Lambert. "Send the horse to harass that cavalry by the river. Let us see if we can stir the Roman eagle from its nest."

Orders were quietly relayed down the line, and, moments later, two troops of Belgic cavalry burst from their concealed positions along the ridge. They were the Red Dragons of the Aduatuci and the Wolf Fangs of the Nervii, each bearing shields emblazoned with the icons of their tribe. They brought their mounts to a full gallop in a crescendo of thunder, the war steeds surging down the slope with heads bobbing like the churning boulders of a landslide. They closed on the lolling Roman cavalry with astonishing speed, iron-tipped lances leveled at their foe.

Remarkably, the enemy horsemen did not scatter at the sight of the onrushing mass. Instead, they wheeled into line to meet them head-on, as if they had been expecting such an attack. The opposing lines came together amid the river, in a cacophony of snapping lances and splintering shields intermixed with the cries of man and beast. Soon, they were a single, indiscernible mass half-shrouded in a violent cloud of white mist and spray. Thrusting points and hacking blades toppled men from saddles in droves. Probing weapons found passages between shield and armor and were withdrawn stained with blood. Those who fell into the shallows desperately groped for the land, many crying out in horror an instant before being crushed by the lethal stomping hooves. A fallen Roman successfully escaped the deadly space, gaining the muddy bank, only to have his head taken off by the lightning-fast sweep of a Belgic longsword. One large Nervii warrior, having lost both lance and sword, swung his shield in great arcs to knock one man from the saddle after another. He seemed unstoppable until three Romans surrounded him and transfixed him with lances like a cornered boar.

The fight raged on, and soon the foamy shallows ran red with blood. The Romans held their ground with determination but were outnumbered and were no match in the saddle against the Belgic knights. When a third of the Romans had fallen, the Roman officer shouted a command, and the survivors broke out of the maelstrom and began to retreat toward the camp. The victorious Belgic horse immediately pursued, but this was not what Ambiorix wanted.

"Recall them!" he said fervently. "We wish for Caesar to come to us, not the other way around."

The horn sounded, and the Belgic cavalry broke off the chase. They wheeled their mounts, and retired back across the river, dispatching any wounded Romans left behind. After gathering their own wounded, they returned to the trees from which they had sprung. Likewise, the Roman cavalry withdrew inside the walls of the camp, and the ford fell silent once again, with a score of dead men and horses littering the muddy banks and shallows.

"Now, let us see if Caesar takes the bait," Ambiorix said, as he and the other chieftains watched eagerly for any signs of retribution from the Roman camp. But as they watched, and the sun continued its march across the sky, it became evident there would be no response.

"My lord!"

Ambiorix turned to see one of his horse guards approaching, sharing the saddle with a man who bled from the temples and who appeared in a half-conscious state. The guardsman dismounted, helped the dazed man down, and brought him before the king. The injured man wore the garb of a Black Rider.

"My lord," the guardsmen said apologetically. "Forgive this intrusion, but this man has just come into our lines. He begs to speak with you."

"What has happened?" Ambiorix said, a cold chill creeping over him as he realized this man belonged to Sedgerick's troop, left with Erminhilt to guard the Roman prisoners.

"Massacre, my king," the man replied between coughs.

Ambiorix felt his blood boil. He did not need any more dismal news today. Out of frustration, he grabbed the Black Rider by the shoulders and shook him, forgetting his wounds. "What are you saying man? Speak clearly! Who attacked you?"

"Roman cavalry, my king," the man replied fearfully. "They attacked in the early hours of the morning, two days ago. They took us by surprise. Killed every man. I alone escaped."

"What of Erminhilt?" Ambiorix said through gritted teeth. "What of the Roman clerk?"

The man's eyes grew wide as Ambiorix's hand moved to the hilt of his sword.

"Tell me!" Ambiorix snapped. "Before I spill your guts on this very ground!"

"Taken, my lord. Taken by the enemy."

Cativolcus gasped when he overheard this, suddenly hysterical. "Erminhilt taken? My dear daughter taken?" His eyes then turned on Ambiorix with venom. "This is your fault! Your fault! Odin curse you, Ambiorix, son of Adalwolf! You have slain her. Oh, Erminhilt! My poor Erminhilt."

But Ambiorix disregarded the babbling old king, just as he ignored the bewildered stares from the other chieftains. He gazed across the valley at the Roman camp, where the enemy cavalry had retired. Caesar must have her, he concluded. Where else could the Roman cavalry have come from? Erminhilt must be there, somewhere within those palisade walls, and the clerk, too. He could easily abandon Erminhilt to her fate – she and her father had been more problematic than useful, of late – but he could not let the clerk get away. He could not let the Roman treasure slip through his fingers so easily. With all that had happened, with his carefully crafted battle plan unraveling before his eyes, he had the distinct feeling he was going to need Raganhar's army of Germans, after all. With discontent and desertion on the rise in his own army, there was little chance it would remain intact for more than a few days. He needed the silver now more than ever. He needed it more than he needed the Aduatuci, the Nervii, and the other tribes – and now he knew what he must do.

"We shall attack the enemy camp at once," he announced.

Fridwald eyed him skeptically. "That was not your line of thinking before, my lord."

"We came here to kill Caesar," Ambiorix answered matter-of-factly. "He lies within our grasp. Let us now seize the day. Let us attack!"

"Do not listen to him!" Cativolcus interjected wildly, as a man gone mad. "Do not listen to this liar! He promises you the head of Caesar, but, mark me, my lords, you'll get the horns before the day is out!"

The rage inside Ambiorix was at the boiling point, and he was about to strike the old man down where he stood, but Fridwald spoke first.

"Be gone, old woman! If you have no stomach for this fight, then go huddle with the camp whores and stand clear of the true warriors! I, for one, rejoice at Ambiorix's change of heart. My nobles will salivate upon hearing this joyous command. They've been itching for a proper fight for far too long. Just let the pompous Caesar lay his eyes on our host, and he and his whole army will piss themselves with fear."

As Cativolcus melted into the background, the other chieftains, either out of shame or genuineness, expressed similar eagerness for the coming fight.

"Listen to me, all of you," Ambiorix said, using a stick to draw a rectangular shape in the mud at their feet. "We outnumber the Romans nearly seven-to-one. They cannot defend everywhere at once. If we attack from all sides, one side must break. When it does, we rush inside and take the entire legion from within. Burchard, you will take your Nervii to the far side of the camp, and attack there. Sweep wide of the Roman missiles as you move into position. Fridwald, your Aduatuci will attack on the left side. The Centrones and the Levaci will take the right. My own Eburones will assault the front. When I give the signal, the whole army is to move swiftly across the river. Move up the hill and take up positions for the assault. Attack as soon as your men are formed."

With a resounding cheer, the chieftains departed to rejoin their brigades. Only Cativolcus remained. He stared dejectedly at the Roman camp as a man with little reason left to live.

"You believe she is within the fort, don't you?" the old king asked feebly, his tone no longer filled with the rage and scorn of moments before. "The gods only know what vile things the Romans have done to her. Perhaps death would have been better."

Ambiorix gave him no answer, quite weary of the old fool's narrowmindedness. It was the same narrowmindedness exhibited by the chieftains of a hundred tribes across Gaul and Belgica ever since the Romans came. The same chieftains who had allowed the Romans to establish their dominance over the land. Now, even with the very future of his people at stake, all Cativolcus could think about was his precious daughter. No wonder he had lost so much influence with the nobles. He represented the meek complacency of a conquered people, obsessed with trivialities and entirely devoid of grand vision.

As Ambiorix climbed onto his horse, Cativolcus was suddenly there, grasping his leg, looking up at him with pleading eyes.

"If she is there, bring her back to me!" the old king exclaimed fervently. "She is my only remaining child, Ambiorix. I beg you, please bring her back to me. I will no longer interfere. The kingdom is yours, just give me back my daughter."

After a pause, Ambiorix offered a grudging nod, then kicked his horse into a gallop. He joined up with the waiting royal guard, and left the old man behind.

XXV

The banners streamed across the river ford.

The banners of the White Wolves, the Spanning Falcons, the Coiled Serpents, and many other brigades moved at the head of the great mass of footmen. The flood of warriors darkened the earth as it emerged onto the far bank and began ascending the slope leading up to the Roman camp. The thirty thousand Belgic spear warriors did not keep the orderly formations of Roman legions, but their approach was no less daunting to behold. The older nobles, in their mail vests and helmets, their faces set in grim determination behind long mustaches and beards, marched in silence in the rear, while the younger knights, eager to show their mettle to both their fathers and their tribesmen, paraded across the front ranks, waving swords and encouraging their men onward with stirring speeches of patriotism. The common soldiers paid little attention to either, most choosing to spend the final moments before battle murmuring to crude carvings hung around their necks or carried in their pockets – representations of their long dead ancestors, who might welcome them in the afterlife this day.

Halfway up the slope, the horns blared again, and the horde of spears separated into four distinct columns, like the stretching fingers of a great hand. The fingers reached out to encircle the fortification until great masses of spearmen had formed up on all four sides.

The host advanced cautiously but steadily, approaching the walls with the murderous repulses before Cicero's fort still fresh in their minds. Oddly, there was little activity to be seen in the camp before them. The Roman workers repairing the palisade had long since scrambled inside, and now the gates were fouled with carts, logs, and other obstructions. Indeed, not one Roman helmet was visible above the wall. Aside from a few figures atop the towers, the camp appeared abandoned.

This was nothing like Cicero's robust winter fortification with solid walls as high as four men standing on end and topped with a platform from which the defenders could rain missiles down on them. The walls of this camp had no fire-step and were scarcely ten feet high, if you did not count the earthen mound on which they stood. Likewise, the ditch before the wall was not nearly as deep. Where Cicero's fort had contained dozens of giant towers, each mounting a deadly missile thrower, this camp had only four towers, one near each of the gates. The towers themselves were simple, two-platform structures, with the top platform stretching out much wider than the tower's base. A few archers and slingers manned them, leaning over the waist-high bulwarks to loose their missiles at the onrushing mass, but the structures were clearly too flimsy to hold engines.

Thus, the remorseless storms of fire and bolt that had vivisected so many Belgae before the walls of Cicero's fort would not plague them here. An infectious joy spread through the Belgic ranks culminating in a great war cry, as each man came to this realization and drew courage from it. Soon the entire host was running toward the walls, eager to get at the enemy inside, eager to slaughter the paltry force the arrogant Roman proconsul had brought with him into Belgica.

The gates were situated in the exact center of each of the four walls. They were not hinged doors but simply pathways, angled sharply at ninety degrees and lined by a palisade, such that any traversing formation would be forced to fight inside a narrow space vulnerable to missile attack from the flanks. Seeing the gates obstructed, and knowing each would be well-defended by the nearby towers, the nobles at the front, barely in control of the Belgic formations, chose to ignore the gates entirely and concentrate their attacks on the palisade walls near the corners of the camp. They set their men to work to force breaches, filling in the ditch and digging out the palisade posts. Many broke out the gladii they had plundered from Sabinus's legion to scrape at the freshly packed mud, working feverishly to tear down what the Romans had spent the previous day building up. The clamoring warriors were so desperate to get inside that the rear ranks became irreparably convoluted with the front, until they were an incongruous mass of veterans and green warriors.

Hovering to the rear amongst his house guards, Ambiorix watched the attacking brigades as they clamored like swarms of angry bees about the corners of the fortification. He would have preferred they remain in loose ranks, allowing only those in front to cluster beneath the enemy walls, but any attempt at restraining them now would only lead to more confusion. They were very near to finishing the job, anyway. He would not stop them now.

Off to his left and right, the massed hordes of the other tribes assaulted the other walls in a similar fashion, all order gone, like packs of ravenous hyenas clawing at a thicket into which they had chased their prey. Like Ambiorix, the chieftains of the other tribes hung back with their mounted knights, allowing their foot soldiers to sustain their momentum. And the soldiers made good progress. In some places, the ditch had already been filled in and they were near to removing a section of the palisade.

It struck Ambiorix as odd that Caesar would allow such an assault against his walls to go unabated. Javelins and stones should be flying over the walls in swarms, and spears thrust through the gaps in the palisade to disrupt the diggers. The only resistance came from the handfuls of archers and slingers in the towers, but even these were no serious threat. Their arrows had felled perhaps a dozen men, and the few fallen had hardly been noticed by their comrades. Ambiorix recognized the slingers by their leather armor. They were mercenaries from the Balearic Isles, but there was scarcely a Roman to be seen among them.

What could be the meaning of such a lackluster defense?

The thought then occurred to him that this poorly-constructed fortification of such reduced dimensions might itself be a diversion. Perhaps the reason so few defended the walls was that there were, in fact, only a few defenders inside. The reported noise that had emanated from the enemy camp throughout the night might very well have been the sounds of Caesar's army departing under cover of darkness. Perhaps, only the Roman cavalry and these scant few defenders remained, sacrificing their lives to buy the proconsul time to escape.

That had to be it, Ambiorix thought. There could be no

other explanation. Caesar was, at this very moment, getting away while his own army piddled at this worthless palisade.

Convinced that he had been duped, and that his only hope of catching Caesar was to immediately break off the attack and pursue at the forced march, Ambiorix was about to summon the other chieftains to him, when a horn suddenly sounded loud and clear above the din of the assault. It came from within the camp, first one horn, then many others. He recognized the distinct tones as those of the Roman cornu, and he could imagine two dozen legionaries wearing the giant circular brass instruments across their torsos and blowing with all their might.

At first, the Belgic troops were unfazed by the enemy horns, so consumed were they with dismantling the palisade, but then a group of freshly painted Roman shields suddenly appeared on the ladders of the nearest tower, and a hush quickly spread throughout their ranks. The shield bearers climbed to the top platform, shielding themselves from view and from the stones and arrows launched at them. Ambiorix saw them reach the top, saw the dozen shields face outward at the edge of the parapet, and then a long wooden pole erected above them. At the top of the pole, a golden eagle, polished to perfection, sparkled in the sun. This was, of course, the eagle of the Ninth Legion. It was one of the most coveted prizes sought after by every Belgic warrior clawing to get inside, and the mere sight of it sent them all into a frenzy. Many shouted curses at it. Many raised swords or spears high in the air and vowed that the eagle flaunted so boldly above them would soon be theirs.

The sight of the eagle changed all Ambiorix's presumptions about the whereabouts of the Roman army, and he now knew for certain the legion had not abandoned the fort. If he had learned anything about Roman pride and honor over the years, he knew it would be a snowy day in

Carthage before a legion willingly left behind its sacred eagle, to which its soldiers were devoted more than they were to Rome itself. Ambiorix had witnessed this devotion first hand during the battle against the Fourteenth Legion, when it had cost him a full three score of his best warriors to wrest that legion's eagle away from the maniacal centurions charged with defending it.

But now Ambiorix was more puzzled than before. If Caesar and his legion were indeed still on the other side of those walls, then what could explain the apathetic defense?

Again, the horns blew, and again an eagle appeared above the tower – a second eagle, to join the first, as if the platform were a stage, and this a carefully choreographed play. The two eagles looked down on the clamoring Belgae like two grim-faced Roman consuls. This second eagle seemed to inspire the attackers more than it confused them, for how much more renown would they achieve were they to seize both prized emblems.

But while his men were inspired, Ambiorix felt a chill slowly creep up his spine. Two eagles meant two legions. But how could that be? His scouts had reported nothing but...*of course!* The sounds in the night had not been Caesar departing, but in fact a new legion arriving. Somehow, someway, another legion had arrived. But where were they? Surely, this camp was too small to contain so many men.

Ambiorix closed his eyes, suddenly understanding that all his actions had played right into the hands of the wily Roman, and he was strangely not surprised by what happened next.

In the center of the wall he now faced, the gate suddenly came alive with activity. Romans dropped over the palisade, some bearing full arms and shields, others carrying no arms at all. The armed legionaries immediately formed a protective screen while the others began working to clear the blockages from the gate. It quickly became clear to Ambiorix that the fouled gates had not been as hopelessly blocked as they had appeared. The obstructions had been placed in a singular order well understood by those now removing them, and they cleared them away with remarkable speed. No sooner had the last obstruction been removed than a mass of fully armed legionaries streamed from the gate, two thick columns of soldiers, at the double step, a tramp of metal and mail with painted shields and javelins held aloft. Ambiorix could not see the other gates, but he surmised, from the wild pointing and gesticulations of the other chieftains, that similar events were happening there, too. He could imagine columns of Romans emerging from all four sides of the fort simultaneously. This was not a disorderly, panic-stricken mob attempting to break out and flee, nor was it a feint. It was a massive sortie of precise order and drill. The hundreds upon hundreds of legionaries emerging from the gate before him immediately formed into two battle lines, facing in opposite directions, with one flank of each line anchored on the wall. Any Belgic warrior attempting to disrupt the assemblage of these units was quickly and mercilessly dispatched by a band of hard-faced centurions who stood by specifically for that purpose.

Ambiorix's initial notion was that such a move was madness. Even with two legions on the field, his own army still vastly outnumbered the Romans at least three to one. But then, he saw the alarm take hold in his own troops, saw the looks of confusion on his nobles' faces, and felt a cold realization overtake him, as a man who just lost his life's fortune in a game of dice. He cursed the fates, cursed his own pride and foolishness, for it was all so suddenly and disturbingly clear to him.

Caesar had played him for a fool.

As a bleeding carcass draws a bear from its lair, the small

camp with its sparse defenses had lured him across the river and had imbued his men with a false confidence, such that they had lost all semblance of order, mixing ranks, bunching up near the walls, like a starving mob outside a granary. It did not matter what orders he gave now, nor if he sent a hundred knights to try to reform them. Nothing could transform that confused mass back into the ordered ranks that would be necessary to face the Roman battle lines. He could do little but watch as the inevitable took place.

The chief centurions bellowed commands and the Roman lines began to advance, each presenting a front of one hundred men with ten ranks behind. The moving fences of elliptical shields bristled with the points of javelins, advancing along the walls in opposite directions, advancing outward from each gate. The Belgic troops in the paths of these formations were quickly thrown into turmoil. Uncertain whether they should face the Romans or continue pressing the breaches, and without clear direction from their equally befuddled nobles, they soon devolved into a mindless throng – a mishmash of veteran swordsmen and green spearmen with no discernable order. The keener warriors saw the danger and fled without orders to do so. The steadier ones turned to face the Romans, attempting to put their comrades in line, but no concerted defense was formed before the Roman formations began pushing into the packed Belgic ranks, compressing them, and toppling a dozen at a time as hundreds of gladii and pila thrust through the gaps between the shields and found exposed flesh. In a few places, the Belgic nobles drew together a handful of warriors and charged against the Roman lines, attempting to force a break in the shields, but any such penetration was short-lived, the offending Belgae quickly stabbed to death by gladii on all sides.

This same chain of events occurred simultaneously on each side of the camp, the Roman lines slowly advancing away from the gates, widening the spaces between them, and leaving a carpet of bloody, twitching Belgic corpses behind. Next, the Roman and auxiliary cavalry galloped out of the gates and hovered near the unanchored ends of the Roman lines to ward off any attempts by the Belgic cavalry at a flanking maneuver.

The Belgic infantry still vastly outnumbered the Romans, but this soon became more of a curse than an advantage. They became so tightly packed that men could hardly raise their shields. This was when the real killing began.

Once again, the centurions barked orders, and the rear ranks of legionaries unleashed their poised javelins in two great volleys that darkened the sky above the Belgae. Thousands of deadly, six-foot-long missiles arced through the air and came down into the heart of the compressed mass. Men screamed in horror as foot-long iron shafts transfixed necks, eyes sockets, shoulders, and chests. A red mist clouded the air above the jostling helmets as severed arteries spurted jets of blood, coating faces and armor, and transforming the tight space into a ghastly nightmare of mayhem and death. Those able to raise their shields in time found the shield suddenly unwieldy and unusable. For each Roman javelin had been constructed with a wooden fastener that broke on impact, allowing the wooden and iron shafts to pivot on the single iron nail holding them together. Instead of a solid pole-like shaft protruding from his shield, the Belgic warrior was left with a flopping, unwieldy appendage, difficult to extract, and virtually impossible to turn around and use on the Romans.

Soon the mob was gripped by an infectious panic as the mud beneath their feet quickly filled with the dead and dying. Men realized their own impotency and cried out in anger and frustration. The few pockets of warriors who had kept their heads and had managed to form up to face the Romans were disrupted by those clawing to get away. Men began streaming from the battle in droves, dashing madly to escape what they believed to be certain death.

"Lambert!" Ambiorix snapped. "Take your knights, and ride down those cowards! Slay them that all may see the price of desertion!"

"Yes, my lord!" Lambert drew his sword and kicked his mount into a run, his men following after him.

It could be salvaged, Ambiorix kept telling himself, as he watched one knight send the head of a terrified boy twirling in the air with one powerful sweep of his long sword. Even with the desertion and the casualties, his army still outnumbered the Romans. There were always opportunities in disaster. If some order could be brought to the brigades, it could just as easily be his men surrounding the Romans. Surely somewhere, on one side of the camp, the Romans were being beaten. But a glance across the field at the other chieftains told him disaster was being met with everywhere. The other chieftains looked back at him uncertainly, clearly as shocked by the turn of events as he was. Even from this distance, he could read their thoughts, hear them now as if they conversed beside him. They were mulling over ordering a general retreat, of leaving now, while they still had armies to command.

Something new caught Ambiorix's attention on the tower – a fluttering, purple cloak, the stoical wearer of which stood beneath the swaying eagle standards. Even from this distance, Ambiorix recognized the slight stature and aged features of Caesar – the proconsul himself. Caesar gazed down upon the massacre and butchery with that same contented, supercilious, abhorrent stare Ambiorix had seen and had loathed so many times in the past. The shields on each side of the proconsul batted away the many missiles and stones flung in his direction, but he seemed unfazed by the danger. The bastard's lips were set in a contemptuous smirk that clearly communicated his confidence that he had carried the day. That stare drove through Ambiorix's soul like a thousand needles. He cursed the gods, not because of Caesar's triumphant expression, but because he knew his opponent's expression was justified.

He had lost. Caesar had beaten him. To try to convince himself otherwise would only add to his folly.

But he was not defeated, nor would he ever be, while he still drew breath. He may have lost the battle, this army might be lost, but there would be others. His people may not be destined for greatness, but he was, and before abandoning the field, there was one last thing he must do to secure that future.

"Ride to the chieftains of the Nervii and the Aduatuci!" he said to two of his messengers. "Tell them to send me every knight they can spare. I need them now! Tell them to come themselves, if they wish."

While the messages were being delivered, Ambiorix rode around the camp in a large circle, his guards galloping behind him. He scanned along the walls, searching for a stroke of good fortune amidst the chaos. He desperately needed one – and he found it. At one spot along the portion of the wall assailed by the Nervii, the Roman advance had been slowed to a crawl. One of the breaches had been successful, the palisade posts either pulled down or hacked in two. The gap was small, perhaps only the width of two men, but many Nervii warriors had already dashed through it, and several more were using ropes to escalade the wall on either side. It would be sufficient for what he intended.

Within moments, clusters of mailed knights from the other tribes began arriving, raising their swords in salute and pledging to follow him to the last. Close to two hundred had answered the call. It would be enough for what he intended.

Allowing his cumbersome cloak to fall to the ground, Ambiorix adjusted his helmet and drew out the rune-adorned sword of his forefathers. There would be one more attack, he thought, and this one would strike a blow that would resonate throughout all of Gaul and Germania.

The Romans had sortied so many troops outside the walls that there could only be a scant few left inside. Ambiorix was taking a gamble that they were vulnerable there – and there he intended to strike. If he found Erminhilt alive, so be it. If he found the Roman clerk, all the better. But those two were not the object of this foray, this mad dash into the very heart of the enemy defenses. This attack had a much more momentous purpose.

Ambiorix glanced once more at the eagle standards atop the tower, and at Caesar, still looking as smug and secure as ever.

"For Odin!" Ambiorix shouted, waving his sword in the air, and then kicking his horse into a gallop.

The knights did the same, following their king as he led them straight for the breach in the walls.

XXVI

The din of battle came from everywhere at once, as if every Belgian old enough to carry a spear surrounded the camp. The whistles of the centurions mixed with the war horns of the Belgae, the clash of steel on steel, of steel on plywood, the cries of the wounded and the dying – but from where Lucius stood with his squad, there was little they could see of the great battle that raged outside the palisade walls.

The fortification had largely held up against the assault. The rows of canvas tents hid much of the camp from Lucius's view, but he could see only one breach in the wall – albeit a serious one – no more than a hundred paces from where he now stood. The breach was being assaulted by an untold number of the enemy, some of whom pushed through the break, while others rolled over the adjacent bulwarks like crashing waves over a seawall. A squad of legionaries and freedmen fought bravely to keep the enemy contained within the breach, but many had been overcome by the torrent of enemy swords and spears and now lay in bloody heaps at the feet of their comrades.

"Juno's teeth, Lucius!" Maximus exclaimed echoing the sentiments of the rest of the squad. "Those lads need us over there! Any more of those bastards come through that breach, and the camp is lost!"

"Very likely," Lucius replied firmly. "But, we stay here!"

This was met with angry stares from the rest of the squad, but they stayed put.

No less than any of them, Lucius wanted to rush to the aid of the beleaguered defenders, but he and his men had been given orders to guard the Belgic prisoners, and they could not simply abandon that duty.

The two legions had spent the night cramped within the confines of the camp. The Twelfth Legion, under Fabius, had arrived near the midnight hour, packing every soldier, cart, horse and mule within the walls such that the enemy would not be aware of the reinforcement come light of dawn. After several uncomfortable hours of waiting, during which the interior of the fort had resembled the crowded hold of an overloaded transport galley, the attack had finally come. At the sound of the horns, the gates had been cleared, and eight thousand legionaries and several hundred cavalry had swarmed out to meet the surprised enemy. In the time it might take a man to count to two hundred, the camp had gone from being overcrowded to practically empty. Only a few defenders and noncombatants remained behind, nearly every legionary being used in the sortie. At the stables, just down the lane of tents, Lucius could see several teamsters fighting desperately to keep a hundred jittery mules from breaking out of their pens. Not far away, stood the hospital tent, where a long line of wounded waited to be seen.

Diogenes was there, somewhere, perhaps within one of those tents, passed out and oblivious to all that was transpiring around him.

Two nights ago, when Lucius and his squad had joined the Ninth Legion, he had expected to be taken before Caesar to recount the exploits of his squad since leaving the fort, and the importance of the information carried in Diogenes's head – but that had not happened. Instead, they had been largely ignored. While Albinus had been summoned to Caesar's tent, presumably to discuss the rendezvous with Fabius's Legion, there came no summons for Lucius or Diogenes. Either Albinus had forgotten to mention them, or he had simply chosen not to.

An impatient centurion, charged with dispositioning the new arrivals, had facetiously refused Lucius's requests to meet with Caesar, dismissing everything Lucius said as the meaningless babblings of a common soldier who had no concept of what items truly rated the proconsul's time. There was an enemy to face, and a battle to fight. Caesar could not be bothered with such trivialities. Diogenes's condition had not helped Lucius's case. The clerk had still suffered from the contusion and had been forced to lean against Lucius to remain on his feet. The contemptuous centurion was not about to bring a man in such a state before Caesar.

And so, Diogenes had been sent to the hospital, while Lucius and his men had been allotted to the provisional century, a mishmash of refugee soldiers relegated to performing the most mundane tasks. A few dozen Belgic prisoners accompanied the army – nobles and questionable knights of prominent families whom the proconsul had ordered apprehended as the legion had traversed the hostile countryside. Lucius and his men had been charged with guarding these prisoners and with constructing the small stockade that now held them.

It was a tedious, ungratifying duty, watching the shifty-eyed Belgae all day, and Lucius was determined that he and his men be assigned to something else, as soon as he found a means to do it. To make things worse, Erminhilt was among the prisoners. After undergoing a series of interrogations, during which she surely had revealed nothing useful, she had been thrown in with the other prisoners.

Erminhilt had kept to herself mostly, sulking in one corner of the stockade, often eyeing Lucius with the pleading look of a victim. The other prisoners were all men, but they had left Erminhilt alone, never once attempting to molest her. Lucius thought this somewhat odd, since he had often seen men in captivity and facing likely execution act in vile and depraved ways. But then he overheard one prisoner telling another in their Belgic tongue that Erminhilt was a chieftain's daughter and the woman of Ambiorix, and realized these facts alone gave her some power over them. If anything, they treated her with a measure of respect.

"Help me to escape," she had pleaded in the dark hours of the morning, when Lucius had walked past the stockade wall opposite her. Her eyes gazed at him sensually through the narrow slits between the posts as if they promised great pleasures should he comply. Lucius stared back at her for a long moment before finally letting out a burst of laughter.

"How long do you think your puny army will last in this country?" she asked, her tone suddenly thick with annoyance. "Ambiorix will deal with two legions as easily as he would deal with one."

"Aye, you may be right, lass. But he's not expecting two

legions."

"It will make no difference," she said dismissively. "Your legions will fail. Caesar will fail, and then you will need me again Roman. I can be helpful to those who help me."

"Is that so?"

"I can convince Ambiorix to spare you." She grabbed hold of the posts between them. "I can convince him to spare your men, too."

"Your lover was not so inclined to be merciful yesterday," Lucius retorted, remembering how the Eburones king had slain Honorius.

"I will persuade him. Ambiorix is a wise king. He can be merciful, and magnanimous, given the right incentive."

"Aye, I've witnessed your skill at that," Lucius said shrewdly.

The comment had obviously touched a nerve with her, but she did her best to hide it.

"He will pay any amount!" she said desperately. "Release me, and he will give you anything you ask!"

"I wish for only one thing." Lucius snarled, weary of her games. "That your whore-spawn lover might stick his neck out the next time I see him, that I may take his head off in a single stroke!"

"You will regret the day you crossed me, Roman!" she had called after Lucius as he walked away. "You will all die here! Your heads will be piled in heaps higher than the wall. Wolves shall scatter your entrails and feast upon your shriveled privates!"

Lucius had dismissed those wild predictions when Erminhilt made them, several hours ago, before the sighting of the Belgic army. Now, with Belgic warriors storming through the breach and no way of knowing how the battle fared beyond the walls, he was starting to think her prophecies might prove true.

The remaining defenders near the breach were facing overwhelming odds now, as a new flood of warriors suddenly poured through the gap in the wall. Lucius considered how effective two or three flaming ballista bolts might be at provoking a panic among the compacted enemy warriors, but that was wishful thinking. Not a single ballista or scorpion was to be found in this camp, both legions having left their heavy equipment behind on this expedition that they might move more quickly across the mud and tangled forests of Belgica.

The prisoners within the stockade had remained largely subdued throughout the morning's action, obviously fearful that the Romans might simply kill them and be done with them if they proved a nuisance. But now, as the captive Belgae peered through the gaps in the stockade, observing the progress of their countrymen at the breach, they began studying Lucius and the other guards with murderous eyes. There was no doubt their docile manner would quickly turn savage should they somehow manage to escape their temporary prison.

A great cry of elation erupted at the distant breach, drawing Lucius's attention away from the prisoners. He looked to see that the centurion commanding the defense had taken two sword thrusts to his mid-section while attempting to close the gaps in his meager line. The sight of this cross-plumed warrior crumpling lifeless to the ground had the double-effect of dispiriting the remaining legionaries and rousing the attacking Belgae. A warrior armed with only an axe, buried the curved edge of his weapon in the head of a legionary, the force of the blow piercing through bronze helmet and skull in a sickening crunch that Lucius heard even from where he was standing. Two more Belgae dispatched other legionaries in a similar fashion. The rest of the defenders quickly lost order and retreated or were cut down where they stood.

It was at that moment, Lucius realized for the first time the Belgae storming the breach were not simple spear warriors. They were nobles and knights, armored in helmets and mail, many bearing swords twice the length of the gladii, which they wielded with great skill and ease. Shrieking like demons from the underworld, they savaged their foe, sending blood and limbs flying with each sweep of their powerful blades. Perhaps two hundred had made it inside the camp, pausing briefly after they had killed the last of the wall's defenders to regain order and collect their bearings. But they were soon moving again, rushing directly towards the stockade of prisoners, defended by Lucius and his few men.

"Get ready, lads!" Lucius said. "Those bastards intend to free these men that they might add to their ranks. We will stop them."

Though he said it confidently, Lucius did not believe for one moment his handful of legionaries could stop the rush of enemy knights who outnumbered them ten-to-one. Lucius was preparing for the worst, but then, when the mass of swordsmen had closed to within fifty paces, they were suddenly assailed from the flank by a line of several dozen legionaries. They were the soldiers of the flying century, a roving unit tasked with plugging gaps in the lines and dealing with any enemies that got over the walls, and they stopped the onrushing Belgae in their tracks. The maze of tents dotting the fort's interior had hidden their approach from both Lucius and the enemy. They were a little late in arriving, but Lucius found them a welcome sight, all the same.

The century worked its way into the knights' path until a wall of shields and pila stood between the enemy and the stockade. The disciplined legionaries fought fiercely, working together to impede the disjointed attack, allowing gaps between their shields just large enough to entice the bolder enemy knights to attempt a breakthrough. The few foolish enough to make such an attempt were quickly gutted from both sides by thrusting gladii. A few managed to skirt around the flanks of the century, but these came at the stockade piecemeal and were quickly dispatched by Lucius and his men.

The skirmish had devolved to a standstill when Lucius heard a man shriek behind him. He wheeled around to see one of his own men struggling to pull himself away from the stockade fence. The legionary had been caught off his guard while distracted by the nearby action and was being held against the fence by several prisoners that had taken hold of his tunic. Before Lucius or anyone else could act, another prisoner extended a crude stake through a gap in the fence and drove it swiftly into the legionary's gullet. As the dying legionary's pulsing blood painted the fence posts, another tumult broke out on the other side of the stockade. Several prisoners had banded together tightly in a small compact column and were rushing at the fence. They used a full two dozen paces to reach full speed, and struck the fence like a human battering ram, putting the full force of their weight behind it. The men in front grunted and screamed as they were crushed to death by the weight of the men behind, but the force was sufficient to break the rope bindings holding the posts together, and the fence gave way. The next moment, every prisoner made a mad dash for the breach in the stockade.

"Slay them, lads!" Lucius shouted above the din. "Slay them as they come out!"

Romans and Belgae converged on the gap from either side, the Romans decidedly outnumbered but well-armed, the prisoners armed only with bare-knuckled fists. The legionaries jabbed their pila low at the prisoners' legs in an attempt to foul the passage with the lame and make it untenable for those behind. Soon, the squirming bodies of the wounded were piled six deep in the narrow passage, but still the others kept coming. Bloody limbs and heads fell in heaps as the gladii sung through the air. Lucius and his squad were but six men staving off three dozen. The press of the prisoners proved to be too great to stop them all, and several managed to dodge past the Roman blades. These escapees did not attempt to help their still struggling comrades, but ran away, presumably to join their countrymen fighting the flying century. Eventually, enough bodies had fouled the break that Lucius and his men got the upper hand. It became clear to those still inside that any attempt to scale the twitching mound would only add their own lifeless corpse to it.

Lucius peered through the gaps in the fence, looking for Erminhilt, wondering if she had survived the tumult, but he could not find her. She was neither among the score of surviving prisoners, nor in the pile of the dead. Had she somehow slipped past him amid the fray? Had she run off to join her compatriots? As much as Lucius would have liked to investigate further, he had other concerns. The prisoners were contained for the time being, but the century fighting desperately to hold back the Belgic knights were slowly being overcome. Five standard bearers had fallen to the enemy swords in rapid succession. Lucius watched as the sixth now cursed at his attackers. The legionary stood helmetless, wildly swinging a crimson gladius, his face so coated with blood that he could not see. The few Romans still standing had been compressed into a small circle of defense around him as the hammering long swords closed in.

If the flying century failed, as it appeared they would, it would be Lucius's duty to see that every prisoner was killed before a single one could be freed. After losing three good men stopping the attempted escape, he would have no compunctions about performing that duty, but his own life would be extinguished shortly thereafter. Of his original squad, only Sergius, Maximus, and Geta remained. They would all die, but they would take many of the enemy with them.

But then, the fates intervened, as if an unseen hand had touched the Belgic knights. They suddenly broke off the melee, backing away from the circle of legionaries. The next moment, Lucius saw that it had not been the fates but the bellowing commands of a bearded knight in a gilded helmet that had called them off. This new warrior spoke to them in an upbraiding tone, as if to chastise them for wasting their efforts on this insignificant band of legionaries. He bad them rally to him, and quickly had the whole mass rushing off with waving swords toward the far side of the camp.

The dozen survivors of the flying century, winded behind the broken remnants of their blood-stained shields, surrounded by dead and wounded Romans and Belgae, seemed just as perplexed as Lucius to this odd change of fortune.

Lucius had instantly recognized the Belgic knight in the ornate helmet and gleaming breastplate. It was Ambiorix, there could be no doubt of that. But why the Eburones king had diverted the Belgic attack so abruptly was a mystery – though Lucius had his suspicions.

Leaving the survivors of the flying century to guard the stockade, Lucius gestured for Sergius, Maximus, and Geta to follow. No more Belgae came through the breach in the palisade, perhaps indicative of the progress of the battle outside the walls. The camp interior was still somewhat in chaos from what Lucius could see between the rows of tents. Small enemy bands had managed to infiltrate the camp in several places by way of escalade, but it seemed most of these were being cornered and dealt with by armed slaves and freedmen. The greatest threat was clearly on the far side of the camp, where Ambiorix had led the murderous mass of warriors. And Lucius believed he knew why the Eburones king had led them there.

"Where in Jupiter's name are we going, Lucius?" Sergius demanded.

"We're going to kill that Belgic bastard!"

How he would kill Ambiorix, Lucius did not know. The enemy king still had several score knights with him, and Lucius had but three men. But he was not about to let that murdering scoundrel get away – for the sake of Honorius, and for the torture his own men had suffered at the hands of the Eburones horsemen. Whether the battle was won or lost, he intended to drive the point of his gladius through Ambiorix's throat, if it was the last thing he did.

At that moment, hooves sounded at the nearest gate, not twenty paces away, and Lucius looked to see a band of cavalry gallop through the narrow passage. He breathed easier when he saw the familiar accoutrements of Roman horsemen. The plumed officer at the head of the horsemen saw Lucius and his legionaries, too, and directed his detachment over to them. Both riders and horses were covered in mud, the tips of their lances red with blood.

"Victory!" shouted the officer. "It is a great victory. The enemy flee on all sides. Our legions have carried the day. We need every man to join in the pursuit. This is no time for hunkering behind the walls, sitting on your arses, men!"

Evidently the officer had not seen the mass of corpses lying all around, nor the blood-spattered mail of the four legionaries facing him. As the horsemen reined in, Lucius recognized the officer as Albinus. Albinus looked down at Lucius disapprovingly, obviously recognizing him as well.

"Legionary Domitius!" he snapped. "Get these men moving! If we let the barbarians escape now, we'll just have to fight them in the spring. Every man is needed."

"Begging your pardon, sir, but you need to come with us."

Albinus looked back at him tiredly, as if he had half-expected Lucius to give him trouble. "Damn it, man, can you not simply follow orders?"

"The battle may be won, sir, but Caesar's in danger, and it'll all be for naught if those barbarian bastards manage to get him."

The tribune gave a heavy sigh. What was this world coming to, when common soldiers did not obey their superiors? Was he a novice to be disregarded so? He would reprimand this upstart and see that some centurion issued punishment, for this reprobate of a legionary must learn his place.

Albinus was about to lay into Lucius with the most severe rebuke, but was stopped short by the sound of a Roman cornu blaring desperately above the din of the battle. It came from the far side of the camp. From the height of his mount, he could clearly see the player of the gleaming instrument standing atop the distant tower. With him, stood a cluster of Roman officers and the two eagle standards of the legions. Albinus knew Caesar was there, amongst those officers, but something was not right. The horn played the distress call, a signal that meant a unit was about to be overrun by the enemy. A handful of archers were also there, urgently leaning over the platform's edge to loose their arrows. They did not shoot away from the camp as one might expect, but at the camp interior directly beneath the tower. Albinus could not see what they fired at because the rows of tents hid his view of the tower's base, but he surmised there must be a mass of the enemy there. If the enemy was there, assailing the tower, then their object was clear, and this damned upstart legionary was right – Caesar was in danger.

Suddenly speechless, Albinus looked down at Lucius in astonishment.

"We must go now, sir!" The legionary implored, looking up at Albinus with eyes that indicated impatience with his hesitation. "There's little time!"

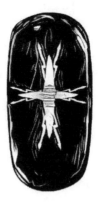

XXVII

Diogenes stumbled around the hospital tent, stepping around the dozens of injured legionaries. He was beside himself with the poor house-keeping practices of the Greek physicians and their orderlies in their rush to tend the wounded. Did they not know how difficult it was to procure bandages and herbal pastes in this country this time of year? They flippantly discarded yards of the vital cloth, cast away scalpels and probes as if they grew on trees, and took no care when removing an expired corpse from a cot, allowing blood and other bodily fluids to freely foul the blankets beneath.

The wounded had been coming in sporadically since the start of the battle, some carried by their comrades, some crawling on their own, many dying only moments after arriving. The survivors all seemed to tell the same story.

The scales had tipped in the legions' favor. The Belgae were being pushed back everywhere. Many thousand were on the run, and all that remained now was to stop the enemy from escaping.

Though dizzy spells still plagued Diogenes from time to time, he was feeling much better, the lump on his head having shrunk to the size of a small grape. The Greek physician of the Ninth Legion had prescribed two more days of rest, but the meticulous quartermaster within Diogenes could never be at ease when waste and disorder abounded, and so he had decided to make himself useful. He moved about the tent gathering up items still suitable for use and returning them to the medical stores and bandage boxes.

The groans of the dying filled the air. There had been so many casualties that the adjacent tents had been procured to accommodate the overflow, and still several bleeding legionaries were forced to light outside in the cold mud for lack of space. Diogenes counted himself fortunate to be spared this fight, but he feared for Lucius Domitius and the rest of the squad. He had not seen any of them since they had ridden into Caesar's camp together, two nights past. All throughout yesterday's march, he had been in such a daze that Lucius and the others could have been walking beside him, and he would not have known it. He had spent most of the trek slumped over the neck of a mule.

Perhaps Lucius and the others were at this very moment amongst the legions fighting outside the walls, Diogenes pondered. He still felt a great debt to the tall legionary who had saved his life on two occasions, and he swore to the gods he would make good on that debt when they all finally rejoined the Seventh. That is, if he rejoined the Seventh. For he had not yet been given the opportunity to impart General Cotta's message to Caesar, and he would have to complete that duty first. Should the battle be won, and the busy proconsul free of distraction long enough to realize the importance of the information he carried, then, Diogenes considered, he would probably not be joining the Seventh after all. The proconsul would most likely dispatch him with a large force to retrieve the pay chests, and once that was done, he would be free of this heavy burden. More importantly, he would have fulfilled his last duty to General Cotta.

Perhaps, he would consider leaving the army. He had served many long years and had brushed with death far too many times, but marching with the legions would not be the same without his old general. He did not relish spending another winter in Gaul, or returning to Gaul ever again. It had been decades since he had seen his native Illyria. He wanted to see the pink flowers in the spring swaying over the fields like so many butterflies, to walk the rocky shores along the turquoise sea, to gaze upon the white-ridged mountains he had known in his youth.

Another wave of nausea came over him, bringing him back to the present with a single breath of the frigid, foul air, and he grabbed a nearby tent pole to steady himself. As he stood there, waiting to recover, a great cry of alarm sounded outside. Men were screaming as though they were being butchered. There were Belgic voices, too. Undoubtedly, the enemy had somehow infiltrated the camp and were killing the helpless wounded where they lay. The hospital orderlies quickly grabbed up their own weapons and rushed out of the tent to defend them, but the clash of steel and more screams told Diogenes their sortie had met with dire results. Most of the men lying about the two dozen cots in the tent were in too bad of a condition to move, and the few that weren't could do little more than struggle to sit up.

Then the flap was thrown open, and a band of blood-spattered Belgae entered the tent. They wore no armor and were armed with an assortment of gladii, long swords, and javelins. The last to enter was the woman, Erminhilt.

Diogenes gasped at the sight of her, realizing these men with her must be escaped prisoners that had thrown in their lot with her. Her stern eyes scanned from one side of the tent to the other, stopping when they discovered him.

"Take him!" She pointed at Diogenes. "Kill the rest!"

Diogenes turned to run, to find a dagger, a gladius, a scalpel, or anything he could get his hands on, determined not to be taken, but to die with these other men. But another dizzy spell sent him tumbling to the ground. The next thing he knew, he was being bundled out of the tent by two Belgae while the physicians and the rest of the wounded died beneath the stabbing blades of the others.

He caught a glimpse of the woman's face as he was carried past her. He had often witnessed some measure of sympathy in her eyes before, but there was no trace of such emotion now, only hatred and a twisted look of contentment, as if she savored the sight of the slaughter.

XXVIII

From atop the tower, Caesar had watched the battle outside the camp unfold. It had progressed as he had expected, his only moment of apprehension coming when the enemy cavalry, backed by several hundred rallied spearmen, led an assault against the flanks of his advancing lines. His own cavalry had been drawn away momentarily, leaving the flanks exposed, but the tribunes commanding the outer cohorts had seen the danger and had pivoted the wings in time to repulse the attack. Repeated charges failed to break them, and the shattered Belgic ranks were swiftly ridden down by the returning Roman horsemen.

The battle had now devolved into a series of large melees. The Roman cohorts had melded with the enemy brigades. Cries of rage and suffering, triumph and fear, emanated from a maelstrom of death and butchery. Roman and Belgian fought savagely, some wielding broken weapons or fragments of shields, some fighting with bare fists. Wounded moved amongst the savaged bodies of the dead, some waving bloody limbs for assistance, some stumbling deliriously as their life blood spurted from stumps of arms, mutilated groins, and opened necks. Pleas for mercy went unheeded by both sides. Wild-eyed, riderless horses darted this way and that, some transfixed with multiple javelins, some trampling the wounded in their maddened state. As in any battle, there were groups of soldiers who milled about this carnage conversing casually, as if they strolled through the marketplace in Rome. These were the opportunists, pausing to plunder the dead, while mere steps away, their comrades fought for their very lives.

A battle is a terrible thing, thought Caesar, but this one was essentially over. The Belgic army was fleeing the field in droves. There was little chance the few thousand remaining could turn the tide. He could see the banners of the legates, Trebonius and Fabius, riding with their adjutants well to the rear of the lines, but close enough to claim their share of the victory. For it was a great victory – one that would resound in the forum in Rome and propel him to greater fame among the populace.

Caesar only hoped he outlived the day to enjoy those accolades.

A new battle had erupted within the walls of the camp. Belgic knights had come out of nowhere – three score howling warriors with blood-stained swords in their hands, and murder in their eyes. Presumably, they had entered through some breach in the walls and had overcome the camp's defenders. Now they assailed the base of the tower upon which Caesar stood, clearly intending to compensate for the defeat of their army by killing him.

The situation was desperate. Caesar's own Gallic

bodyguard had formed a ring around the base of the tower and now endeavored to fend off the enemy knights. It was a vicious melee, the ancient enemies slaying one another with a barbarity burgeoned by generations of hatred.

Looking down on this wild fight, Caesar could scarcely discern his own bodyguard from the enemy. He saw only a mass of dented helmets and swinging swords against the shadowed earth. But as the fight progressed, the outnumbered Gauls were eventually isolated into small groups and overcome. All of them were slain, but they had exacted a terrible toll on their enemies, sending more than half of the Belgic knights to the underworld. Scarcely two dozen remained when the crimson long sword was withdrawn from the mailed breast of the last twitching Gaul.

"You must go, Caesar!" the tribune Quintus said fervently as he and another man hefted one of the coils of rope stacked in one corner of the platform. The ropes were always staged in the towers as a means of escape in the event the tower caught fire, but the young tribune clearly intended to use them now to facilitate his general's escape. The outer edge of the platform extended beyond the palisade wall below, and here the two men tied off the rope and tossed the slack end over the side such that it dangled to the ground just outside the camp.

"You must climb down, my lord!" Quintus urged again. "We will cover your withdrawal!"

The enemy knights had already fought their way onto the lower platform, a square of planking half as wide as the upper platform. A handful of men struggled to hold off the Belgic warriors, but were proving to be of little consequence. Caesar shared the upper platform with only Quintus and another adjutant, and the two men bearing the eagle standards. All others, including the archers, had gone below to serve as human obstacles to the encroaching enemy. Earlier, Caesar had released the contingent of centurions that normally guarded the eagle standards, that they might lend their veteran swords to the battle outside the walls. Now, he wished those hardy centurions were here.

"Please hurry, my lord!" Quintus exclaimed as the tower vibrated from the scuffle on the lower platform. "There is not much time!"

Caesar did not respond. He stared through the opening in the floor at the bloody skirmish below. The tribune's assessment was not amiss. The meager defenders were being slaughtered by the long swords of the wild-eyed enemy.

He could escape, of course. He could simply take the rope offered him and climb down. It was a long drop. He was not as agile as he had been in his younger days. More than likely, he would lose his grip somewhere along the descent and break a limb in the fall. But, once outside the palisade wall, he could easily retreat to the safety of his victorious legions and live to fight another day.

But how would his image – his auctoritas – endure such an act? What damage would it do to this no-nonsense, Homeric hero-like persona he had carefully crafted and nurtured over the years? He was to be the antithesis of the stingy, self-serving senate – a leader who would get things done, and who would share with the people the riches of their great empire. Were he to leave now, no distracting news, no amount of propaganda, no clever wording in his reports, could conceal the fact that he had run. The truth would eventually reach Rome, probably embellished ten-fold, and how his opponents would savor it. They would fashion their own proclamations to be read out in the forum.

Great victory in Gaul. Proconsul injured while fleeing. Bodyguard and staff fought to the death while defending the eagle standards.

That would never do. He would rather die under the Belgic swords than suffer such shame. Escape was out of the question.

Caesar's sword had remained in its sheath for the entire campaign, but he now drew it out. A tentative look from Quintus indicated the tribune understood his general's intentions, and he drew his own sword as well.

One of the enemy knights on the platform below caught Caesar's eye. The man had a blonde-gray beard and wore fine armor and a fanciful helmet. He directed the efforts of the others and appeared to be their superior. From time to time, he glanced up and met eyes with Caesar in a hateful stare, as if he wished nothing more than to take Caesar's head.

It had been many months since Caesar had laid eyes on Ambiorix, but he immediately recognized the features of the Eburones king. In the few moments Caesar had to prepare to defend himself, he considered how foolish his opponent was to risk leading such a foray inside the camp. Should a fortunate blow manage to kill the enemy king, the revolt would surely wither and die. Of course, Caesar admitted, he himself had committed an equally brash move in personally leading this expedition into Belgica. Now, it seemed, Ambiorix's risk had paid off, while his own had led to his demise.

The last defender of the lower platform was a Cretan archer, whose insides spilled onto the blood-stained planks after the stroke of a Belgic sword sliced him open from hip to hip. The screaming archer was bodily lifted in the air and tossed over the side to the elation of the knights on the ground. Ambiorix and the knights with him began to climb to the upper platform, some upon the ladder leading up through the hole in the floor, some upon the tower supports.

With upturned faces, the knights on the ground cheered on their ascending countrymen, expecting the body of Caesar to be thrown to them next. But their buoyant expressions quickly transformed to those of alarm as the sound of rumbling hoofs filled the air. An instant later, a score of Roman horsemen spilled around the corners of the nearby tents, charging at a gallop, their lances leveled. The enemy knights turned to meet this new threat, but too late. Many had sheathed their swords or had stabbed them into the ground while watching the progress of their comrades above. Only a few were ready when the horsemen drove into them. A series of thumps signaled the deflection of lances by hastily raised shields, but a great many of the deadly iron tips found their way past these defenses and drove deeply into mail and flesh. A moment later, the cavalry and swordsmen were embroiled in a tangle of flashing steel, screeching beasts, and stomping hooves.

The disadvantaged swordsmen fought valiantly. One knight managed to side-step a lance thrust, bringing his sword around in a back-handed sweep that broke the back of his attacker, the Roman eques falling limply from his mount. Two Belgae had taken hold of a horse's reins while another drove his blade into the neck of the beast, killing it in a torrent of blood. The helpless rider fell with his mount and was quickly hacked to death. But these were by far the exceptions. The horsemen had the upper hand, their bloody lances probing in downward thrusts, finding the exposed necks and arms of their enemies.

Caesar was elated at these events, but knew in his heart the horsemen were being delayed too long by those below, and would not be able to stop Ambiorix and the other knights from reaching the top of the tower.

Then, suddenly, he heard a wild shout, loud and clear above the din of battle.

"Ambiorix! Ambiorix!"

Caesar looked to see the shout had come from a tall legionary who had been riding double with one of the horsemen. He bellowed up at the Eburones king, his scarred face savage within his helmet. The next moment, the legionary leapt from the saddle, took hold of the base of the tower and began climbing quickly, hefting himself up from one support to the next with flexes of his massive arms. In three breaths, he had gained the lower platform. While the two enemy knights there moved to engage him, three more legionaries began climbing the tower from the opposite side. One, a giant of a man, slipped and fell into the melee below, but the other two managed to hoist themselves up and reach the lower platform. The tall legionary, however, did not need their assistance in dispatching the two knights who now faced him. He nimbly ducked the sweeps of their long swords, and, while low, drove the point of his gladius through the extended thigh of one of his foes. The knight grimaced in pain, then screamed when the blade was ripped out, severing arteries, muscle, and flesh. Straight from the bloody and mangled leg of the first knight, the gladius was buried in the groin of the second, then withdrawn covered in gore. The tall legionary then stood back while his dying victims toppled over the side.

Through the opening in the floor, Caesar could see that the three legionaries were now masters of the lower platform. They were a scraggly lot, but he knew from their icy stares and self-assured movements that these were fighting men, veterans, killers. None of the three had shields. Each wielded only a gladius, notched and stained red from their earlier victims this day. But Caesar lost sight of them when Quintus hustled him to one corner of the platform. Quintus and the others had been fighting off the enemy knights on the ladder, but then realized these were merely serving as a distraction while the Eburones king and four other knights climbed over the outer edges. To avoid being surrounded, Quintus had moved Caesar to the corner, and now he and the others formed a defensive semi-circle around the proconsul such that the enemy could only approach them from one side.

Quintus, wearing a fine bronze cuirass bravely stepped in the path of the Eburones king, swinging his gladius wildly in short chopping strokes. He had no shield, and the reach of his blade did not allow him to get close enough to his larger opponent without putting himself in great jeopardy. Ambiorix clearly knew this, and held his position, waiting for the right moment when the tribune inevitably ventured too close. When the moment finally came, the long sword moved with the speed of a lightning bolt, sweeping in a high powerful arc that ended half-way through the tribune's skull, helmet, forehead and eyes split by a bloody chasm.

The three remaining men with Caesar stepped in the place of the fallen tribune, preparing to fight to the death, but the Eburones king and his four knights paused as a voice boomed behind them.

"I'm going to kill you, Ambiorix, you son of a whore!"

It was the tall legionary again, flanked by his two comrades. They had climbed up through the opening in the floor. Caesar concluded that they must have made short work of the knights on the ladder, to have reached the upper platform so quickly. Now, it was Ambiorix and his men who were surrounded. Seeing the tables turned, one of the standard bearers made a lunge at the back of one of the Belgic knights, but soon found out his foe, while surrounded, was not impotent. A sudden, back-handed sweep of the knight's sword removed the top half of the Roman's head, and he dropped to the floor dead.

The attack of the three legionaries, however, was not so easily dealt with. The knights drew up in a protective screen in front of their king, and the clash of swords began. Through a series of jabs, parries, and sweeps, the three legionaries engaged the four knights in a nearly equal fight that employed nearly every square foot of the platform. Ambiorix had retreated to the corner opposite Caesar, watching as his men fought on his behalf, a sureness in his eyes that they would prevail. But these were no ordinary legionaries, and when the tall one with the facial scar knocked one knight over the edge and buried his sword to the hilt in another's throat, all within the space of a heartbeat, Ambiorix's eyes suddenly showed concern.

In that moment, Caesar realized the tall legionary with the scarred face, was the same man who had arrived in his camp with Fabius's cavalry, two nights ago, and now he remembered the name – Lucius Domitius – a legionary with whom he had crossed paths on more than one occasion, and often when the moment hung in the balance. Obviously, this Lucius Domitius had a grievance against the Eburones king that seemed of a personal nature, because he snarled the same phrase again through gritted teeth as he fought off another knight.

"I'm going to kill you, Ambiorix!"

The Eburones king seemed equally shocked that this berserker legionary would address him by name, but he had a very short time to consider it. Lucius Domitius's blade opened the jugular of yet another one of the knights, the warrior clutching his spewing throat before Lucius, with one solid kick, sent him tumbling over the side to his death.

The remaining knights were fighting for their lives

against Lucius's companions. Now, nothing stood between him and Ambiorix. Lucius smiled sinisterly, his face assuming a demoniacal nature covered in the blood of his foes. There was fear in Ambiorix's eyes. The hunter had become the prey.

"You cannot run from me, you Belgic turd!" Lucius taunted him.

Ambiorix held his sword at the ready, but he clearly had no desire to face this madman in single combat. As Lucius approached, Ambiorix began backing away until his back touched the platform's bulwark.

Then, another voice rose above the din, shouting something in the Belgic tongue. It came not from the platform, but from below. It was the voice of a woman.

Ambiorix took his eyes off Lucius for a moment to glance over the edge. Then, without a moment's hesitation, he hurled his sword at Lucius with all his strength. Lucius was unprepared for this, and lost his footing dodging the twirling steel. By the time he was back on his feet, Ambiorix was gone. Only a taut, twitching rope remained where the enemy king had been standing.

"He is escaping!" Caesar shouted from the opposite corner. "Stop him, legionary!"

Lucius darted to the platform's edge and peered over the side. On the ground below, just outside the palisade wall, several Belgae sat mounted on Roman horses. They waited as Ambiorix quickly made his way down the rope. Lucius instantly recognized Erminhilt, who sat defiantly upon her mount, returning his stunned gaze with a sinister smile. Some of the others he recognized as prisoners from the stockade. But before he could register all of this, two of the men below, armed with bows, sent arrows flying at him, and he was forced to duck behind the bulwark. The straining rope was right beside him, and he wasted no time in parting it with one hack of his gladius. An audible crash of metal told him Ambiorix had fallen, but the sound had been too soon after the severing of the rope to have been fatal. As Lucius heard the hooves of the horses departing, he looked over the edge and saw the band of Belgae riding away. Ambiorix rode with them, now helmetless and appearing to be in extreme pain. Before Lucius had time to curse his ill-fortune, he noticed another rider, this one with his hands bound to the saddle, his horse being led by Erminhilt.

It was Diogenes. He was battered, but he was alive – and he was their captive.

"Damn it, man!" Caesar was suddenly beside him, also watching the riders flee, his face twisted in frustration. "Had you cut the rope first and satisfied your curiosity after, that miscreant would not have gotten away. We might have ended this revolt, right here and now!"

Lucius did not respond as Caesar lightly struck the bulwark several times in vexation, staring after the departing enemy king. Then, without a single word, the proconsul whirled and left the platform, descending through the hole in the floor.

Maximus and Sergius, having slain the other two knights, now joined Lucius.

"Lucretia's chaste arse, Lucius!" Sergius grumbled, looking at the opening where Caesar had disappeared. "You'd think some bloody gratitude was in order. Give me the word, and I'll accidentally drop my gladius on the bastard."

Lucius smiled, but shook his head. "Geta?"

"He's alive, Lucius," Maximus reassured. "I saw him down below. Looks to have broken a leg, but he made it."

"Seems senseless," Sergius said, gazing at the distant riders. "We come all this way, only to have that fool of a clerk taken right from under our noses."

The same thought nagged at Lucius, but the loss of Diogenes, and the information he carried, did not grate on him nearly as much as the lost chance to kill Ambiorix. He had been mere steps away from driving his gladius through the Eburones king's heart, and yet he had failed. He did not give a goat's fart that it irked Caesar. The proconsul could go to Pluto's Realm, for all he cared. But for Honorius, an upright man murdered like some common criminal, as his own father had been murdered, he had failed, and now he chafed at the prospect of missing perhaps his only chance to avenge the ill-fated tribune – to settle the score.

Honor, that notion at which Lucius had so often scoffed, demanded it – and honor must be upheld.

XXIX

The battle was lost.

An endless stream of broken refugees crossed at the ford, some even risking the icy depths to swim to safety. The field beyond was a scattering of disoriented refugees, a ripe harvest of death for the Roman cavalry who rode everywhere at once, it seemed, breaking up any warriors attempting to rally. They could not possibly cut down all the retreating Belgae, but they kept the panic alive, the threat of their blood-stained lances stirring it anew wherever it began to abate. It was clear these troops would never rally again, would never come together as a single army, for all stripped themselves of any guise of soldiery as they fled. Desertion and their distant farms were their only objectives.

"We must withdraw, my lord Cativolcus," a knight

attempted to get the attention of the old king who gazed upon the disaster across the river as if gazing upon the ruin of the world.

"And who is to blame for this destruction?" Cativolcus mumbled, "It is not Ambiorix. No, not him. Not that pretentious son of a Sugambrian whore. He is not to blame. He only did what the people begged him to do, after all – throw off the yoke of Rome and return the Belgae to their former glory."

"My lord?" The confused knight impatiently held onto the reins of the king's mount, unsure whom the king was addressing. "We must go, my lord! The enemy horsemen will be across the river any moment."

Cativolcus looked back at the knight as if he were a child holding a deflated udder ball, and he began to laugh maniacally. "Who has brought this destruction on us, young man? Not Ambiorix, not the people – but I. The blame lies with me. Cativolcus the Brave, Cativolcus the German Slayer, son of Carolus, descended from the long line of kings entrusted with the protection of our people – overcome by a fanatical love for my daughter."

"My lord, please."

"She is the daughter of my dear, beloved wife, long-since departed. Why did she die so terribly young? Why did she leave me to walk this earth a ghoul haunted by her image in the face of my daughter? And that face and her fondness for Ambiorix kept me from doing my duty, from defying that degenerate who has now led our people to their utter destruction!"

"We must go now, my lord!"

"Go?" Cativolcus turned on him, his face twisted in a scowl. "Go where? All is lost. Caesar will turn his terrible vengeance upon us. He will make our people suffer for what we have done. He will make us an example to all of

Gaul. This is what happens to those who spit in the face of Rome. I, for one, will not grovel before Caesar, only to have my neck wrung as the Romans cheer. Draw your sword! Draw your sword and slay me! Do it at once!"

But the knight refused this order. Having given up on his attempt to save his king, he mounted his horse and galloped off, leaving Cativolcus alone in the grove of trees.

Then, something caught the old king's attention. A band of horsemen splashed through the ford, turned abruptly downriver, and began riding away, taking a different path from that of the vast flood of refugees. Before he lost sight of them in the foliage, Cativolcus saw among them a woman with flowing dark locks and a stature he would have recognized from miles away. It was Erminhilt. She rode, following her lover Ambiorix as a sheep follows a shepherd.

"She lives!" Cativolcus proclaimed in a moment of euphoria. "She lives!"

But the moment did not last. A harsh grimace overshadowed his features as he pondered the world she now inhabited, and the fate that lay in store for her. She would live the life of a refugee, a princess without a kingdom, and the willing whore of the wretched Ambiorix, who would exploit her devotion to his gain, and her ruin, as he had the devotion of the Eburones people.

The Roman cavalry were now killing men on this side of the river, and were working their way up the slope. The old king knew he had only moments before they reached him.

"No matter," the old king said with a sly smile, half mad, half becalmed. "I have brought a special ale for this occasion."

He reached into a pouch at his belt and removed a small vial. The Druids of the woods brewed concoctions for such times, born of the sacred yew deep in the Black Forest, a special mixture to bring an end to all suffering. He wished to be conveyed swiftly from this world to the next, and he prayed his forefathers would accept him in the great hall, but he doubted they would. For he had led his people to ruin, and he had allowed his love of a woman to cloud his judgement.

He had been weak, and the gods only respected the strong – like Caesar.

Cativolcus gazed across the valley at the distant Roman camp and raised the vial as he would a tankard of ale.

"To you, great Caesar!"

He then tipped back the vial and felt the acrid mixture slide down his parched throat.

"You are the victor," he coughed in a whisper. "May you someday know defeat! May you know the pain of a father deprived of his daughter. May you die confused, in a world you cannot compre….comp..."

Cativolcus, king of the Eburones, tried to speak, but he could say no more. The witch knew her craft well. The poison was swift.

XXX

It was a warm, breezy day, when the cohort of the Seventh Legion entered the small hamlet on the northern edge of the Eburones lands. Budding trees and flowers came to life a little more each day under the welcome rays of the climbing sun. Spring had returned, but there would be no festivals celebrating it this year, or for a very long time in these lands.

Halt!" The primus pilus bellowed to the cohort, bringing the column of trail-weary legionaries to a stop in a hamlet consisting of little more than a few farmer's huts and barns. It was hardly discernable from the half dozen other settlements they had visited this day. "Fall out and search, and be quick about it!"

The long, black and white feathers of the chief centurion's traverse plume exuded authority. He was, indeed, the very embodiment of the merciless might of the Roman Empire. He sat atop a docile army mule as it were Bucephalus, gazing imperiously upon the pitiable inhabitants as the legionaries set about searching the dwellings, confiscating weapons, taking prisoners, and delving out punitive measures.

The few half-starved beasts left in the fields were gathered, along with a collection of equally emaciated slaves. The slaves made no effort to resist as they were shackled to the train of carts, and had no reason to, since they were essentially exchanging one set of masters for another. They would be sent far to the west to be sold to the tribes that had remained loyal to Rome. There was little resistance from any of the villagers, either. A troop of auxiliary cavalry had reached the hamlet hours before the cohort and had already subdued the restive ones, as evidenced by a giant oak from which a dozen bodies swung in the breeze. Most were men. Some were boys. The women of the village had been reduced to hollow-eyed ghouls, having already been raped by the Gallic auxiliaries. They appeared in a daze as they, too, were loaded onto the carts, destined to live the rest of their lives as slaves.

At one point, a figure burst from one of the huts, a lad who had managed to hide from the cavalry, but who had finally been discovered by the probing legionaries. The lad could have been no more than sixteen, but was old enough to swing a sword, and thus old enough to be a threat. He made a desperate dash for the woods, but was quickly ridden down by the lingering Gallic horsemen who laughed at his pleas for mercy as they ran him through with half a dozen lances.

This was the dirty business of soldering, the part Lucius despised. These people were ultimately to blame for the massacre of the Fourteenth Legion. They had followed their king in his defiance of Rome, knowing full well the consequences. Even still, Lucius could not partake in the atrocities, nor did he have to. There were more than enough demonic men eager to participate. The painful memories of his youth were ever at the forefront of his thoughts during such times. Often, he would try to intervene in such slaughters, but the men's blood was up, and there was no stopping their vengeance this time. Many had lost good friends in the revolt. Many had not. But all seemed eager to hold every breathing Belgae accountable.

Such scenes had become commonplace over the past weeks, ever since the spring thaws. Caesar's legions, now fully equipped and reinforced, ranged along the various roads and wagon cuts running through the land of the Eburones, slaughtering, raping, and pillaging. A trail of fire and smoke lay behind the legions wherever they marched, and mercy was extended to few.

The Seventh Legion was a part of this punitive expedition. After several months licking its wounds from the casualties sustained during the winter siege, and after receiving hundreds of new recruits from Spain, the Seventh had been bolstered to nearly three quarters of its full complement. Nearly every soldier had received commendations for their actions during the siege, and Quintus Cicero, awarded the laurel wreath for his *intrepid leadership* and his *unswerving devotion to his men*.

If so many had not died, Lucius thought, the praises heaped upon Cicero would be almost laughable.

"Get to it, Lucius," Jovinus said, breaking him out of his moment of reflection. "You and your squad search that farm over there."

Lucius had not yet gotten used to seeing his friend in the cross-plumed helmet of a centurion. Jovinus had been officially appointed to the position months ago, but still seemed somewhat out of place in his new billet. The new men from Spain gazed upon the medallions adorning Jovinus's chest with awe and respect, but Lucius still saw the scraggly legionary with whom he had marched into Gaul four years ago.

"Yes, sir. We'll get right on it," Lucius saluted half-mockingly. "Come along, lads."

The farm was larger than the others, and the hut well off the road. Lucius and his squad approached the hut warily, fanning out to search the well and stable, and livestock pens. A woman stood just outside the door watching their approach, while a hunchbacked elderly man, who appeared half-mad, and who talked to himself, dug in the bare field with his hands, crying with elation whenever he came up with a bit of grain or a worm.

The woman wore a dingy, tight scarf upon her head, such that Lucius could not tell the color of her hair, but, as he approached, he quickly recognized the proud stance, and the way she stood with her arms crossed. Though she now wore the rags of a peasant, and seemed much thinner, it was indeed Erminhilt. Her eyes indicated that she, too, recognized him. She made no effort to run, but simply greeted him in a supplicant fashion, dropping to her knees and clasping her hands before her face.

"Is that the bloody wench who betrayed us?" Sergius nudged Lucius.

"Shut up." Lucius replied, eyeing the woman coldly. "You and the others search the hut. Leave her to me."

Erminhilt appeared much different than she had on that day in the midst of the battle, when she had looked up at him on the tower. Then, she had a victorious, almost spiteful, air. Now, she seemed a shell of the woman she once was, a shadow of her former self, a survivor of much pain and suffering. After staring at each other for a long moment, while the rest of the squad rifled the hut behind her, she finally spoke.

"Will you, too, take your revenge, Legionary Domitius?" she sobbed numbly. "Will you defile this body as so many others have? I would prefer you slay me and be done with it."

"How did you end up here, lass? Did your bastard lover leave you?"

"He abandoned me after the battle. Put me off, took my horse, and left me to fend for myself in a wood crawling with Romans. He is a liar and a tyrant. I despise him!" She spat on the ground.

"Aye, he's as sly as a fox, that one."

Ambiorix was the most wanted outlaw in the Roman Empire. All winter, troops of cavalry had combed the countryside in search of the elusive king, but he had proved as slippery as the morning dew. He had remained one step ahead of his pursuers, sometimes escaping a village only hours before the Romans arrived. Caesar had ordered several such villages torched and their inhabitants slaughtered for aiding the fugitive king, but it had made little difference. Ambiorix was still at large.

"By some miracle, I avoided capture and made it here," Erminhilt said distantly, as if reliving her winter trek. "These past months, I have dedicated my existence to the care of my poor father, but I knew someday you Romans would come seeking your cruel revenge. And, here you are."

"We found poor Diogenes," Lucius said. "What was left of him, anyway."

Her eyes darted to the ground remorsefully and she covered her face. Was it all an act?

After the battle on the Henne so many weeks ago, Lucius had not immediately rejoined the Seventh, but had connived his way onto the expedition sent to recover the remains of the Fourteenth Legion. The wolves had taken their toll on the month-old battlefield, leaving very few of the seven thousand dead legionaries in a state that could be identified with any finality. Lucius had joined the expedition hoping he might stumble across the hidden pay chests, but they were not to be found. He did, however, find Diogenes. The clerk's body had been one of the easiest corpses to identify, having been dead for only a few days. He had met a most gruesome end, tied to a tree near the crumbling walls of the burned-out winter camp and made to suffer in a manner only devised by the most sadistic of minds. It had clearly taken him a long time to die. It was one of those images that would have given even the most hardened soldiers pause.

"Your lover tortured that poor bastard – tortured him for hours." Lucius sighed. "But, I suppose that means he never found the money." Lucius watched her eyes closely. He was testing her.

"Never say that again!" she said with venom. "I do not care what you do to me. Slay me if you wish, but do not say that again! Ambiorix is not my lover. I hate him!" She gestured to the adjacent farms, now billowing great clouds of smoke after having been put to the torch by the ransacking legionaries. "Look what he has done to these people. The Eburones are no more. They will fade into the dust. I curse the name of Ambiorix. I curse the day he was born!" She then appeared to collect herself and added solemnly. "I am truly sorry to hear about Master Diogenes. Had I known he would meet such a fate, I never would have taken him. I only sought to secure my father's release."

"And is that your father?" Lucius gestured to the old man hunched over in the field.

She nodded. After a long pause, during which she seemed more uncomfortable than before, she said, "He was released shortly after the battle, but his treatment in captivity has reduced him to little more than a child," she glanced over her shoulder at the old man who seemed oblivious to the nearby Romans as he dug for snails and grain. "I have lost everything, Legionary Domitius. My father is all I have. His mind is gone. He is no threat to you. Do not deprive me of the last precious thing I have in this life. Do not let them take my father from me."

"Lucius, what in Jupiter's name is the delay!" Jovinus said, marching impatiently toward the hut. Evidently, he did not recognize the woman.

After staring at Erminhilt for a long moment, during which her eyes were filled with despondency and supplication, Lucius made up his mind. "I wish to spare this farm, Jovinus, and these people."

"You what? That's not your bloody call to make, Lucius!"

"Do this for me, Jovinus. For an old comrade."

"Damn it, Lucius, no! I extend you enough favors as it is!"

Jovinus's outburst caught the attention of the centurion of the cohort who casually steered his horse over to them.

"Now, you've done it," Jovinus muttered to Lucius as the senior officer approached. "Just let me do the talking."

The primus pilus sat stiffly in the saddle, a polished vine branch under one arm. With the same disapproving expression he had assumed when dispositioning countless other farms, he examined the habitation before him, the hut, the old man in the field, the disheveled woman, and then finally the upturned faces of Jovinus and Lucius.

"What have we here, Jovinus?" the centurion said in a taciturn voice. "Why are these structures not burning, and why is that woman not in chains like the others?"

"A slight delay, sir." Jovinus smiled apologetically. "It'll be done forthwith, sir. Don't you worry, sir."

The centurion stared at Lucius inquisitively for a moment, then asked. "This is Legionary Domitius, is it not, the one who –"

"Yes, sir," Jovinus interrupted fretfully. "The one who knows his place, and who'll do exactly as he's told, without question. Yes, sir. And he'll fire this house and apprehend this woman, just as he's been directed, sir."

"This woman is an ally of Rome, sir," Lucius spoke up suddenly, looking up at the centurion and ignoring Jovinus's hand motions to remain silent. "She suffered terribly under the rule of their king."

Appearing more amused than annoyed, the centurion said skeptically, "Not so terrible to have a house such as this, legionary. Surely, she belongs to a prominent family."

"She is a friend of Rome, sir. Noble or peasant, it makes no difference." Lucius pointed to the old man in the field. "Her father was tortured for refusing to raise his sword against us."

After looking at the distant old man, the centurion chuckled. "It appears that fellow has not raised his sword in a very long time." He then paused for a long moment as if considering the request, and then sighed. "Oh, very well. I suppose the gods would frown on us if we did not extend mercy where it is due. I will take your word for it, legionary."

The centurion extended a hand to a clerk who stood nearby toting a large canvas satchel. The clerk produced a rolled sheet of paper and handed it to the centurion along with an ink stylus. After scribbling a few words on the paper and marking it with his signet ring, the officer handed the paper to Jovinus. "Mark the estate, Jovinus, and then reform your century. We've another half dozen miles to cover today, and I have no desire to be the last cohort in camp."

"Yes, sir," Jovinus replied grudgingly.

"Thank you, sir," Lucius said, though the centurion had already kicked his mule back to a walk and was headed toward the road where the cohort was preparing to resume the march.

"Here!" Jovinus said angrily, slapping the paper against Lucius's mailed chest. "Be quick about it, and get your arse back in line."

As Jovinus marched away with the rest of the squad, Erminhilt smiled appreciatively at Lucius, tears in her eyes. Lucius removed a hammer and nails from one of the pack mules and then affixed the notice of clemency to a post at the edge of the farm.

"This piece of paper will protect you and your possessions, from any Roman units that might come along. Do not lose it. See that it is well cared for. Your lives depend on it."

She knelt before him in obeisance, taking his hand in hers and kissing it several times. "You are an honorable man, Legionary Domitius. May your Roman gods bless you for this. You have my gratitude. You have it until the end of time. Bless you. Forgive me for any harm I have caused you."

"You had little choice, lass." Lucius said genially. "Were my father a hostage, I might have acted similarly. I bear no grudge against you."

Lucius shouldered his kit, bid her goodbye, and then rejoined the ranks of passing legionaries. Erminhilt stared after him as he marched away, smiling and waving whenever he looked back over his shoulder.

She was still staring long after the Roman column had

disappeared, but her smile eventually faded, replaced by the stoic resolve of the undefeated. She then turned to meet the gaze of the old man in the field. He no longer slumped like a broken man, but stood up straight and tall like a warrior. His perfect blue eyes blazed with intensity and were accompanied by a furtive smile that even now, after all they had been through together, sent a surge of desire coursing through Erminhilt's veins.

XXXI

"**M**y lord says he has many reasons to distrust you," the German warrior said from atop his mount, staring down at Ambiorix in the torchlight.

"Perhaps Lord Raganhar has forgotten about the silver I sent him, not a fortnight past."

"Some silver, yes. But not all that was promised. Again, my lord waits, and again you make empty promises."

"I, too, have waited," Ambiorix replied assertively. "I have waited for the Romans to come into our lands. Now they are here, pillaging the land, encumbered by baggage trains, their legions spread across many hundreds of miles. The time for us to strike has come at last!"

The German regarded him skeptically, and with a measure of amusement bordering on disrespect, but Ambiorix ignored it.

"Tell Raganhar I will meet him at the Druid's Tree near Tarentel in four days. He shall have the rest of the silver as promised. Now go!"

As the German horseman rode off into the darkness, Ambiorix felt a surge of confidence he had not felt in some time. It had been a long, wearisome winter, but things were about to turn in his favor, now that he had finally managed to convince Raganhar to bring his army once again to the shores of the Rhenus.

The fates were with him. They had to be, considering how close he had come to disaster earlier this afternoon.

He had donned the disguise of the mindless old man, knowing the Romans were more inclined to spare the elderly in their march of devastation. But, in the end, it had been Erminhilt's unique charm that had saved them — that and the influence she still had over that daft legionary, the same bastard who had come so close to killing him atop the tower all those months ago.

He had taken due precautions, paying several peasant boys to warn him if any Romans approached the village, but the miscreant urchins must have lost their nerve and fled, because the first indication he had of the enemy's approach was the sight of auxiliary cavalry in the village square. He had played the part of the senseless old fool in front of the Gallic horsemen and their Roman officer, enduring their kicks and their spit while Erminhilt did her best to satisfy them with her figure. Eventually, she had produced a small sack of silver denarii, and this had satisfied the horsemen such that they left. Then the Roman infantry had arrived, and, once again, Ambiorix had been sure their game was up. To flee would have meant certain capture or death, so they had been forced to continue in their roles, and fortune had favored them by perplexing that fool of a legionary. Erminhilt had played her part perfectly.

Ambiorix had also been fortunate to have kept his dozen mules confined within a sink hole a mile from the village, deep in the forest, and well hidden from the pillaging Romans. That precaution had paid off, and now, as the train of animals waited outside, he and Erminhilt hastily packed provisions for the journey ahead of them. They packed everything left of importance, for they would not be returning to this place.

In the scant light of the lantern, Ambiorix could see that something weighed heavily on Erminhilt's mind. He suspected he knew what it was, but he did not want to discuss the matter again.

"Should we not flee, my love?" she said finally, gazing at him with imploring eyes. "Let us go far to the north. We can sail across the sea to the jagged lands, where no Roman will ever find us."

"We have already been over this," he said firmly. "We shall go to our friends in the land of the Menapii, and from thence cross over into Germania. We are going to deliver the silver to Raganhar, just as we planned."

"Listen to reason, my love," she crossed the room and stood beside him as he stuffed a satchel. "Our people are being led away in droves. The Romans will send them to distant lands. They will never return. Only the lame and old remain. The Eburones will cease to exist within a generation." When he made no acknowledgement, she reached out and tenderly touched his arm. "Were my father still alive, he would encourage us to —"

"Your father!" Ambiorix snapped, angrily. "Your father was a senile old fool. We would not now be criminals in our own land, had he allowed me to lead our people without interference. I should have done away with him long ago!"

"Ambiorix, my love, it is over."

"It is not over! I am destined for greatness, regardless of what happens to our incompetent people. I will be high king. I will! If you no longer believe that, then you are free to be someone else's whore! Be off!"

She glared at him, gritting her teeth and clenching her fists as if she might strike him, but then turned on her heel and crossed to the other side of the room, burying her head in her hands and sobbing.

It was not over. Did she not see? This was the dawn of a new kingdom. Now that he had the means to buy Raganhar's army – a German army, a *real* army – he could face the legions properly. The other Belgic chieftains had been cursing his name these past months, but they would curse him no more. When they saw his mercenary army, they would fall in line, or they, too, would be counted among his enemies. He would muster a new army, twice the size of the last one, and destroy Caesar's legions one-by-one.

Erminhilt had, perhaps, outlasted her usefulness. Once he had joined with Raganhar, there would be no time to coddle any frivolous emotional attachments. He was about to tell her this, when he heard two of the mules braying outside.

Something had disturbed them.

Ambiorix wore no armor, and his sword lay sheathed on the far table. He was just moving to grab the weapon, when the shabby wooden door to the hut suddenly burst open, and a tall figure entered the room. It was the legionary from this afternoon, the scar on his face prominent in the dull light of the lantern.

The legionary held a javelin in both hands, extended to prevent Ambiorix from reaching his weapon on the table. Seeing that the legionary could have easily killed him, but did not, Ambiorix stepped back, raising his hands in surrender, but Erminhilt was not so easily pacified. She screamed in a maddened fury, her face twisted into a demoniacal scowl as if to vent all her anger on this man. She rushed him from the side, a dagger held reversed in one hand, but the legionary was prepared for her attack. With one quick rotation of the javelin, he struck her across the face, stunning her, and then delivered a solid blow with the butt end to her unprotected head, knocking her to the floor.

An instant later, the point of the javelin was again pointed at Ambiorix's belly, quelling any opportunistic temptations. The legionary met his confused expression with a contented smirk.

"Well, Roman," Ambiorix said in Latin, sensing the possibility of making a deal with the man. "You have tried to kill me before. I can only assume you are not doing so now, because you desire something from me."

"I do," the legionary replied succinctly.

"My mules, perhaps?" Ambiorix ventured, then pointed at the unconscious Erminhilt on the floor. "Or perhaps the woman? You are welcome to them both. You are welcome to take anything I have, if it will buy my freedom."

"How about silver? How about three hundred thousand denarii?"

"But I am a king without a kingdom, Roman. I have little more than the clothes on my back."

"Oh, I think you do." The legionary eyed him shrewdly. "I've already searched those mules out there, and you're not fool enough to hide it in here, otherwise my lads would've found it when they rummaged through this place earlier today."

"As I said, Roman, I haven't a single ounce."

"You're a mule turd, Ambiorix – a lying mule turd. I

know exactly where you've hidden it." The legionary gestured to the lantern on the table. "Grab the light, and step outside."

Ambiorix had no choice but to do as he was told. He walked out into the night, the sounds of the forest insects reverberating across the fields.

"Go on." The legionary nudged him in the back with the point of the javelin. "Out there. Keep walking."

The legionary directed him out into the dark field adjacent to the hut.

"You see," the legionary said behind him as they walked. "You and that whore didn't fool me earlier today. The only reason I didn't blow your cover was because I couldn't figure out if you had managed to make the clerk talk. But, a few miles down the road, after I'd had time to think it over, I realized that you had. That's far enough, I think. Stop here, and turn around."

Ambiorix turned to face him.

"You were rooting around here today, pretending to dig up snails and worms, but I think you were protecting your treasure. It's buried here somewhere, and you're going to dig it up for me. You're going to dig with your bare hands. If it takes all night, and well into tomorrow, I don't care. You can lead me right to it, or you can dig up this entire field trying to avoid the true spot. It will only mean more labor for you, and the result will be the same. It is your choice. What will it be?"

After a long pause, Ambiorix finally nodded. "You are right, Roman," he said in a dejected tone. "I will attempt no more deception. It is here."

"Then I suggest you start digging."

Ambiorix walked to the spot where the earth was still soft, where he knew the remaining chests were buried. He knelt, and began to dig. The legionary seemed fairly pleased with himself as he stood there watching him. And why shouldn't he? It was not every day that a common soldier got to watch a king toil like a slave. But Ambiorix did have one more ploy, and this he intended to be the last one he would ever need to play on this Roman. He dug slowly, pretending to not be accustomed to such work, pretending to need frequent rests. Eventually, the legionary got bored and complacent enough that he stabbed his javelin into the ground and took a long drink from his waterskin. At that moment, Ambiorix began digging faster, for it was not only Roman silver that lay beneath the soft earth. He had also buried something else. His heart leapt in his chest as his probing fingers finally touched cold metal – not the metal of commerce, but the metal of war.

Ambiorix wrapped his hand around the hilt of the buried long sword. In one motion, he drew it out and swung it in a high arc at the lounging Roman. But the Roman was not as distracted as he had let on, and about mid-way through the wild swing, when Ambiorix's momentum was too great to stop it, he saw the Roman pull something from his belt in a lightning fast move then step to the side. The sword missed, striking the soft ground, and while Ambiorix was over-extended, a sharp pain suddenly flared in his side. He then realized the Roman had pulled a pugio dagger from his belt and had buried it just beneath his ribs, the blade penetrating up into his lung. The blade was withdrawn and inserted two more times before the legionary backed away.

As Ambiorix struggled to remain on his knees, the sword fell from his limp hand. Each breath was more difficult than the last. Through blurry eyes, he saw the legionary walk around him and pick up his long sword. Then the legionary stood before him, balancing the sword in his hand.

"You may have forgotten," the legionary said, looking down upon him. "There once was a man named Honorius. You slew him while his body was wracked by a poison concocted by your whore. Do you remember?"

"I will be high king!" Ambiorix wheezed. "I will be king over all."

"Then go be king in Valhalla!"

The sword sang through the air. The next instant, the head of Ambiorix, with its features frozen in terror, rolled into the pit, coming to rest between the partially excavated chests full of coins.

XXXII

Erminhilt awoke as the eastern sky turned from black to gray. Her shoulders hurt, and she soon realized why. She was seated on the ground, tied to a fence post. A few steps away, she saw Lucius cinching up the satchels on a mule, singing a light-hearted tune to himself.

"What are you doing?" she said.

Lucius peered over the top of the laden mule's back and smiled at her. "Good. You're awake."

"Where is Ambiorix?" she asked instinctively, then instantly realized such a question would not serve in her best interest. When she spoke again, she assumed the pitiful tone of a victim. "Why am I bound? Untie me."

"I am normally sympathetic to women in plight," Lucius said. "But you have been deceitful at every turn. The last time I spared you, three of my men were killed, not to mention what happened to poor Diogenes." He drew his sword and walked toward her.

"Do not kill me! Please! Please! I am a friend of the Romans! All that I said was true about my father! Ambiorix forced me to be with him! I always hated him!"

"Save your breath, lass. I don't kill helpless women – not even a heartless witch-whore with the tongue of a demon."

Her face flushed at the insult, the pitiful victim now all but vanished, her noble breeding getting the better of her. She looked at him defiantly and spit in his direction. "There! That is what I think of your mercy!"

"Oh, I didn't say anything about mercy, lass," he smiled. He then raised the sword as if to silence her, but then turned and struck the notice of mercy from the post nearby. He tore the papyrus to bits, and let the wind carry it from his hand.

"What are you doing?" she demanded.

"You remember the seven thousand Romans of the Fourteenth Legion, the men your pig-nosed lover betrayed and slaughtered?"

She looked at him with annoyance, but said nothing.

"Well, it just so happens the entire Fourteenth wasn't massacred that day. There were two centuries that survived – two centuries who did not perish with their comrades, because they had the good fortune of being on special duty in the Aedui lands at the time. Those lads belong to the Eleventh legion now, but they're still fairly upset about the way their mates were handled, as you can imagine. In fact, Caesar was so worried they'd leave this country in ruins, he took the precaution of stationing them at the rear of the column, guarding the baggage. They were about a day behind us, so they should be along directly – just after sunup, I suspect." He paused and looked into her eyes. "Those lads come from the Po Valley. I've heard they're little more than savage Gauls in Roman armor – eight score dirty, Gallic legionaries, deprived of revenge, and forced to settle for the leavings of the legions marching ahead of them. But I fancy they'll be somewhat pleased to come across you."

Her defiant expression melted into a look of horror as she realized what he was saying. She began to squirm in her bonds. "No! No! You can't! Take me with you! Please! Take me with you!"

Lucius smiled at her. "Not this time, lass."

Erminhilt screamed at him, cursed him, begged him for mercy, offered him anything he desired, but Lucius ignored it all. Sighing heavily, he grabbed the reins of the lead mule in the train, turned and walked away.

Her screams still resounded across the barren fields long after the last mule had disappeared into the gray morning haze.

Made in the USA
Monee, IL
16 August 2021

75751069R00173